BACKSTAGE PASS

RILEY SCOTT

BELLA
BOOKS

2016

Bella Books, Inc.
P.O. Box 10543
Tallahassee, FL 32302

This is a work of fiction. Names, characters, businesses, places, events and incidents are either the products of the author's imagination or used in a fictitious manner. Any resemblance to actual persons, living or dead, or actual events is purely coincidental. The publisher does not have any control over and does not assume any responsibility for author or third-party websites or their content.

Printed in the United States of America on acid-free paper.

First Bella Books Edition 2016

Editor: Cath Walker
Cover Designer: Sandy Knowles

ISBN: 978-1-59493-490-2

About the Author

In addition to having published poetry and short stories, Riley Scott has worked as a grant and press writer and a marketing professional. She holds a degree in journalism. A chunk of life spent in the Bible Belt has given her a close-up look at the struggles facing the LGBT community in Small Town, America, and she strives to bring these to light through her writing. Riley's love for fiction began at a young age, and she has been penning stories for over a decade. She is a proud New Mexican with a passion for her partner (who, if you'll note, is listed ahead of green chile), green chile, dogs, and lively literature. She lives in Albuquerque with her partner, two beloved dogs, and a cat who was part of the package but isn't so bad once you get to know him.

Other Bella Books by Riley Scott

Conservative Affairs
Small Town Secrets

Dedication

To the readers who want to take a walk on the wild side and let their rebellion show, this book is for you—and of course for my love, my muse and the rock star of *my* heart, Heather.

Acknowledgments

Writing a book like *Backstage Pass* required a great deal of research—and attendance at several rock concerts throughout the past few months. Thank you to my friends who tagged along and made these experiences both memorable and informative. Additionally I would like to extend my gratitude to my fellow Bella Books authors whose insight and advice has served to make me a better, bolder writer. Special thanks to Erica Abbott, whose wisdom, humor and guidance stuck with me through writing some of the most difficult parts of this story. Thank you to Cath Walker for working hard to polish this story and to all of the Bella team for commitment to producing top-notch literature. And thank you most of all to the love of my life, whose patience and love during writing days—where I refuse to leave the house, speak in jumbled half sentences and drink enough coffee to become a frazzled mess if disturbed in the slightest—will always be appreciated.

CHAPTER ONE

Melissa Etheridge crooned out of the speakers in Christina's room as she set to work packing the last of her essential items. As the remainder of the evening sun streaked through her curtains, she let out a sigh and sat on the edge of her bed, a mix of nervousness and excitement swirling in her head.

She belted out the lyrics, singing along to Melissa's tune and trying to drown out her muddled thoughts. Though "Nowhere to Go" was the opposite of her current problem, the words were soothing and sang about finding home and a place in the arms of a kindred spirit.

She took a deep breath and glanced into her closet. It was difficult to decide what to take and what to leave behind when entering a world so different from her own. Forcing herself to pay attention, she sorted through clothing. She didn't want to appear as if she was trying too hard to be edgy—or too professional. There had to be some mix.

"Brit," she called out to her roommate down the hall. "Can you come help me for a minute?"

She waited until she heard footsteps, trying her best to don a game face, one that said she was ready for whatever she was about to conquer.

"What can I do for you," her peppy, blond roommate asked, poking her head into Chris's room, "aside from returning this little guy?" She held out Paco, Chris's tiny dog, as if he were a peace offering. His tan fur stood up in tufts from his recent bath, his ears drooped, and his big brown eyes made the perfect "sad puppy dog" look complete.

"Hey buddy," Chris said, taking him into her arms. "I'm sorry. He must have sought refuge in your room. He hates it when I pack. Typical Chihuahua."

"I know," Brittany said with a shrug. "Don't worry about a thing. We are going to be just fine while you're out on the road, living it up."

Brittany reached out and patted her on the shoulder, looking closely at Chris. Her touch was tender, her smile soft. Her gentle approach told Chris her game face was failing miserably. Chris looked into Brittany's sky-blue eyes, smiling at how they sparkled in the light, exuding warmth and a touch of mischief. She also remembered those blue eyes shining with desire and longing—and brushed the thought aside.

"I don't know if I should have accepted this opportunity," Chris admitted quietly, again taking a seat on the bed.

"Come on," Brittany encouraged, sitting next to her. "You were so excited when you found out they chose you. In fact, you didn't stop talking about it for a week. It's a once in a lifetime chance, remember?"

"You're right," Chris said, nodding and trying to resume her initial confidence. "There were several firms up for the job and they chose mine. And beyond that, my boss put *me* on the task." Even to her ears, her voice sounded more like she was making a grocery list than recounting her greatest professional accomplishment.

"You are a PR superhero," Brittany said, her bright smile spreading across her face with ease. "You're the same woman who single-handedly saved the mayor's transportation project from public doom. You made the kid who smashed the windows of his school into a model citizen when his rich parents hired you. You turned around the reputation of that tech company whose products blew up in consumers' hands. And most importantly, you represented…" Brittany paused for dramatic effect and used her fingers to create a drum roll on the bed. "Superstar baseball player, Tom Stella, in his doping case."

Chris listened as Brittany regaled her accomplishments, savoring the way Brittany viewed her. It was incredible to be so loved, so entirely accepted and applauded all the time. It meant even more because she knew Brittany had seen her at her worst and still saw her in that light.

"Seriously, I've seen you take on some of the toughest cases—the most intense crisis situations—and leave everyone smiling when you walk off the scene," Brittany continued. "Whether you're working your magic with words and penning crafty statements or staging publicity events, you are the *best* at what you do. You've got this. It'll be cake for you and not only that, you also get to party with a rock star."

"That's the part I'm worried about," Chris said, giving voice to her fears. "I know I can turn things around for this girl. She's clearly smart, she's talented beyond all belief, she puts on great shows and she's beautiful. She's a household name who sells out the biggest venues, but she's just done a good job of running her name into the ground. I can work with her and I have little doubt about that. I'm just worried that I don't really know how to behave in that world."

Brittany laughed and the sound helped calm Chris's nerves. "You know exactly what to do," she said with a wink. The move was subtle but served as another reminder that Brittany's friendship was more. "You're going to have wild sex parties and snort some blow."

"That was one time," Chris said, her joke easing the tension completely. As they both broke into a fit of giggles, Brittany stood and looked at Chris's closet.

"Is this what you wanted help with?" she asked, pointing. "Trying to find the balance between the stripper and the businesswoman?"

"You know me too well," Chris said with a shrug. "I just don't want to look like I'm trying too hard, in either direction."

"Just go and be you," Brittany offered. "You're the coolest person I know and you're my favorite party buddy, as well as my favorite PR professional. Just go and rock it." As she spoke, she flipped through the closet, selecting a few items that seemed to fit the bill perfectly.

"These," she said, holding up a pair of faded, ripped jeans and a tight black shirt, "are for the evenings, the night shows. And these," she added, holding up a pair of darker jeans and a red, silky, scooped-neck blouse that showed too much cleavage to wear on a normal workday, "for when you need to dress up. Also be sure to take a pair of slacks and a jacket, just in case you have to go on camera. You never know if the girl is going to go off the deep end and need you to comment on her behalf."

"I knew you'd save the day," Chris said appreciatively, standing to give her a hug.

"No," Brittany said, pulling back from the hug. "I'm just the style guru. You're going to be the one to save the day. Now, stop doubting yourself, put this stuff in a bag and go kick some ass. But most importantly, go have a blast."

Reassured, she knew Brittany was right. There was no need for her to go into this with anything other than her usual confidence and optimism. There was a reason that they had chosen her and she was going to prove them right, whatever it took. Until then, she was going to snuggle Paco for another night and try her best to get a good night's rest.

"Have I showed you the schedule?" she asked, prolonging the interaction for a while longer. She was going to miss her best friend—the constant in her life who made her feel at home in the world. She thought again about Melissa Etheridge's song and how she sang of asking someone to dance with her forever. Confusion lingered in her mind as she eyed Brittany, wondering if that was why she would miss her.

She noted Brittany's smile and felt her heart flutter. She couldn't tell if it was out of familiarity and warmth or something deeper and unsettling. Regardless, she would miss this—the ease with which they spoke, the tender hugs. She would even miss the longing glances and tension-filled moments as they felt out exactly what their relationship or lack thereof looked like.

"I think you've showed me six times, but run it by me again." Brittany's laughter filled the room as she sat down on the bed again. She reached over and patted Chris's shoulder, and the touch sent shivers through Chris's body. Things would never be the same between them again. But she couldn't figure out what they should be. She glanced at the schedule, hoping that her time on the road would provide some clarity for their current situation. Either she would miss Brittany and know she was the one, or she would find freedom and new connections in new places.

"We start out in Austin, and we hit most major cities in the southwest over the course of a month." She harnessed her attention to the matter at hand. "And that's just if Susan thinks I've done what I need to do after a month. She could make me stay two, three or even more months. If I stay for the full two months they've got scheduled, that will be twenty-four shows, eight weeks and seven states. She's playing three shows a week and covering a lot of territory. For some unknown reason, we go from Texas to Arizona, back to New Mexico, back to Arizona for a concert she is doing with the kid who won *American Idol* last year, then California, Nevada, Utah and finally Colorado and Oklahoma. At this point, it's impossible to even guess where I could end up, let alone what weather or timing will be beyond those two months. It's exhausting to even put it into my planner."

"Then ditch the planner and just enjoy the ride."

"Easier said than done," Chris said, shaking her head.

"I know. Pack for the long haul but be optimistic. Maybe you will be back in just a few weeks." Brittany patted her on the knee and stood. "One more thing," she added, standing in the doorway. "You might want to start listening to something a little more hardcore. Something tells me your girl is going to like it more if you can sing along to her songs."

"I can growl, yell angrily, shoot whiskey and tell the world to fuck off with the best of them," Chris said, brushing it off. "Besides, we both know that I'm a fan."

"Yeah, I know," Brittany responded, winking as she walked out the door. "Don't show her just how often you fantasize about her while you're out there on the road with her. It'll add to that big ego of hers and make you seem like a bit of a lovesick pup."

Chris laughed, shaking her head and shutting her door. One thing she was sure of was that she was definitely not going to let Raven know just how big a fan she was, or how much she had crushed on the singer throughout her late teens and early twenties—for the last decade of her twenty-eight years. The rest she could figure out along the way.

"Go get 'em, champ," she whispered the words to herself, smiling sadly and wishing that her dad was still around to give her his usual pep talk before every big life event until he had passed away two years ago. She cued on his strength that still lived in her. She lay down on her bed and closed her eyes, letting her excitement about tomorrow come back and her anxiety subside.

* * *

Thankful for the dark light in her bus bathroom, Raven looked into the mirror, taking special note of how her eyeliner was smeared down the side of her face, making her brown eyes look even darker. Her long, dark hair was a tousled mess, its natural waves refusing to cooperate. She tried unsuccessfully to pick through the strands with her fingers. With a sigh, she moved on to the next task. As deftly as her hangover would allow, she cleared the black goop from her face with a makeup remover wipe, her clean face showing off angular features that were often termed 'exotic' in the press.

She wanted to laugh about it and would have done so if she had an audience. However she could barely manage to keep her eyes open. She removed the rest of last night's makeup and expertly reapplied another coat.

"Never let them see you weak or unprepared," she whispered to her reflection. "Even if it's just for rehearsal," she added to no one in particular.

The beating on the bus door came again and she wanted to tell Frank Karnes—her manager—to go to hell. She took a deep breath instead and glanced in the mirror, thankful that her bitchy face needed no extra coaching today.

"What?" she asked angrily, throwing the door open to Frank's hand hanging in midair.

"You're late," he said, his bald head gleaming in the afternoon sun, the lines of frustration showing out of the side of his sunglasses, and his wide forehead wrinkling even more than usual. "That's what." His gruff tone indicated that he was in no mood for nonsense today.

The corners of her lips turned up slightly at the thought. Aside from the roar of a crowd, the powerful riff of a quality song or the way that she knew that no matter what she did, he would stand by her side, there was little that brought her as much delight as his little panic attacks over nothing.

"It's not a big deal," she said with a shrug. "We all know that we're going to play the same set as last night and we killed it last night. I've got this. Besides, tell Pete that he should practice without the rest of us. He's the one struggling."

The mention of her bass player's flub only made Frank scowl more. "That's enough," he said. "You can't do a show without them. Keep that in mind before you start hurling insults."

"I know, I know," she said, holding her hands up as if she was being assaulted. "We're a team and all that jazz. I'm just saying, we're going to be fine tonight. We'll rock the hell out of Austin. They'll never know what hit them."

"You're playing to a huge crowd," he said, raising an eyebrow at her and pointing around, emphasizing that she was the headliner for Austin's biggest music festival of the year. "I just want to make sure you're as amped and prepared as you need to be. This is a music-loving city, and you'll be on stage for thousands who paid high-dollar prices for those tickets."

"I *am* pumped," she said, not allowing her facial expression to show just how excited she was. She was as happy to be living her dream as anyone could have been, but that didn't mean she was going to give them all the satisfaction of knowing it. "Let's go have some fun. Isn't that what this whole thing is about anyway?"

He eyed her sideways. "Not too much fun," he added, pulling off his sunglasses for a moment. "We can't have another night like Chicago. I'm all about you kids having a blast out there. That is, indeed, what this is all about, but you also have to remember that news spreads like wildfire and I can't have your face plastered about with bad publicity like it has been lately."

The mention of her latest scandal caused her to stiffen. As she had told him before, it wasn't her fault that kids had a fascination for putting their every encounter on the Internet. But she wasn't going to get into that argument again.

"It'll be fine," she said, reaching up to pat him casually on the shoulder. "After all, that's what people expect from us—sex, drugs and rock 'n' roll. I wouldn't want to let my fans down." She winked at him before turning back into her room for a moment, grateful she had opted to spend the extra money on a large bus with private rooms.

"I thought you were ready," he called out, his voice rising in frustration.

"I am," she said. "Just give me a minute to use the restroom. I'll be right there and we can have a little fun with the rock 'n' roll part of that bit."

She heard his sigh as she shut the door in his face, leaving him back outside her world for a moment. Taking one last minute to herself, she eyed the Red Bull on the table and gave it a second of consideration. Knowing it wouldn't be nearly adequate, she slipped into her bathroom and reached into her cabinet for the small locket engraved with her initials, the one thing that had survived through all the moves and all of the chapters of her life. She looked at it, remembering the day it had been given to her by her father on her fourth birthday. She shook her head, wondering how some memories held such clarity even twenty-three years later.

Running her fingers across the hard metal of the heart-shaped necklace charm, she slipped a nail in the crevice and carefully opened it up, before pouring out a line. One quick snort and she leaned back.

Finally awake for the day, she smiled into the mirror and headed out the door.

"Let's go make some magic, Frank," she said, putting her arm around him as they walked toward the building.

Looking up, she had to smile. This was what she lived for. A blue-sky day with white puffy clouds and right now, they seemed to come to life. And she knew she'd feel even more alive when she belted out the opening lines of her latest hit.

"We have a guest today," Frank said, looking down in her direction, clearly oblivious to the magic she was experiencing.

"What kind of guest?" she asked, not letting his news blur her good mood. She glanced up at him briefly, noting the way worry seemed to cloud his eyes. She wanted it to fade and wished he felt as good as she did. She glanced away, not wanting to either see his anxiety or absorb it.

"You remember our conversation about hiring a public relations firm, right?" His voice was steeped in caution, as he quietly, but pointedly, enunciated each word.

Her heart raced, as she recalled the conversation, a combination of anxiety and frustration seething within her. Just because she had slipped up once didn't mean she needed a nanny. Her latest mistake had been splashed about social media and plastered on the cover of every gossip rag, making her look like some kind of fool. To think that some outsider could come in and fix it was ludicrous. Her fans had moved on and so had anyone with a brain. It was the game to be a little wild. She was no exception to the rules of rock 'n' roll. Anyone who looked back on the history of rocker scandals would see that she was the norm. She was what she was expected and trained to be. No one with any talent slipped through this fast-paced world of fame and entertainment without a few bumps along the way. She was just fine and she didn't want someone with a pretty résumé joining the so-called "team" just to snoop around in her personal life. That would only make matters worse and interrupt how she was running her life and her career. This was no one else's business.

"You know I don't want to do that," she said. "I don't need it. I'm fine. I'm who my fans expect me to be and I don't want to be some Barbie doll version of a rock star. We have too many of those. I'm not a bubble gum pop singer or one of the Golden Girls."

"Don't start in on that again," he said, pulling away from her side and turning to face her. "I know that's not who you are and we're not going to change your image. We're just going to clean it up a bit. We can't have incidents anymore. We can't afford them."

"Sales didn't drop a bit," she said, sticking to her guns and shaking her head. "Not even a dip. I have checked every day since then."

He raised an eyebrow at her and cocked his head to the side, seemingly questioning her intensity. "You have?" he asked after a moment.

"Of course I have," she said, shrugging it off. "This is my career. It's my art. I wanted to be sure I was making the right decision to forgo the agency and I am. I'm fine."

When his eyes again showed signs of worry and his brow furrowed, she glanced at the ground. It was too painful to see legitimate concern in his eyes. "Look at me," he said gently, giving her no choice but to comply. When she lifted her eyes to his, she saw the softness of a father figure and the pang in her heart was palpable. "We both know you're *not* fine, honey. Talented as hell? Without a doubt. But fine? No. And I want to help you with that. We all do. This is for your own good."

"It's just so the public has something they can digest," she said, shaking her head and refusing to let her feelings get in the way. "I appreciate you, Frank. You know that. But I still don't want to do this and I'm not going to. I'm not going to have some outsider come in here and tell me how I need to look, what I can and can't say, and who I'm supposed to be. If you remember, our last public relations chump lasted three weeks. That bastard gave me a list of words I couldn't use."

"And you used plenty of the words in telling him where he could shove his list," Frank said, trying to keep his amusement out of his tone.

"And I'll do the same to this one if you insist on making me even meet with them. But I don't want to do it."

"At least meet her," he said. "This time, we stuck to the guidelines you requested. I know that the last one fell through, but we didn't listen to your criteria then. This time, we brought you in a young woman, about your age—she's twenty-eight. And she's someone who can understand you as a person. I interviewed her personally. Unlike the others, she's actually a fan of rock music. She's been instructed not to interfere with who you are or change you. She's simply here to make your public image more appropriate and clean. She's one of the best in the game with a long list of successful client cases in her portfolio."

"I'll meet her," she said, "but rest assured, she won't last."

"We'll see about that," he said, placing his arm around her and directing her toward the stadium. The move clearly cut the discourse short, but she was sure he was just as tired as she was of having the conversation. Nonetheless, she wasn't giving in.

CHAPTER TWO

Thankful that the plane ride had passed uneventfully, Chris looked around at her surroundings. After a quick stop at the hotel to drop off her things and freshen up, she went to the Frank Erwin Center. Luckily, the band was staying an extra night in Austin, so she was afforded something that would become a luxury—staying in an actual room instead of on the group's bus.

She looked down at her dark skinny jeans, blue blouse and peep-toe heels. Taking a deep breath, she smoothed her hands on her jeans. She had made the right choice in wardrobe. Not too classy, but not slouchy either.

As the guitarists and drummer jammed out onstage, the hot, dry air enveloped her. The star of the show was yet to grace the practice area, even though the sound and light crew were hard at work setting up equipment with the band.

Wringing her hands together to keep her palms from getting too sweaty, Chris tried not to focus on her racing heart. *This is business*, she reminded herself. *You're a professional.*

Listening to the music, she smiled. There was nothing like strong rock to set a mood. They sounded crisp and well-practiced. The men showed raw talent. Yet they were having fun as they played, their passion for their craft seeping through every chord, every note.

"You've got this," she reminded herself as they played the final note of their warm-up number. No amount of pep talking could still her nerves or keep her from feeling a volatile mix of anxiety and excitement. On one hand she felt like the teenage girl waiting to meet her celebrity crush. On the other, she felt suddenly unsure about whether accepting this opportunity had been the right move. She had done her research. The poor guy who had previously taken the position had been dispensed with quickly.

Perhaps no one could tame the beast that was Raven. She took a deep breath and silently went down a mental list of all of the clients she had pulled from the wreckage of their own stupidity. She vowed this one would be the same.

She craned her neck toward the doorway where she had seen the infamous Frank Karnes exit minutes before, but couldn't see anything. She wanted to introduce herself before he ducked out, having recognized him from his years in the industry. But he had been quick to leave and his expression signified he was on a mission. *Just like a diva to keep them all waiting*, she thought. Glancing around, she decided that standing in wait was ridiculous. Instead, she chose a chair close to the stage and let the guitar riffs carry her away to another less stressful place.

"Glad to see you at least have good taste," the raspy voice jolted Chris back into the moment, causing her to open her eyes and refocus.

Raven stood in front of her, in the flesh. Chris managed a smile as she stared into deep chocolate-brown eyes. Raven's dark hair was disheveled, slight waves all the way down the middle of her back. Her angular face still held its astounding beauty, but her mouth showed no signs of a smile and her eyes no sign of amusement. Nonetheless, she was easily the most beautiful woman Chris had ever seen.

Standing, she regained her composure. "Good morning," she said, letting her smile deepen and hoping her cheeks didn't betray her by blushing. "I'm Christina Villanova. I'm going to be handling some of your public relations efforts moving forward."

"Raven," she responded, offering her a hand but stubbornly remaining stiff and unapproachable. "We'll see if you pass the test." Chris marveled at just how tall Raven was in person and how quickly the words seemed to tumble out of her mouth, as if her world was moving faster than everyone else's. Raven stood a solid half foot taller than she did, yet Chris held her ground, refusing to be intimidated by her stature or her coldness.

With that, Raven turned and took the stage.

"I'm sorry," Frank started, but Chris held a hand up to stop his apology.

"No need," she said. "It's fine. I'm used to it. Most people don't want help or think they need help. I didn't expect any less. I'm Christina, by the way."

"Frank Karnes," he said, extending his right hand for a formal introduction, although the two of them had spoken on the phone and corresponded via email for weeks.

"Nice to finally meet you," she said, accepting his handshake.

"Likewise."

She smiled warmly at Frank, thankful that he clearly had her back, and took her seat again. Still jolted, she took a second to reflect on what had just transpired. She had expected something a little different—not from a professional perspective, but certainly as a young girl who had admired the rocker since she had come onto the music scene almost a decade ago. As an eighteen-year-old, Chris had marveled at the star who instantaneously took the world by storm.

On stage, Raven transformed before her eyes. Gone was the sullen and quietly combative woman she had just met and in her place stood someone confident and fun-loving—the woman she admired. Clad in nothing more than a pair of jeans, a pair of Converse and a plain red V-neck T-shirt, she looked stunning—even more so than she usually did, with her hair and makeup perfected for the stage.

"It's about time you got out of bed," her drummer teased.

"That's enough out of you, stick boy," she shot back, sticking her tongue out at him childlike, innocent and free from the pressures of the world. "I didn't have to show up early, Paul. I *know* the new song." Her voice held a tease that made the other members of the band smile as she cast her eyes to the bassist.

"That happened one time," Pete the bassist said, offering nothing more in explanation than a shrug.

"Yeah, one time," she said. "During your solo part of yesterday's practice, thus why we didn't unveil the song last night."

"I've got it down," he said good-naturedly. His sheepish grin showed hints of embarrassment. "You left me plenty of extra practice time today to get it down pat."

"Good," she said, giving him a wink. "Don't let me down." Chris watched as she turned to her guitarist. "What about you, Joe? Are we good to go?"

"You know it," he said, nodding even though he seemed somewhat nervous.

Chris couldn't help but wonder what their day-to-day lives must be like and if she was always as intimidating as she seemed this morning—or if this was just a show put on for Chris's behalf, to let everyone know that she was, indeed, the boss.

"We're ready to rock, bro," she said, nudging her guitarist on her right. "Hit it." Her voice came out as more of a growl than anything and her lips curled up into a villainous grin. As the beat swelled, Chris watched in awe. Almost as if she noticed Chris's positive reaction, Raven turned her attention to the front row. "You're in for a treat, PR lady," she said, offering a seductive up-and-down look and winking. "You're about to hear the song we finished on the road just a few weeks ago and it's going to rock your world."

Despite her better judgment Chris smiled back. She didn't want to fuel the fire of Raven's arrogance, but she felt helpless against it. Her charm dripped off her every word, even in condescension, and Chris knew that's how she always got her way.

The drumbeat had her entranced already and when the guitar joined in, Chris knew she *was* in for a treat. The music came alive around her, reverberating off the walls and making the huge stadium feel more like a grunge garage—quaint, yet rebellious.

"Who are you," Raven sang the opening lines, closing her eyes and moving to the beat. Gone was the chip on her shoulder. This was real. This was what people needed to see off stage. "Who are you to tell me how to live my life?"

As the beat intensified, Chris listened to the words, uncertain if they had been directed at the backlash of her latest scandal, or if they were about something deeper. As the chorus neared, Raven was half-screaming, half-growling the lyrics, her deep, throaty voice striking every chord within Chris's body.

"Maybe if you looked inside," she sang, making the deep notes seem effortless as she jumped up and down to the beat onstage. "Maybe if you looked inside yourself for once, maybe you'd see what I see, yeah maybe you'd see, that you're the same as me."

The words seemed to ignite something within Raven as she gave a full performance to an empty stadium. When she turned her eyes in Chris's direction, Chris could have sworn they seemed to catch fire and burn into her soul. "Maybe you'd see there's a demon in you, yeah I can see clearly, it's the same one that's eating at me."

Raven sang out, letting her voice reach its deepest octave. "Staring at us in the mirror, those bloodshot eyes, a cold ghost of what was, try my demons on for size."

When the guitar solo took over, Raven cast her one final, unreadable glance before moving to work the other side of the stage. Even without a crowd, she was in the moment, focusing her entire being into perfecting her routine. Chris hoped that, at some point in the future, Raven would dedicate as much energy and investment into her persona, her people skills, as she did at perfecting her craft. Regardless, she had to admire everything about the performance—and the words that she knew had come directly from Raven.

Chris was a fan of singer-songwriters and that had been one of her major draws to Raven early on. Every lyric was penned by the rocker herself and every word of this song seemed to scream a cry to be understood, to be left alone and to express her inner turmoil.

Raven sang, her eyes closed as she moved to the beat.

As the song came to a close, Raven and her guitarist stood back to back, both pouring every bit of themselves into the last notes.

"So, what do you think?" Raven asked, raising an eyebrow in Chris's direction.

Put on the spot, Chris wanted to say that she saw a rare vulnerability in Raven's questioning smile as she waited for an answer. However she quickly decided to forgo *that* response, knowing it would only alienate her from Raven even further.

"It's powerful," she said. "It's the ultimate, 'fuck off, I do my own thing' anthem, jazzed up a bit with a little bit of fun and made much deeper with the fact that you're drawing a parallel with the struggles we each face."

Raven eyed her quizzically for a moment, keeping her eyebrow raised. Finally, she nodded. "I like the analysis," she said slowly. "Thanks."

Raven seemed to work hard to keep her tone neutral and her expression cool, but Chris could tell the compliment had meant something. Raven's eyes shone brighter, despite her tight-lipped nod. Chris shook her head, wishing the rocker didn't feel such a need—for whatever reason—to shut herself away from showing any emotion. She seemed bitter. That much was crystal clear. What could leave someone with the world at her fingertips angry enough to push away gratitude for a compliment?

Raven had left Chris's mind reeling. Throughout the rest of the rehearsal, Raven ignored Chris, going on with the show as if no one but the band was present. Chris hoped that would stick. She didn't want to be the outsider, the one who disturbed the process. She wanted to blend, to become part of the team, at least for the time being until she could handle Raven's affairs from afar. As it was now, she was on the road for an indeterminate time and was going to have to make the best of it.

"However long it takes to fix it, that's how long you'll be gone." She replayed her boss's words in her head. Judging by the awkwardness so far, she hoped she could pull out her Wonder Woman skills and right this wrong quickly, so she could go back home and return to admiring the singer from a distance. Currently, Raven was a little like a bear—cool from a distance, but more than a little unnerving up close.

"And that's a wrap," Raven said after the last song. "Raven out," she said dramatically, dropping the microphone from her hands with a smile.

"You've got to stop doing that," her guitar player said, swooping in behind her to grab it from the ground. "I get to listen to the sound guys bitch about it every time."

"It's fun," she shot back as she exited the stage. "I've got to meet with Frank anyway and we all know I can't keep him waiting."

On stage, Paul the drummer moved close to Raven's side for a hushed conversation. After a moment, Raven nodded and pulled him in for a hug. Curious, Chris watched the interaction, likening the pair's interaction to siblings.

"I'm ready Frank," Raven called out, nodding in his direction.

Chris watched as Frank let out a sigh beside her and she wondered what made him stick around. It couldn't be the money. He was one of the most sought-after agents in the business and could be with anyone he wanted. But he stayed, taking what could only be described as the ribbing a daughter would give her doting but overprotective father.

He stood and went to meet Raven as she exited the stage.

"How was it?" she asked quietly, but not quietly enough to be out of Chris's earshot.

"You did great," he said, placing a hand on her shoulder. "I love the new stuff."

As Chris observed the exchange she tried to piece it together. In order to do her job—and to settle her curiosity—she needed some answers. She needed to cut through the bullshit and find the source of problems, figure out what made Raven tick and determine how Frank and her band seemed to be able to get past Raven's veil of bitterness. That was exactly what she needed to tap into to gain her trust and show the public a softer side.

Even from an outsider's point of view, it was clear that Frank and Raven fulfilled something within each other—something that presumably they didn't get elsewhere. Everything she had seen and read on the band from their quirky social media posts to the behind-the-scenes videos they often shared seemed to suggest the entire band formed a dysfunctional family unit. It appeared to her that Frank also played a role in the family. When they turned to walk in her direction, she had more questions than answers, but figured those would come with time. For the time being, she had a job to do and she was going in blind.

"Let's all go grab a drink," Frank said as they approached Chris, still sitting. "We can talk and get to know each other a little bit."

"Are you going to make me look good?" Raven asked, her mood somewhat softer now, but still holding an edge.

"I have every intention to do just that—but more than that, I'll help you look good to yourself," Chris said, smiling and hoping that Raven felt her sincerity. She wanted to do more than offer a publicity stunt. She always wanted more. She wanted to actually help people help themselves.

Raven nodded at her and turned to walk back toward the bus. "I like her more than the last guy," Raven said to Frank, talking about Chris as though she wasn't there. "At least she's not a stammering idiot in a suit telling me to go to church."

Frank laughed and shook his head. "You'll have to excuse her," he said. "She's a little rough on newcomers, a little untrusting."

"She says 'fuck,' and she's not afraid of an afternoon drink," Raven said, continuing her verbal assessment. "She's not nearly as bad as the guy who said no drinking before a show."

"Was he Puritan or something?" Chris asked, loudly enough for Raven to hear, several paces ahead of them already.

Without turning around, Raven let out a laugh. The sound rang through the air, making Chris smile. She felt she had made a connection with the woman.

"Something like that," Raven said. "I'm going to stop by my room. I'll meet you both outside on the side patio in a bit."

"She sure knows her way around the place," Chris commented to Frank as she scanned the area for a patio. Finally up ahead in the distance, she spotted a couple of umbrellas.

"She's been around this circuit for a while. She knows pretty much every venue big and small and this is one of her favorites. It's a large venue that brings a crowd of rock fanatics," he said with a shrug. "In no form or fashion is she new to this. It's just that lately she's found herself in a bit of trouble."

"Why is it all so recent?" Chris asked. "I mean, was she always this heavy into partying?"

"Partying, yes," he said, his gray eyes darkening and his worry lines increasing. "They all are. Partying is one thing, but this, not so much."

"Do you know why it's been a recent thing?"

The question hung in the air as Frank shook his head. He opened his mouth as if to speak, but shut it quickly. One thing was clear. Whatever Frank knew, it was between him and Raven. His loyalty kept his lips tightly shut. And whatever he knew, she was going to have to either figure it out on her own—or just do her job the best she could while being kept in the dark.

Keeping pace with Frank, she let him take the lead when they reached the patio. He crossed the concrete and tapped gently on the concession stand window.

"We're closed until six," a woman's voice called, before briefly opening the window and glancing out. "Oh, hey Frank," she said, her smile stretching across her weathered but kind face. Her blue eyes lit up and Chris noted how she looked like someone's good-natured grandma. "How have you been?"

"Pretty good," he said, smiling at her in return. "Could we grab a few beers?"

"Anything for my favorites," she said, "I'll bring out a pitcher in a minute. Y'all go ahead and take a seat."

"They must retain concession stand workers pretty well," Chris noted as they took a seat.

"That's not a concession stand worker," Frank said, smiling at her. "That's Connie. She's the general manager of the grounds here. She just pitches in and helps with all set up. That's kind of the Texas way. But I'm sure you're used to that in Houston."

"I get it," Chris said, the statement about Texas warming her heart. "I'm from Texas—born and raised. My dad was also from Texas and that's kind of how he approached life. Her kindness reminds me of him."

Nostalgia washed over her, taking her back to when her dad was just a phone call away and when her favorite singer was a muse in her mind, instead of a mouthy pain in her ass. Shaking the thoughts aside, she followed Frank's gaze to Raven walking up to meet them.

"She really is a good girl at heart," he said quietly.

"I know she is," Chris agreed. "I just want her to know it as well."

"You and me both," he said, before directing his attention to Connie as she brought them out a pitcher and glasses.

As he thanked her, Raven took a seat next to Frank and directly across from Chris. The intensity with which she stared was marred only slightly by the way her eyes glassed over after a second. She opened her mouth like she was going to speak, but suddenly burst into a fit of giggles, proving what Chris knew to be true. This was going to be unlike any job she had ever taken on.

CHAPTER THREE

Staring across the table, Raven took in the woman who had flown in to save the day like a superhero. She wanted to hate her, but her bright eyes and unassuming smile made that difficult from the get-go. Chris ran her fingers through her perfectly straight and chicly styled blond hair and Raven watched, even more perplexed.

She had to admit that instead of hating her, she was intrigued. There was an innocence behind the southern drawl that had drawn Raven in like a bee to honey. She wanted to know more about her and she wanted to talk to her one-on-one. She wanted to see what made those eyes light up, to be the one behind that smile. But she also knew that doing so would be playing with fire. This woman wasn't on her side. She was the enemy. And even if she was attractive, she was the one who had come—like they all did—to change her, to make her more presentable.

"So what's on the agenda?" she asked, giving her curiosity a break. Pouring a beer, she glanced from Christina to Frank, waiting on one of them to speak. "Isn't this the part where you want to know all about me, where you ask me a million questions and then tell me to straighten up?"

The hesitancy in Christina's eyes made her look like a wrangler, gently approaching a wild beast. Raven wasn't sure if she should be flattered or insulted by the look. She chose to take it as a compliment and proceeded. "I'll save you some of your questions," she said when neither of them spoke up. "Yes, I drink. I occasionally smoke, if the drinking has hit me just right. Yes, I've done a drug or two in the past." She had grown used to the lie. "No, I'm not addicted to any substances. Yes, I occasionally sleep around, but so does any woman and it's not anyone's business who I fuck. Yes, I sleep with women—and the occasional man, if it suits my mood. No, I don't plan on changing. Yes, I'll continue to say 'fuck' in my songs and yes, I plan on having a drink or two before I hit the stage. Did I cover it all?"

"I already knew all of that," Christina said with a shrug. "But I didn't come here to badger you with questions."

"Why did you come here then?" Raven asked, wanting nothing more than to be left alone—or to have met Christina in some other circumstance. As she watched Christina lick her lips, her mind went wild with what it would feel like to have those soft and plump, pink lips pressed up against hers.

"I came here because you need public relations help," Christina said, breaking through Raven's musings. "I came here because I rebuild images. It's my job. I don't change people. I don't give orders. I don't make any adjustments other than rebuilding a flawed image."

"Make me look good then," Raven said, the words coming across more like a challenge than anything. "Make me *look* good, but don't ever ask me to change." She lifted her glass in a mock "cheers" effort and then gulped it down before pouring another. "I refuse to change. I am who I am and that's what I tell all these girls to hold true to. People look up to me for that. And it's not about that, but it's about being the voice of being who you are. Since I rose to fame, that's what I've preached. It's what I've always believed. I'm the spokesperson for the weirdos, for the girls with guitars, for the kids who don't quite fit in or know where their place in this world is, for the people who—even as adults—just don't quite fit the molds of society. I'm that and I won't ever change. I'm a firm believer in letting those quirks define you, not in letting society change you. For that reason, I'll be great with measures that make me look good, as long as looking good doesn't change who I am."

"I wouldn't ask you to change," Chris said slowly. "You're the woman who has entranced millions, the one who has helped girls across the nation deal with heartache or find their own identity or their own unique way of expressing themselves. You're the face on posters in countless rooms, I'm sure, and millions have fallen in love with your music and your form of expression. I wouldn't change that."

"You sound like you think you know me," Raven said, tilting her head and casting her eyes over the rims of her aviator sunglasses to look at Chris.

"No," she said, offering a smile and deepening the moment of eye contact. "I just know some girls who benefitted from your music and I want to make sure you stay true to that image, to that pedestal that so many put you on."

For a second, Raven nodded her head, but the agreeable behavior wasn't to be long-lived. She still didn't like this. She had heard too many sugarcoated speeches from PR reps to buy this. Even though this one seemed sincere and even though her sea-green eyes sparkled in the sunlight, she couldn't let herself be duped into believing that it was different. They all started like this—grand promises and soppy words. But if you gave them an inch, they took a mile and before long, they wanted to parade her out into the world in a dress, at the White House, hosting parties at schools, you name it. This wasn't going to be any different. Without another word, she pushed her glasses back up on her nose.

"Do we want to talk about guidelines or boundaries?" Frank asked after letting the silence hang for a moment.

"Boundaries?" Raven asked, turning in her chair to face Frank.

"Yeah, boundaries," he said, nodding decisively. "After this stop, you'll both be staying on the bus, which even though it's luxurious and has some private space, we all know it can get a little cramped. Chris, you will be pleasantly surprised though. I have been in the industry a long time and I have spent a lot of time on buses. This one is the best there is. Custom built. If you were imagining bunk beds and weird couch sleeping situations, you don't have to worry about that. We have rooms and it's probably the biggest bus you'll see on the road, ever—at least in our time.

"While you will have places to retreat to and to recoup, it *is* cramped. Pete, the bass player, and Joe, the lead guitar, agreed to bunk up in order to give you a room of your own, so you will have space. Paul, the drummer, will keep his space. But when I say you have your own room, I'd like you to imagine a closet. You will have your own closet-sized space, but you will have your *own* space. I just want you to be prepared for how you will be traveling. It'll give the two of you a chance to connect. It always makes for better PR when someone knows your goals and motivators. Nonetheless, Raven, if you want to set times where you need your own time, let's lay those out on the table, just so we don't have any disruption or frustration."

Raven glanced sideways in Chris's direction, considering the thought. She had set times when the last PR guy wasn't to be allowed in her bus, like right after a show when she was entertaining those she had selected as VIP guests or taking a minute or two to come down from the exhilaration of performing. This woman seemed to be able to take things in stride though and Raven wanted to see if she was really up to the test. She clenched her jaw, weighing her answer. If this woman really was going to last, which Raven doubted, she was going to have to be all in or all out. Raven was up for the challenge of making her run for the hills—as long as Christina was up for the challenge of sticking around.

"She can come and go as she pleases," Raven said, addressing Frank, and purposely leaving Christina out of the discussion. "It's going to be her home for the next little bit anyway, or for as long as she chooses to stay. At her discretion. Whatever she thinks she's game for seeing or experiencing, she's welcome to join in."

Frank's eyebrows knitted together in obvious concern, but Raven ignored it. If there was something she didn't want to see, she was going to have to be smart enough to keep her distance at times. He gave her his infamous "no nonsense" look and she smiled in return, reading his unspoken warning.

"Don't set traps for her," she could hear him saying, as he had said time and time again to her about various "helpers" they brought along.

"It will be fine," she said, answering before he could voice anything. "I think she's up for it." She winked at him, before turning back to face Christina.

Christina's demeanor hadn't changed and she remained smiling. "I'm up for anything," she said, her true feelings easily slipping through the false bravado, as her words squeaked out an octave too high. "I wouldn't have taken this job if I wasn't up for a challenge or an exciting ride."

Raven knew that the words held a jab at her, but instead of being offended, she was pleased that, if nothing else, this one could match her wit with a little backbone. Even more than that, she was happy that Christina didn't think it would be a walk in the park. That had been a downfall of many before her.

"Let's do it, Christina," she said, reaching across the table to shake on the deal.

"Call me Chris, please," she said, returning the handshake.

As her fingers entangled in Chris's, she felt an electrifying shock race through her body, leaving every nerve tingling. Chris's hand gripped hers tightly and she briefly considered hanging on to the touch, but relented and let go.

Frank cleared his throat, bringing Raven out of the moment. She felt a flush sweep across her cheeks and was thankful for the large lenses of her sunglasses.

"I guess I should be going to get my head in the game and get ready for tonight," she said, chugging the rest of her second beer and standing. She gave Chris one last look before turning to walk back to the bus. She wanted to linger, to ask more and she wanted Frank to leave the two of them alone for a bit.

"In a different time and a different place," she whispered to herself, forcing her mind to view Chris as what she was—not as what Raven would like her to be.

Nonetheless, as she crossed the distance across the parking lot, she couldn't help but replay Chris's southern drawl in her mind and revel in the apparent gentleness—combined with just enough sass and tough edges—of the woman.

Once inside the sanctuary of her bus, she was relieved to find Pete sitting on the couch.

"Are you all finished up and ready to rock?" she asked, taking a seat beside him.

"We're ready," he said, offering her a swig of the bottle of whiskey in his lap.

"Not right now," she said, waving it away. "Thanks, though."

He looked at her curiously, prompting further response.

"I just want to make sure I'm on top of it all tonight," she said, shrugging off any further questions.

Unfortunately, Pete didn't take the hint. "It's that hot PR girl, isn't it?" he asked, nudging her with his elbow and smiling from ear to ear.

"Who said she was hot?"

"I did," he said, "and so would anyone with eyes. After watching her interact with you at rehearsal, I think it's safe to say she plays for your team."

"She *definitely* plays for your team," Joe called out from the back of the bus.

"So you were listening in?" Raven asked, laughing at the way these two often teased her with a one-two punch.

"Of course I was," Joe said, sticking his head out into the hallway. "I just want the best for you. And I agree she's hot but definitely likes the ladies." He winked before disappearing.

"Thanks," Raven called down the hall. "I picked up on that as well," she said, turning her attention back to Pete. "They tried to get someone my age with shared interests. Makes you wonder if they placed an ad somewhere looking for a lesbian in her midtwenties who was attractive enough to make me walk a tighter line."

Pete's playful grin grew. "So you admit she's attractive?"

She laughed, trying to play it cooler than she felt. "It has nothing to do with her," she said. "I just like performing in Austin. It's always a rowdy crowd and they're fun. I want to give them their money's worth."

"You always do," he said, standing and heading toward the back of the bus to his small "room."

"Thanks," she called out, genuinely grateful for the compliment. Although Pete was the newest member of the band, he had been part of it for six years. Like the others, he was like a little brother—always there to lighten the mood or defend her honor as needed.

Her head still swimming, she lay back on the couch in the common area of the bus, thankful to have a moment of peace and quiet. There was no doubt that having Christina around was going to change things. It always did. It was an all-or-nothing commitment on their part and it was one that had always gone to hell in a handbasket.

Sure, she usually helped set it ablaze, but that was beside the point. The fact remained that—no matter how hot this girl might be—she didn't want her here.

She took a deep breath and started to hum the opening line of her new song, hoping the distraction would take her to another place. After mentally going through the words, she stood and grabbed the pack of cigarettes off the counter. Stepping outside, she lit one and took a deep drag. She inhaled the nicotine and let it sit deep in her lungs before exhaling a plume of smoke behind her.

The weight of her current dissatisfaction filled her to the brim and she tried to sort through the feelings. Whether it was a quarter-life crisis or something deeper, she had yet to figure out. Frank was right. She *wasn't* fine. But she still couldn't place what had sent her reeling so often for the past several months. Try as she might, she still couldn't sort through her turmoil. It was too heavy for the moment, so she took another drag wishing the burden of failures to leave her be.

She heard the footsteps before she saw Christina's approach and she felt her nerves tighten.

"Please don't start in on how bad this looks on my image," she said, turning around to face the newcomer. "It's futile."

"No," Christina said, offering a shrug and a gentle smile. "I was actually going to ask if you had an extra."

"You smoke?" Raven asked, narrowing her eyes to look the woman up and down.

"I quit," she answered, the dimple on her cheek lighting up in a mischievous smile. "At least that's what I tell people. I stopped about five months ago, but every now and then, when I'm stressed out, I crave one. I smelled it and I came to see if whoever had that smoky goodness could spare one."

Still confused, but more than willing to cooperate, Raven pulled one from the pack and handed it over, lighting it once Christina had pressed it to her lips. Seeing her lips wrapped around the cigarette made Raven's mind run wild again. She wondered if they felt as soft as they looked and if that sweet smile was even sweeter when they pulled away from a kiss.

"Thank you," Christina said, taking a long drag and offering her a smile.

"So, I'm guessing there won't be any of the talk about how I should put on a better front for the kids and not smoke?"

Christina shook her head, taking another drag. "Not from me," she said, exhaling. "I mean, I believe that everyone makes adult decisions. I'm not here to transform you. I'm just here to make sure that the public sees the best sides of you and that parents aren't running and screaming, ready to reenact the Salem Witch Trials after their kids come to see one of your shows."

"What classifies as an adult decision?" She knew she was playing devil's advocate, but if this woman was the real deal, the one who was going to stick around, she was going to have to be up to the job.

"I suppose that depends on who you ask," Christina answered, her words coming slowly, thoughtfully, as if she was taking extra care to place them just right. Raven appreciated the gesture, waiting patiently as Christina took her time. "I'd say that an adult decision can be anything really, anything that we would rather not have the public be a part of. You are an adult and you can do what you please, but there are some things that we don't often showcase to the younger generation—drinking heavily, drug use, smoking, casual sex and the like. I want you to be you, but it doesn't really matter what I want, because it's your life. It's just my job to try to deliver a positive image to the public. What goes on behind closed doors doesn't really matter, unless it gets out into the public eye."

"Are you talking about the thing with Snapchat?"

"Among others, yes," Christina said, nodding and looking away for a moment.

"I know it looked bad," Raven said, sighing heavily. "But I won't apologize for it."

"We don't have to talk about it now," Christina said, holding her hands up to stop Raven's explanation. "In fact, I don't want to talk about it before your show. I want you to be at the top tonight, ready to go. We can talk tomorrow and we'll hold a strategy session. We can determine what you are and are not willing to do from the things I propose before we tackle any of it."

Raven wanted to believe her, but she couldn't. She just shook her head. "Fine. But I'm not apologizing. I didn't do anything wrong."

Raven saw a faint flicker of defiance in the woman's eyes, but Christina formed her lips in a tight line and nodded. "I'll see you after the show," she said. "Thanks again for the smoke." With that, she turned in the opposite direction, her cigarette still in hand.

Her frustration grew with each step Christina took away from her. She wanted to understand the woman like she understood most people. At the core, she believed that most people were fairly one-dimensional, but there was far more to Christina and her gentle approach.

She threw the cigarette on the ground and smashed it under her sneaker, shaking her head and hoping that, at some point, the earth beneath her would feel a little steadier than it had today.

Ever since Christina arrived, everything seemed tilted, muddled and unsure. And she felt as though she had even more to deal with internally than she had when she woke this morning.

* * *

Surrounded by the haze from the fog machine, she closed her eyes and took a deep breath, only to open them and revel in a sight of which she'd never tire. Smoke curling around her face and seeming to dance in the light as the show kicked up, she let herself feel it, let herself get lost in the beat of the drum, in the swirl of neon lights accosting the crowd.

With Paul kicking off the show in a drum solo, she felt it all in the depths of her being—every beat, every light flash, every second a reminder that she was right where she belonged. Tapping her foot and beating the microphone against her leg in sync with the drum, Raven knew that this was going to be an incredible night—one for the books. She allowed herself a glance to the front row for affirmation and she knew that her feelings were justified.

Swaying to the beat and grinning from ear to ear, she saw a group of young women tapping their beer cups against each other, basking in what could only be described as unadulterated ecstasy. Joe and Pete joined in, making the music swell and come to life. Not wanting to dull the pulse of electricity raging through her body, her mind betrayed her and curiosity won out as she glanced back to her "VIP" guest of the evening. She looked to the right of the stage, willing those concerned, but striking green eyes out of her mind. When she couldn't shake the memory of how they had bored into her soul earlier in the day, as if she was reading every thought and instead of judging, asking nicely to be let inside, she glanced to find Christina in the crowd.

As she searched, she recalled Christina's words about trying to be the person her fans thought she was. She remembered the sadness in her expression as she had turned away, cigarette in hand, knowing that Raven was exactly who Christina didn't want her to be. Like a moth to a flame, she spotted her at the left of the stage. She masked her move with a covert wink to an enamored male fan in the front row and continued to tap her foot along to the beat of Paul's pounding on the drum.

There, in the middle section of the front row, she fixed her eyes on what was quite possibly the most intriguing, most perplexing and most beautiful sight she had ever seen. Closing her eyes and moving with the music, Christina was on her feet, wearing a smile comparable to that of a child at Disney World for the first time. If there had ever been an inspiration factor—a muse—Raven was pretty sure she had just locked in on it.

Thankful for her cue, she needed no further urging. Belting from a deeper place than any she'd felt in recent years, she immersed herself in the music.

"Tonight," she sang, letting her raspy voice hang in the air, reverberating in the smoky haze. "Let's burn it down, let's forget the price of fame."

As she sang, she simply couldn't fight the urge to look back at Christina's section. To her surprise—and much to her enjoyment—Christina looked more at home than Raven had seen her so far. Gone was the out-of-place and uncertain woman filling the PR job, and in her place was a confident woman, at one with herself and the music. Her blond hair was swaying and no longer perfectly in place as she danced, and her face was the symbol of pure joy as she sang along, never missing a beat. The woman was free, at peace and so alive. Raven was certain she had never seen a more emblematic vision of what it meant to feel the music.

"Let's get lost in it all, get lost in nothing short of you screaming my name," she sang out, for the first time singing to one person and only one person, caring only that Christina felt the words. As though the entire crowd had faded into the distance, she stared, riveted by her newly discovered muse. She serenaded Christina as though she was singing the last song that would ever cross her lips.

Completely unfazed by Raven's attention, Christina was oblivious, seemingly lost in the music and entirely unaware of how she had enraptured the star of the show. Fueled by her apparent disinterest, Raven moved closer to the edge of the stage. Moving her body sultrily to the rhythm, Raven's voice easily cascaded over the sensual lyrics of one of her favorite numbers.

She crooned and with each line, she rotated her hips with the words. "Don't waste a minute baby, grab the gasoline, 'cause I know this destruction is what you love, you love seeing me come undone; light it up, watch it burn, rip the sheets, make me squirm. Light it up, make it rage, let's blow up the night, with you calling my name."

When Christina finally looked in her direction, Raven felt her body flare, turned on by the admiration of those sparkling green eyes.

Biting her lip during the guitar solo, she watched as Christina continued to enjoy the show, undeterred by Raven's undivided attention. As Raven danced across the stage, the two locked eyes. When the final beats hit, she winked and turned her back, reluctantly understanding she had to entertain an entire crowd tonight. Briefly glancing back over her shoulder, she took in the depth of Christina's smile and knew she would do everything in her power to have the woman as an audience of one—at some point. For now, she had a few more songs to sing and she had a crowd full of screaming fans.

From the back of the VIP seating section, she heard the first of what would likely be many marriage proposals of the night. "Marry me, Raven!" a man called out from the right of the stage. She shimmied her chest in response and pulled the microphone up to her lips.

"Maybe," she said, huskily. "We'll talk about your benefits backstage after the show and see if this truly is a match made in heaven." With a wink, she shot Paul a nod, urging him to move forward with the next song, as the crowd erupted in laughter.

Through her regular set list, she felt at one with the crowd, completely at ease with everything. She was invigorated by the crowd's urging, their swaying during her ballads, their jumping in her fast-paced rocker jams, their admiring eyes intent on her performance, their sheer awe with how the band meshed. As she performed, it was as if the rest of the world slipped away and all that mattered was the music. When it came time for the new song, she nodded to the boys, smiling and giving them her best silent encouragement.

"You all are in for a treat," she said into the microphone, her voice somewhat hoarse from having added a few extra growls and yells for the crowd. Texas masses required a little more oomph than some. "We're about to share something with you that only our bus guys, sound crew and a few others have been privy to. How do you feel about that, Austin?"

She waited, urged on by hundreds of screaming voices. "Good," she said, smiling widely at the crowd. "That's what I was hoping you'd say. In that case, here's our latest song. It's a heartwarming little ditty called 'Demons,' and I think it might just bring a tear to your eye." She paused for a moment to let her joke resonate. "On second thought, fuck that. It might just make you get up on your feet and sing out like the freaks that you are."

Anticipation tingled her every nerve and she felt high as she glanced from face-to-face in the crowd. These moments—about to unveil something that she had poured her heart and soul into—were always a bit exhilarating, yet laden with anxiety.

"*You are Raven*," she spoke the words within her head. "*It doesn't matter what they think.*"

As if on cue, Paul hit the drum. She closed her eyes and let herself get lost, putting aside everything—the struggles of the past few weeks, the pressure, her own ego and definitely the thought of those hauntingly gorgeous green eyes. Tonight, she was here to do her job. She was here to entertain and to amaze.

CHAPTER FOUR

Even though the stadium lights had come on and the band had long since left the stage, Chris couldn't bring herself to move from her seat. Around her, she heard people shuffling to the exit, yet she stayed sitting, staring dumbfounded at the stage.

It was no wonder people across the globe fell in love—or at least in lust—with Raven. The adrenaline from the talent and magnetism she had just witnessed still coursed within her, making her question how she had never made it to one of Raven's concerts before. From beginning to end, slow to fast songs and through each ebb and flow, each interaction with the audience, Raven had bared her soul to her audience. Perhaps this was the only way she could interact openly and honestly.

Raven had probably made every fan in the room feel as if she was singing directly to them, as if she was their best friend. It was a feeling that Chris wished she could hold onto. As she looked at the microphone stand that had been in Raven's hand, she wondered how one person could hold so much charisma and such pure talent—and be a such a spoiled brat.

Though she wanted to hold Raven on a pedestal, Chris figured it would be much healthier—and much wiser for her sanity's sake—to recall how guarded, bitter and rough around the edges Raven could be in person.

Bringing herself back to the moment, she glanced around to see that the seats around her were mostly empty. At the end of her row, a man looked as stunned as she felt and it seemed that he wouldn't be moving from his spot anytime soon. She laughed to herself, shaking her head and again wondering what it was that the girl had that made everyone so crazy.

Making her way to the bus, Chris found herself singing along to one of Raven's sexier songs. As the lyric "rip the sheets" came off her tongue, she forced herself to stop and straightened her shoulders. She was not here to be a fan or to be sucked into the bizarre situation. She was here to do a job—to make the rest of the world see a new side of the bad girl who had given voice to their inner turmoil and made them all think about walking on the wild side. Though they resonated with her rebellion, she needed them to see a cleaner image and a well-rounded woman—not just an edgy and talented, but damaged rocker.

At the tour bus, Chris wasn't quite sure what to do. This was going to be her place of residence soon, but she wasn't sure if she should just go straight to her hotel room for the night or stop in to congratulate Raven on a great show. Standing outside, she listened to the blaring music inside and heard a mix of excited voices. She looked around, wishing there was some sort of rule book for how to respond in these situations, or at least wishing she wasn't so awkward right now.

"Got a light?" she heard a man's voice in the darkness to the left.

She jumped, startled out of her own thoughts, glancing in the direction of the voice and relieved to find Paul the drummer standing beside the bus. His lanky frame leaned against one of the tires as he ran his hand through his shaggy, sandy-blond hair. He smiled, looking every bit like the goofy boy-next-door, which put her at ease. She laughed at her jumpiness and reached into her pocket, fishing out the lighter she had pulled from her purse on the off chance that it might make her more relatable to the crew. She had watched enough of their videos and behind-the-scenes footage to know they all smoked, so had come prepared.

"I've got a light, if you've got an extra cigarette."

"Fair trade," he said, flicking one out of the pack and handing it to her in one smooth motion.

"Thanks," she said, offering him a light before lighting her own cigarette.

"What did you think of the show?" he asked, standing beside her. Even in the darkness, she noted how at ease he looked, as though posing for an album cover. Despite his tall and thin frame that would have looked awkward on most, he was poised and held a smile that spoke volumes about his self-confidence. She wondered whether this coolness was something that they were all born with, or something they adopted as they spent more time together living the rock star life.

"I've been to a lot of concerts," she said, taking a deep drag and exhaling it. "But none have ever moved me quite like tonight's. It was the most incredible show I've ever seen."

"Glad to hear it," he said. She admired the way his smile lit up like a little boy's grin. "We've hit a really good meshing point lately and it's made for better shows than we've ever put on before. I'm happy to hear that you really enjoyed it."

"Well thanks for putting on a great show," she said, nodding her head in approval.

"She's pretty amazing, isn't she?" he asked, as if sensing the direction of Chris's thoughts.

"That she is," Chris admitted, unsure of how much she should actually say, but deciding that she might as well befriend the band guys as well since she was going to be cohabitating with all of them soon enough. "She really knows how to give the crowd everything they wanted—and perhaps a whole lot more than they ever anticipated."

"She knows how to give that to us too," he said with a laugh. "Just wait until you're on the bus every night. I'm sure you'll catch a glimpse of it tonight at the after-show bus party, but you'll be in for a treat when you get to experience her full force. She's goofy, fun-loving and sweet and she will shock the pants off you that way. She's so much more than she ever lets any of the others see, but I'm sure you'll get to see it."

"I hope so," Chris said, a smile taking over her lips. "I want everyone to have the chance to see her at her truest self. I want for her to stop hiding behind a façade of bitterness."

"Oh, she's plenty bitter too," Paul said. "But there's a softness beyond that shell. Come on in and you'll see."

"I don't know if I should," Chris said, her earlier qualms recurring.

"Of course you should," he said, shrugging. "It's the after-party. You don't want to miss it."

"I don't even know if I'm invited," she said, her brows furrowing, as she felt every bit like the awkward kid in junior high who wasn't invited to the dance.

"We don't throw invitations out around here." She heard a husky female voice behind her and turned to stare into Raven's dark brown eyes. "You're one of us for now. That means you're invited. Now, come on in and party your ass off."

Chris wanted to retort but bit her tongue. Instead, she opted for a smile, crushed her cigarette on the ground and followed Raven into the bus. She glanced back at Paul, who simply nodded and winked at her, as if to reassure her she was making the right decision.

Even though she had heard all the commotion coming from the bus, she wasn't prepared when the door swung open. Inside there were far too many bodies crammed into the small space. Feeling as if she was at a nightclub, she marveled at how much the simple bus had been transformed. There were people smoking a joint on the couch, and others grinding together to the fast-paced music streaming out of multiple speakers. Raven was greeted by adulation wherever she walked.

"Want a drink?" Raven called back at her as Chris stood in the doorway.

No longer caring whether or not it was professional, she knew she *needed* a drink. She ignored her inner turmoil and nodded.

"Come on then," Raven said, waving her over to where she stood in a mix of people. Chris obeyed the order and made her way through the mess of writhing bodies until she stood next to Raven at the bar. "What would you like?" Raven asked. Before Chris could answer, she felt Raven's arm go around her waist and pull her in close. Her breath caught in the back of her throat and her heart pounded. Feeling intoxicated, she looked around and saw that Raven had merely saved her from being crashed into by what could only be described as a drunk frat boy on the loose.

"Careful, Justin," Raven called out. "How many times have we had to tell you not to accost the pretty girls?"

"Friend of yours?" Chris asked with a laugh.

"No," Raven said, shaking her head and lowering her voice so no one else could hear. She leaned in closer and whispered in Chris's ear. "He's one of our roadies and he's a little out of control."

"Oh," Chris said, nodding her head, even though she wanted to ask if any of them were really *in* control.

"Anyway, now that I saved you," she said with a wink, "what can I mix up for you?"

"Tequila," Chris said, not wanting to step too far outside her comfort zone.

"Tequila and what?" Raven asked, a smile spreading across her lips.

"Tequila and lime on the rocks," Chris answered, noting the glimmer of amusement in Raven's eyes.

"Sounds like a party girl drink to me," Raven said, nodding in approval. "I like it."

"I've always figured, why mix when you could drink something good enough to stand alone," Chris said, having experienced the reaction to her favorite drink quite often. "If something is good enough, it doesn't need a mixer."

"I'll trust your judgment on that and mix myself one too," Raven said, grabbing the bottle. Chris's eyes widened at the sight of the bottle of Don Julio Real.

"She's a rock star. Of course she can afford a three-hundred-dollar tequila." Chris silently reminded herself where she was and

wiped her sweaty palms on her pants. She watched closely as Raven mixed the two drinks.

"Cheers," Raven said, clinking her glass to Chris's.

Chris reciprocated, smiled and took a drink. "God that's good," she said, bringing the glass back down from her lips.

"Yeah. It is," Raven responded, her voice somewhat breathless. "Hot."

"What?" Chris asked, certain she had misunderstood her words.

"Nothing," Raven answered, her words tumbling out quickly. "You can hang out with me if you feel more comfortable, or you can make some friends. Your call, but either way, welcome to my party."

"Thank you," Chris said, glancing around the small space to view her options. "I'll hang out with you for a while."

"Good," Raven said, seeming truly happy about the prospect. "Let's introduce you around."

Thinking she was going to shake a few hands and make small talk, Chris followed her until she stopped at the front of the bus.

"Everyone, listen up," Raven called, her raspy voice sending Chris's heart into flutters, making her feel like a frightened child. "I want to introduce you all to Christina. She's a new part of the crew and she'll be with us for a while, so everyone make her feel welcome."

There were a slew of "Hey Christina," and "Hey girl," greetings but she felt out of place. Although she had attended her share of big-name parties, this was a different breed of partiers. She stood and smiled, even though she felt like she had been thrown to the wolves. Perhaps this was some kind of test by Raven to see if she would make the cut. Straightening her shoulders, she nodded around the room, making eye contact with her new acquaintances. It was time to cue on her skills typically used for addressing crowds, talking with the press or meeting new people, regardless of how different these people might be from her normal environment. "Hey everyone," she called confidently before taking her seat.

"There you go," Raven said, reaching down and patting her on the shoulder. The touch put Chris at ease as Raven's intentions became clearer. Not malicious but welcoming. “You’re one of us. If you want to make that last, blend in. Make friends and be one of us.”

Chris nodded and she couldn’t quite tell what switch had flipped, changing Raven from cold to warm so suddenly over the course of the show, but she genuinely felt welcomed into this strange new world. She finished up her tequila, much to Raven’s delight.

“Want one more and then we’ll go dance?” Raven asked, before downing her own drink and heading for the bar. She gave no time to hesitate or resist the offer, so Chris took the drink once it was poured. “Good girl,” Raven said. “Now, let’s dance.”

As Raven pulled her to the tiny area where everyone was dancing, she heard the clamor around her. “It’s time,” a man’s voice yelled. “Put on the song.”

“What song?” Chris asked, leaning closer to Raven, noting the electricity that pulsed through her veins at the sheer touch of her hand.

“My *favorite* song,” Raven said.

“Cherry Pie” by Warrant flooded through the speakers. Chris watched, delighted as Raven transformed before her eyes, downing her glass of tequila and throwing her head side to side with the beat, her long, dark-brown hair flowing through the air. Every straight teenage boy’s fantasy, Raven dropped to the ground and slid across the floor to the music, before popping back up and moving her hips seductively in Chris’s direction. She raised an eyebrow and motioned to Chris to “come over.” Chris couldn’t have resisted if she had wanted to.

Never certain of her own dance moves, Chris downed her drink and danced over. Their bodies moving together, she could feel her arousal building as each move Raven made looked like raw sexual energy.

“That’s it,” Raven whispered in her ear, “move with me.”

Their hips circled to the rocking beat and Chris was no longer certain if it was the blur of the alcohol flooding her senses, or the proximity to Raven that was making her feel alive and ten feet tall.

Others danced, talked, sang and smoked around the two of them. But Chris didn't care and to her surprise, Raven seemed as entranced as she was. Time stood still as they moved in sync.

When the song came to a close, Chris felt like it had ended too soon. Forcing her breathing to return to normal, she glanced awkwardly around the bus, feeling as if she was unclothed in front of everyone. No one seemed to notice anything out of the ordinary, so she tried to relax. She had just been dancing—nothing more. Yet if these people could have read her thoughts…

A man reached up and passed a joint to Raven, who took a deep drag.

"Thanks man," she said, offering him a devilish smile. "Want some?" she asked, offering it to Chris.

Chris considered it. She hadn't smoked pot since college. "Never mind," Raven said, before she answered. "You can have some later if you want it. I'm not going to pressure you into anything you don't want to do."

"Thanks," Chris said with a nod. She couldn't figure Raven out. She had pegged her for the peer pressure kind of person, but Raven was proving to be decent through and through. "By the way, where's the harder stuff? I thought this was supposed to be a crazed, drug-laden type of shindig."

"Sorry to disappoint," Raven said, winking again. The wink seemed to come so naturally and Chris envied it. She figured if she could wink like that, there would be little work she'd ever have to do on anything. "We're a cleaner bunch these days."

Chris raised an eyebrow and smiled. She didn't believe that for a second, but she was having a good enough time that she wasn't going to challenge the claim. "Fair enough," she said.

"I'll be back in a few," Raven said. "Have fun until then. Make yourself at home. Pour yourself some tequila, dance, party like a rock star."

Feeling a little more at ease, Chris poured another drink and took a spot next to a couple of middle-aged women on the couch.

"So you're the new girl?" one of them asked, reaching out a hand. "I'm Monica and that's my husband Todd over there," she said, pointing off to the corner of the room where a man was controlling the music. "He's one of their regular sound guys."

"Nice to meet you, Monica," Chris said, offering a smile.

"I'm Joanna," the other woman said. "Just an Austin lady out enjoying the good show and after-party."

"Nice to meet you as well," Chris said.

"What do you do?" Monica asked her, looking her up and down.

"PR," Chris said, not sure how else to put it, or if she should even try. "I just started today."

"Well, in that case, welcome to the party...and good luck," she said, raising her glass in a toasting motion. "Hopefully we will see you again down the road. We travel with the band and although we don't party like we used to, on special occasions we'll come—like tonight. For the most part, we travel in a caravan behind the bus with the rest of the crew and keep to ourselves at hotel after-parties but Austin is always such a fun show, so we thought we'd celebrate...Anyway good luck."

Chris understood the doubt that filled the silence between Monica's words, but she brushed it off knowing she was the underdog who could prove them wrong.

She made small talk with Monica and Joanna for what felt like an eternity, every once in a while glancing back toward Raven's bedroom. Her mind went wild with what could be happening behind that closed door but she forced herself to focus on something else.

When she saw Paul stand to go outside, she stood as well. Desperate for escape, she followed him outside.

"Same trade as last time?" she asked him, hoping he wouldn't see her as a mooch.

"Sounds like a deal," he said, offering her a cigarette. "Needed to get out of there?"

"Does that make me pathetic?" she asked, raising an eyebrow at him.

"Not at all," he said. "I think it makes you human. Not all of us were made to withstand that much at once. In fact, I think that's why I like smoking so much. It gives me the chance to come out here and forget about all those people—at least for a minute. Don't get me wrong, I like them and all that. I like the lifestyle, but sometimes you just need a breather, a moment to yourself to get right with the world again."

"I like that philosophy," she said. "I'm not ruining your alone time, am I?"

"No," he said, quickly dismissing the idea with a shake of his head. "You're one of us. You heard the girl in there. We'd all like you to stick around. We could use some consistency in a few areas and I think you could be the pin that holds it all together. So take your moments to yourself—or with me if you need to smoke it all away—and then go back in there confident. Don't hide, don't shirk away from it all. Just be yourself and take as many alone moments as you need to deal with it all."

"It's just a lot at once," she said. "It's kind of a different world from what I'm used to."

"What are you used to?"

"Suits, ties, skirts, heels, professional behavior, fluorescent lighting, meeting rooms, presentations, folders, being on top of your game always, never letting on that you have bad habits or vices, and everyone acting like they're a polished replica of themselves," she said with a shrug. "Sure, we recognize that we're just real people. We're not always these overinflated versions of ourselves and while there are egos to deal with, it's not like this, where one person seems to be the sun to everyone else's planet. It's more we hide behind the cape of our professional titles and our accomplishments. We don't talk about personal things, we never broach each other's personal space and it's kind of a cold, corporate life. It's nothing like this."

"And how would you define *this*?" he asked, pointing back to the bus.

"Wild," she said, shaking her head. "It's tantalizing and intoxicating—even without the booze and pot. It's like college, but with adults and it's magnetic, like it could suck you in and make you never want to leave—never want to go back to the mundane. It's a different world entirely. Even though I've only been here for a day, it feels like those suits and heels are a thing of the distant past. Here, they don't matter. And here, nothing can touch me. It's like being seventeen again, but with the freedoms and rewards that come with being an adult. It's amazing. It's also dangerous, but beautifully so, like a fire dancing on the wind."

"That was pretty damn poetic," he said, eyeing her carefully.

"I'm a wordsmith," she said, shrugging off the compliment. "It's what I get paid to do in part. I write statements and press releases that support building a positive image. It could be described as creative writing, but I also have the help of tequila tonight."

They shared a laugh and he shook his head. "You're pretty funny. You know that?"

She laughed and looked off into the distance. "I can be. You know, when I'm not out trying to play good cop, bad cop with some untouchable rock star, treading the waters between friend and ally or enemy and authority."

"You don't seem to want to be the authority," he noted.

"I don't and I'm not," she said. "I just hope she sees that."

"She will in time," he said. "She's had a rough go of it with some who have traipsed in here, vowing to save the day and only succeeding in pissing her off and ruining a few shows."

"I don't want to do that," Chris said, letting the smoke linger in her lungs.

"You won't," he said. "I have faith in you. Besides, you've immersed yourself into her world more in a day than most have done in their entire time representing her."

"What do you mean?"

He pointed to the cigarette in her hand. "You're partying with us, aren't you?"

"I hope that doesn't send the wrong signals," she said, the alcohol allowing her words to tumble out freely and unfiltered.

"Not at all," he said. "At least not to her—or to the rest of us. It shows us that you're legitimate in your promise not to change her."

"She told you about that?" Chris asked, not sure whether to be flattered that she had been the subject of band gossip or unnerved that nothing in this place was secret.

"We're a family," he said. "Especially her and me. We've been friends for a long time. Besides, although you're here for *her*, we're all kind of a package deal."

Chris nodded, taking the words for what they were. He was right. There was a very communal feel to the whole situation. From everything she had read and heard about Raven, relatives were never mentioned. In the absence of a family, Chris assumed that the band and Frank functioned as such in these close quarters. "Where did she go, by the way?" Chris asked, finally giving way to her curiosity and deciding that she could trust Paul as much as anyone else at this point.

"She's probably taking some of her 'alone time' right now," he said, using air quotes to emphasize the point.

"And what does she do in her alone time?"

"Ask her," he said. "I'd venture a guess that it changes night to night."

"Ah," Chris said, letting out a steady stream of smoke. "So alone time might not necessarily be *alone* time."

Paul smirked at her. "Jealous?"

"No," Chris answered as quickly as she could get the word out. "She's a grown woman. She can do what she pleases."

"I do think she's in there alone tonight, for what that's worth," Paul said, laughing with ease. "At least I didn't see anyone else go back there."

The door of the bus opened behind them, causing Chris to jump. She scolded herself silently, noting that she was going to have to get a better grip on remembering her surroundings, even if she had been drinking.

"Look at you," she heard Raven's voice call out, sounding like a songbird in the night. "I thought you didn't smoke much these days."

"I'm going to regret it in the morning, I'm sure," she said. "I'll end up sounding like one of those eighty-year-old ladies who hasn't left the casino in months and my throat will burn. But it just felt right in the moment."

"God, if I had a nickel for every time I've uttered that phrase," Raven said, letting out a throaty laugh as she lit up beside Chris.

They all laughed and Chris tried to still her mind's wondering just how many times Raven *had* uttered that phrase. She decided she didn't want to dwell on that thought. There would be no circumstance under which developing anything more than a professional relationship with Raven would be acceptable.

"Are you enjoying your first big party?" Raven asked, nudging Chris's shoulder playfully, her eyes twinkling and appearing cognac-brown under the light of a flood lamp. Chris marveled at their beauty, previously unaware of how brown eyes could change so much. "And why is your glass empty?"

"I'm just taking it a little easier," she said. "But I'm certainly enjoying myself."

"There *is* no taking it easy," Raven said, draping her arm around Chris's neck. As she leaned closer, Chris noticed that her eyes looked a little glassier than they had before she had disappeared.

The realization hit her like a ton of bricks. It hadn't been "alone time," nor had it been time with another human being. It had been time with the type of friend that Raven needed to stay away from if she was going to not only reinvent her image, but if she was going to stay alive. Period.

Gone was the girl who had been so free of peer pressure and in her place stood a party-hard rock star, ready to bring anyone along on the ride with her.

"What do you say?" Paul asked, cutting into her thoughts. "One more and then we all go home?"

She laughed. "I thought this was *home* for you all."

"It is," Raven said, her words tumbling out of her mouth like rapid fire. "And it will be for you too in just a couple of days. For now, let's finish up your welcome party the right way. You have to taxi back to your hotel room anyway, so you've already got a built in DD. You're set and there's no reason you shouldn't have one more with us. Let's go."

"Okay," Chris agreed, inexplicably pulled to Raven.

"You have amazing eyes, by the way," Raven said as she threw open the door to the bus. "Now, let's get this green-eyed beauty a cocktail."

The words danced all over Chris's heart and made her emotions jump like a live wire. Her smile grew and she was thrilled to have the compliments tossed in her direction. Raven was raw, she was bare and she was ready to tell the world exactly what she felt.

As Raven poured them all another drink—tequila on the rocks—Chris noted her rapid speech and shaky movements. No doubt, this was far from her first rodeo on what Chris assumed was cocaine. But it was clear that this must be highly powered coke, or she must have taken far too much. The thought of her overdosing sent Chris's heart rate through the ceiling.

She accepted the drink and tried to smile at Raven's toast.

"Here's to the heat—not the kind that ignites and burns down shanties, but the kind that delights and burns panties," Raven said, her dimple twinkling with each word as she raised the glass into the air.

Chris watched with eyes wide, surprised that the crude toast didn't shock her. She guessed she was saturated with shock value. It was clear that there were many sides to this woman—and this side simply wanted to do nothing more than bristle against anyone who stood in her way of her rough edges.

"Cheers to that!" Joe called, sidling up beside the pair and offering his glass for a toast.

"And cheers to your first day," Pete added, throwing his arm around Chris and joining the group.

She raised her glass to theirs and smiled.

"We're a team now," Paul added with a wink. The five of them stood huddled, glasses raised in the air and Chris nodded. In unison, they raised the glasses to their lips and Chris let the alcohol slide down the back of her throat, her eyes never leaving Raven. She wanted to stay, not for her job, not for anything other than to make sure that Raven was okay—that someone with so much potential, with so much ahead of her, didn't give up the fight too early in some type of "accident."

"Are you okay?" Raven asked, sliding over to stand right beside her and in so doing signaling to Paul that he was free to do as he pleased with the rest of his evening.

"I'm fine," Chris lied. She chose her words carefully, not wanting to push Raven away by being over solicitous. "Are you?"

"I'm great," Raven said, a sloppy smile spreading across her face. "I know you agreed to one more drink and you've already drunk it, but would you like to dance with me just once more?"

It was as good an excuse as any to stay with her and make sure she was fine for just a little longer. There was no denying she had enjoyed their previous dance, so she nodded her head and Raven grabbed her by the hand much to her reluctant delight.

"Here," Raven said, grabbing the bottle of tequila and adding another splash to Chris's glass. "You'll need this for what we're about to do. Trust me." She winked as she walked over to the deejay, not letting go of Chris's hand. She whispered something in his ear and judging from his mischievous smile, Chris decided Raven had been right about needing more tequila.

She took a long drink as the speakers bumped with the opening beats of a song that Chris couldn't place at first. Chris stared mesmerized as Raven walked over to the wall, glancing back with a dazzling grin and turning on a dime to slide her body down the wall. Moving her hips to the beat and shimmying her chest seductively, she gyrated like a seasoned stripper, keeping eye contact with Chris through each movement.

Singing every word, Raven never missed a beat. The singer belted out a line about a "porn star dancing," and Chris had no doubt that she was watching exactly that. Regardless of whether or not Raven was clothed, Chris was watching Raven make love to her through dance.

When Raven reached out to pull Chris into her striptease-like moves, Chris wanted to pull back. But overtaken by Raven's charisma, she gave in. As the song ended, Chris knew she had to get out of there. She was feeling far more than she should have—whether thanks to the tequila or thanks to Raven's sheer sexuality. She couldn't stay. And thankfully Raven looked as if she was coming down. Her eyes had cleared somewhat and Chris assured herself that she would be just fine come morning.

Gathering her things, she looked around the room, noting that no one showed signs of stopping. She was out of her league. She hadn't partied all night in years and it seemed like that's what these people had in store.

"Thanks for tonight," she said, patting Raven awkwardly on the shoulder. "I'm going to head back to the hotel. I'll see you in the morning."

It looked like Raven might protest, but she nodded. "Have a good one," she said, adding a wink to the end of it before waving and turning back to the bar.

Out in the night air, Chris walked quickly to catch her taxi, wanting to put the night behind her. She didn't want to dwell on anything—not her feelings, her worries about Raven's well-being or her doubts about whether or not she was in over her head. She just wanted to be, to let loose and enjoy the fact that she was blissfully drunk.

CHAPTER FIVE

The afternoon sun beat down on her fair skin and though the blue bonnets bloomed nearby, their sweet scent couldn't calm her. The worst of the massive hangover from the night before had passed through her system, but she still felt both exhausted and nervous. Moving onto the bus was proving more of a commitment than Chris had anticipated. It was a total surrender of privacy and even more than that, it brought her closer to any potential trouble.

Even with her head pounding, she had made sure to take advantage of the hotel gym before surrendering that luxury. She looked down at her arms and flexed, hoping that her usual morning Pilates regimen would be enough to keep them sharp throughout this project. She would miss her CrossFit workouts as much as she would miss her freedom. Though it had been her choice, it was a sacrifice.

She stood nervously wringing her hands together, vacillating over making a grand entrance to her new home. Squaring her shoulders, she smiled confidently and reached for the door handle. Before she could pull it, it swung wide open in front of her. In a blur, Raven bounded down the steps, rapidly punching numbers into her cell phone. She offered a nod in greeting in Chris's direction but looked right through her.

Chris stepped back into the shadow of the open door.

"Mel," Raven answered her phone, putting her left hand on her hip as she paced back and forth. "I just saw something online and I need you to tell me if it's true."

There was a pause in the conversation and Chris took a moment to take in Raven's appearance. It was clear she hadn't quite begun prepping for the day just yet. Clad in a white tank top and blue boxer shorts with green four-leaf clovers, Raven was barefoot and makeup-free with her hair in a messy bun. Even in her natural state and with worry lines creasing her brow, she looked stunning. Chris couldn't tear her eyes away. Her voice sounded hoarse and gravelly, as if she had just woken, but her eyes were wide, burning with intensity. Watching, Chris's curiosity was piqued.

"There's a kid—Ryland Morrow," Raven said, picking up the pace as she walked a line on the pavement. "I keep an eye on a few message boards from homes—you know, the type of homes we both know a little too well. I pay special attention to blogs and social media pages of the homes in Detroit *for obvious reasons*..." Chris cocked her head to the side, watching as Raven took a deep breath. "Anyway, I watch for updates of kids who might need a hand more than others. I saw an update today on this kid in my old home. I know he's not one of yours, but I'm hoping you can help me out." There was a brief pause, while Raven listened to the person on the line. "You've heard of him?"

My old home. Chris played the statement again through her mind, the stark reality behind Raven's many façades more apparent with each passing moment. She refocused on Raven who still paced side to side in front of her.

As Raven's expression changed from concerned to thankful and back to concerned, Chris wished she could hear the other half of the conversation. "Yeah, that's what I read...I also read about the cancer. Tell me it's not true."

Raven listened, her expression turning somber in an instant. "Uh-huh," she said slowly. "I see…" her voice trailed off and she looked off into the distance, the Austin sun rising high in the sky, heat beating down already, even though it was still early. "I want his phone number, please."

Raven shielded her eyes from the sun and let out a sigh. "I know it's not typical protocol, but we both know I have my reasons—especially when it comes to kids in *that* place."

Raven reached into the waistband of her boxers, pulling out a pen. Scratching numbers on the palm of her hand she thanked her friend. Chris stared, confused and curious, as Raven took a deep breath and sat on the ground. Looking to the horizon, a single tear slid down her cheek.

"Frank is inside," she said, not turning to directly face Chris but clearly addressing her, nonetheless. "Make yourself at home and get started with him. I have to take care of a few things." Her voice was thick with emotion.

"Thank you," Chris said, taking this as her cue to make her way onto the bus. Inside, Frank was pacing much the same as Raven. He held up a finger in her direction, before turning his attention to the phone at his ear. Not quite sure where she was supposed to go with her luggage, she set it at her feet and took a place on the couch.

"What's up?" Paul's voice filled the room as he emerged from the hallway. He was the most approachable person here, the one with a talent for putting people at ease. He sat his tall lanky frame beside her, offering his goofy, reassuring smile.

She shrugged, smiling at him and enjoying the simplicity of what was likely to be the calm before the storm.

* * *

Raven had worked out the details the minute she had read the post about Ryland. Now it all seemed a blur.

"Ryland…seventeen…CNS tumor…fifteen percent survival rate…"

Those details had been heartbreaking enough, but to know he had no one had filled her with a rage against the universe and a pressing need to do something. As she waited for him to answer the phone, she hoped he would let her help. After talking briefly with an angry-sounding woman at Home Again, Detroit's roughest, nastiest foster care system, she waited for Ryland to pick up the phone. Her mind flashed back to the large house, complete with angry voices, stern rules and no love. She wondered if it still smelled of tapioca pudding and stinky feet, and if Mrs. Johnson—the meanest woman she had ever encountered—still ran the place. Her thoughts were interrupted when she heard a boy's voice on the other side of the line.

"Hello," he said, his voice low but still youthful enough to sound as if he was purposefully trying to make it deeper.

"Hello Ryland." She smiled to keep her voice light and upbeat. "This is Raven Daniels. Most just call me Raven. I wanted to call you, because I saw your video and I heard you like rock music."

There was a brief pause. "Is this a joke?"

The question was expected. Through the eyes of a foster kid, a large portion of life could seem like a bad episode of *Punk'd*. Most kids in Ryland's situation had learned at an early age not to trust anyone. God knows she certainly had.

"It's not a joke. It's me." She cleared her throat and began to sing along to one of her most famous choruses a capella to prove her point. When she finished, she didn't have to wait for his response.

"Damn!" he exclaimed, childlike exuberance evident in his voice. "It *is* you! Wait, is this because I have cancer?" His voice dropped in an instant.

Had it not been such a serious situation, she would have laughed about how much this kid already reminded Raven of herself at his age.

"It's actually about the fact that you are in a position I was once in—trying to take on the world on your own at seventeen. And like me, you have a passion for music. The cancer thing I can't understand but the rest I get. And I want to help. I don't want you to be alone in this and more than anything, I want you to have the chance to play in front of a crowd. Like I said, I watched your video, where you were playing guitar and singing. I've watched it about fifteen times. You're pretty damn good, kid."

"Thank you," he said, his hushed tone conveying both disbelief and genuine gratitude. "What do you mean play in front of a crowd?"

"I want you to join me and my band onstage at one of my shows."

"Are you…are you kidding?" he asked. "I mean, is this one of those 'in case I die' things? I don't want to sound ungrateful. I'm just curious." His words fired at rapid pace.

Cynical too young, she thought, shaking her head. "Not at all. This is because I want you to see how amazing and exhilarating it is to play for a crowd of screaming fans. I want my fans to know how talented you are. That way, when you're in treatment, remember that feeling and fight like hell to survive and feel it again."

For a minute, he said nothing, but she could hear soft sniffling.

"I'm on your side. I think you have what it takes," she added, giving him a while to compose himself. "I'll get permission from your heavies, sign whatever papers I need to sign, fly you out to my next stop in Phoenix, you and I can have lunch and then we'll warm up with the band. You will play with us in the show, if you want."

"Thank you," he said again, his voice struggling to maintain composure and act tough. "That would be so awesome."

They talked through schedules and details. Raven was certain she wanted to do this before he started his next round of therapy in two weeks. He was well at the moment. Her heart soared when, as long as it was approved, he agreed to fly out of Detroit to make it in time for her concert in Phoenix on Thursday night.

After talking to the appropriate authorities, she hung up. The process would have been much harder with many homes that adhered more strictly to procedure and with a child who wasn't almost a cast-aside adult, but she was thankful. With a few clicks on her phone, she purchased his flight and sent him the information. The kid had four days to get packed and prepared.

She knew it wasn't much in the grand scheme of things, but she hoped it would show him a reason to fight and give him hope that he wasn't in the battle alone. She often scrolled through message boards from these homes. The pages were littered with short blurbs, photos, personal details, looking more like a flyer for a used car lot than anything else. Even so, she read each post wishing there was some way she could help. Today, when she had read Ryland's story and saw his video, she knew she could finally do something to make a difference. On a mission, she bounded back to the bus.

"We're having company in Phoenix," she announced on the bus. Excitedly, she told them all about Ryland. She watched their reactions to the video on her phone, jaws dropping as they listened to a seventeen-year-old, self-taught kid play better than many of the professionals they knew. When the song ended, she looked around the room to a slew of affirming smiles.

"Good work," Frank said, reaching up to pat her on the shoulder. She nodded, keeping it together until she glanced at Paul grinning at her in pride. He knew and understood the driving force better than anyone. He knew where she came from and why this was important to her.

Having been her best friend during her years in foster care, he knew. While he had been afforded the stability of his own family, he had been her sounding board through all of the hurt and pain that went with being tossed from home to home. And he certainly knew of the neglect and verbal abuse she had endured. She felt the sting of fresh tears in the corner of her eye, as she silently gave him a half smile and looked away.

"That's great," Christina chimed in. Raven turned her attention to the slender blonde, noting her genuine smile as well as her sharp, high cheekbones, which suggested she hadn't been eating or sleeping enough. Even so, her green eyes sparkled in the light. The words were tumbling out of Christina's mouth too quickly for Raven to keep up. "We could get the press to cover Thursday's show. I could send a release tomorrow morning so it hits their desk first thing on a Monday morning. That would give them time to get crews out there to cover the show."

"No," Raven cut in authoritatively, holding up her hand to quash the idea before it took off. Her movements silenced both Frank and Christina. "This is about Ryland—not about publicity. I just want to help him. I won't cheapen that with a press release."

For a split second, it looked like Christina might protest, but she nodded. "No, you're absolutely right and that makes me incredibly proud to work with you."

Christina smiled up at her and Raven offered a half smile in return.

This was for Ryland only. This was for a kid who had nothing and no one—except for cancer and a dream. She recognized his need too much not to help.

* * *

For the first time in several months, Raven was up before either an alarm or a knock on the door. Her heart fluttered and her excitement tangled with nervousness in the bathroom. As she applied her eyeliner, she let herself consider all that today meant to her. She refused to let Ryland's visit drag her down her own memory lane. This was his day and she wouldn't cheapen it. She had come a long way and so would he.

She took a glance in the mirror, caring more what she looked like this morning than usual. Not that she wanted to impress or dazzle—she simply wanted to be who she needed to be. Today, she was the adult and she hoped that she could pull it off. Nodding to herself, she turned and walked out into the open area of the bus. Paul stood waiting by the door, dressed and ready to go.

"I need to do this part alone," she told him, shaking her head.

For a second, he looked hurt. He turned his head to the side, raising an eyebrow, questioning her insistence.

"Yes."

"Why?"

"He's been in and out of foster homes. I did some digging and made a few calls. He's been tossed around since he was a toddler and has caused some trouble. Some family took him in a couple of years ago and the only thing the lady reported was that whenever they tried to get close to him, he pushed back and started getting into trouble at school. Eventually the family gave up. He's not the trusting type from what I've heard and will probably be a little gun-shy if anyone pushes too hard." She gently elbowed Paul in the ribs and smiled. "I once knew a kid like that back in the day."

"I know. I know."

"Judging from how I was and this kid's rap sheet, you and I both know that he likely has the propensity to run if ambushed. Hell, we know that I sure did. Even you did for a while as some sort of teenage rebellion despite living with your parents. Chances are, he's no different."

"He might be and I worry about your safety."

"He's not a monster," she said, placing a hand on her hip and holding her ground. "I won't budge on this. He's a kid. A foster kid. With cancer. I'll be fine and he'll be happier if he's not bombarded by all of us at once."

Paul narrowed his eyes, grabbing the door handle as though he might block her way out of the bus.

"Don't you dare," she said sternly. "You know I'm perfectly capable. I'll be bringing him back here after I pick him up and get to know him just a bit. Then and only then, can you step in and play big brother. Maybe you can bring him some fun snacks. We all know that's how you won me over back in the day—bringing stuff too frivolous and expensive to be found in a home with thirty other kids. Bring him gummy bears. Those were always my favorite."

She sidestepped him and made a beeline for the door.

Once in the cab, she directed the driver to the airport. Just as she wanted this to be an authentic experience for Ryland devoid of any publicity stunts, she wanted him to feel comfortable.

Her mind drifted back through the years and she remembered in vivid detail the way her palms would sweat and her voice would shake when she'd received too much attention. She also remembered the way she could turn into a snotty little brat, her jagged edges warding off anyone who ventured too close. She remembered the way she had hidden behind her microphone. It was for protection and she had relied upon it at least until she had become emboldened, realizing that she could keep the world at arm's length with her behavior alone.

There was little doubt in her mind that Ryland would be in the same boat. Dealing with most of these kids was a bit like approaching a wild animal.

The cab pulled up curbside to a young, tall, blond-headed boy in faded jeans, a black Rolling Stones T-shirt and a backward cap. Leaning casually on his guitar case with his duffel at his feet, he looked side to side, taking in his surroundings. Raven threw open the door.

"Ryland!" she called out, waving at him as she approached.

She stopped in her tracks when he turned, nodded and broke into a wide smile.

"Yes," he said after a moment, extending his hand for a handshake. "It's nice to meet you."

His voice was gentle and she marveled at how polite he was. At seventeen, she was anything but polite. This kid was something special.

"It's nice to meet you, as well," she said, returning the handshake. "Let's grab your stuff and go get some food. After a five-hour flight, I bet you're starving."

He nodded again, his smile a mixture of starstruck awe and confusion.

"What's wrong?"

"I just..." he started, but shook his head, grabbing his bags instead.

"It's okay," she coaxed.

"I just guess it's really strange to actually meet someone famous," he said, shrugging and smiling sheepishly. "I've always been a big fan of your music and this is great."

"I'm very happy you're here," she said, walking around the car to get in beside him.

On the drive to the restaurant, she was careful to only talk about superficial things. There needed to be no talk of cancer, no talk of their mutual background. Instead, they needed to focus on fun things. After all, that's why he was here, to give him a break from the brutal reality. She listened as his words tumbled out quickly.

They talked music and cars and food and before she knew it, two hours had passed. They had finished lunch in a blur and she clung to the fact that, even if just for a day, Ryland was going to get a taste of a life worth fighting for.

"Are you ready to join the band?" she asked, when they arrived back at the bus.

He turned, looking out of the cab window, his eyes widening as he took in the sight of the massive vehicle. "This is what it's like?" he asked, his voice now nothing more than a whisper.

"This is what it's like," she affirmed. "At least, after a while. There's a lot of time prior to this stage, where it's basement playing and hopping around from club to club, begging people to let you play your music, even if they don't pay you. Once you hit it big, you get to travel around and play at incredible venues. There are also other options for touring. You could fly from spot to spot. But this is what it's like for me. And what it could be like for you some day."

"It's real." His voice held disbelief as he reached up to touch the glass of the car window tenderly.

"It is," she said, putting her arm around his shoulders. "It's real and from the way you play, it could be real for you too one day. Tonight, it *will* be real for you."

He turned back to face her, his face set and hardened as stone. He held his breath and set his jaw to keep tears at bay, but Raven could see the moisture building.

"Don't worry about it," she said, reading his nonverbal statement of gratitude and again patting him on the back. "Let's go have some fun."

She walked a few steps behind him, marveling at the way he was seeing this world for the first time—and recalling how she once held that same look of wonder, back before this was normalcy, back when all she had was a backpack, a couple of outfits and a guitar.

* * *

Taking advantage of a rare quiet morning, Chris had indulged herself with pampering. Raven didn't want her tagging along, so she had opted for an at-home—or on-bus—facial, foot soak and manicure, all in her tiny, shoebox-sized room. They had arrived in Phoenix a night early so Raven could be rested and have the day with the boy. That had meant an entire day, parked in front of the night's venue and an entire day in which the crew and driver had made a run for it.

They had all poured from the bus at first light, as if they were sailors in port for the first time in months. She was left to her own devices. Of course, she could have opted to explore the city like the others, but her energy was drained. Desperate for rest, she had chosen a morning of solitude.

When she heard the car outside, she peeked out the window. A smile spread across her face as she watched Raven and the boy laughing together. They looked like a tight-knit family, a brother-sister duo having a day of fun together. Here was the rough-around-the-edges, show-no-weakness woman letting down her guard and dancing, roughhousing and cutting up with a teenage boy.

Chris stayed in her room. It was impossible not to eavesdrop in these close quarters, but she didn't want to break up their moment. And she didn't want to miss out on this unguarded, soft side of Raven.

"Tonight, when I play with you, are you going to tell the crowd why I'm there?" she could hear Ryland's voice coming through the walls. It was deep, making him sound much older than he was, but his exhilaration made it obvious that he was still just a boy.

"I sure am," Raven answered, with a laugh. "I'm going to tell them that you're my friend Ryland and that I invited you out here to join us so the rest of the world could hear the incredible music you make."

"You're not going to mention the cancer thing?" His tone turned more hesitant and Chris waited for Raven's response.

"Of course not," she answered quickly. "That's not what this is about. This is about the fact that I've heard you kill a guitar solo better than Slash. I've heard you rock it and I think you've got a future in this. That's what this is about. It's about you having a chance to fully shine."

"Thank you." Chris could barely make out his whisper.

She felt a pang of guilt strike through her gut. Raven was right. Chris *had* wanted to make it more, make it a publicity stunt, but Raven's heart was in the right place. This was a poor, helpless, innocent kid facing a devastating disease—not someone to exploit. She reminded herself that she had perhaps been a little too quick to judge Raven and maybe a little too focused on her own motives.

Leaning against her door, she listened to the ease of their conversation. They started playing together. A melodic, beautiful sound filled the air, as Ryland played the guitar and Raven sang along to a cover of Warrant's "Heaven." The powerful chords and soulful vocals created a haunting rendition.

Ryland joined in the vocals and the pair belted out the touching lyrics about not needing to be a superhero as long as they had love. They sang of being closer to heaven within that connection, of loss and of never giving up on that love. It seemed like an odd choice to duet with a kid who didn't have a home, or the connections the song spoke of, but as the song progressed, Chris replayed the revelation that made the song even more powerful. Home wasn't a place. Heaven wasn't a place. It was this. It was what the two of them were sharing right then and there.

When the song came to a close, Chris knew that Raven had also been right about the kid's talent. The two of them went to meet the band for sound check. She looked out the window to watch them exit, Raven's arm draped around his shoulders as they walked in step with one another.

Chris wiped at her tears. This was an emotional situation and Raven was handling it like a professional, like someone whose heart was big. Even more than that, the two of them seemed to have a genuine connection, something Chris hadn't been sure Raven was capable of forming.

The show went off without a hitch and Ryland was a natural on stage. Raven had been right. Even more surprising to Chris though was Raven's genteel approach where Ryland was concerned. Instead of being the party-hard rock star, she had ushered all those wanting to party after the show to a nearby hotel and had opted to take Ryland out for dinner by herself.

Throughout her quiet night on the bus, having also forgone the opportunity to party, Chris smiled as she reflected upon the exchange she had overheard between the two of them following the show. Not only had Raven encouraged the boy in his dream to pursue music, but she had insisted that he keep in touch—a clear indicator that this was far from a stunt.

CHAPTER SIX

A loud banging jolted Chris out of a deep sleep and as she rose quickly, the sun streaming through the curtains intensified the pounding in her head. Unsure what had woken her, she sighed heavily, realizing that according to her alarm clock she should have had at least another half hour to sleep. She heard shuffling down the hall as the rest of the crew rose as well. Knowing one of them would handle it, she contemplated going back to sleep but then thought better of it.

"I'm too damn old for this," she muttered, her hangover worsening with every move. She was far too old to be partying like the college kid she once was and she was too old to be sleeping on a bus.

Chris stretched her sore muscles and smiled despite the pain. She might be too old, but she had to admit she was having fun. It had been a week-long party, with only that one night off during Ryland's visit. As it was, she had been drunk to hungover more times this past week than she had since college. With as much focus as her tired body would allow, she stretched and did her workout—something she had adapted to such small living quarters. When she finished, she glanced in the mirror on the back of her door, wishing she had been able to work with as much tenacity as she did in the gym back home.

Shaking her head, she made her way to the bathroom. She recalled the previous night and every night since she had arrived and chuckled as she pulled herself together to look presentable before she joined the rest of the band for the day ahead. It was going to take some time to adjust. But it was amusing.

When she opened her door, her eyes widened. Even after a few days on board, she hadn't adapted to the lack of boundaries. Standing in the shared space of the bus in nothing more than his boxers, Joe was eating a bowl of cereal while watching YouTube videos on his phone.

"Morning," he called, a dribble of milk coming from his lips.

"Good morning."

Joe chewed, swallowed and eyed her curiously. "Are you all ready for your big day of girl time?" he asked.

"Ready as I'll ever be," she said, nodding and turning to head into the bathroom.

"You better be ready." She heard Raven's voice behind her. "We've got a full day of bonding planned. Frank even made me block out normal practice times, so I'm yours all day."

Chris laughed easily at the silly faces Raven was making. "I'll be out in a bit," she said. "And trust me, I'm ready."

As she shut the bathroom door behind her, she heard normal ribbing between Paul and Raven. The two behaved more like brother and sister than co-workers. Looking around the small space that served Raven, Paul, Pete, Joe and now Chris, she figured they probably couldn't help it. Paul had also alluded to a long history between the two of them. The bus seemed to enhance that connection.

Enforced bonding was what today was all about. Even though things had been going much more smoothly than Chris had expected, she still needed to get below the surface with Raven. She doubted she would ever reach the depths of the demons that tortured the girl—and after seeing just how hard she could party, Chris wasn't quite sure she wanted to. But to understand her, to know what made her tick, she need to be let in, at least in some level. Most importantly, she needed to know what capacity Raven had to connect with people, aside from music. If she was going to do this job properly, she needed to present a *new* Raven of sorts, one who gave back and cared about the world around her, instead of a woman who simply existed to create music and wreak havoc on the general population whenever her tour bus rolled into town.

Chris brushed her teeth, put in her contact lenses and prepared for the day. Staring in the mirror, she noticed that she had aged a year in just a matter of days. She wasn't sure if it was the late nights, the partying or the fact that anxiety seemed to have overtaken her every thought today. Sure, she had spent plenty of time in conversation with Raven and she had never been left to fend for herself for too long at any of the parties. On that level, they got along well, but it was merely alcohol-fueled banter.

Today would be different. It would be a test of sorts and she was anxious about it.

She took one last deep breath and a long glance in the mirror, silently nodding to herself that she could—and would—do this. She would be successful.

"If there's anything in the world you know, it's people," she whispered aloud to herself, needing the additional affirmation. She slung her purse over her shoulder and walked outside, gesturing to Raven that she was ready.

Wordlessly, Raven nodded at her and grabbed her clutch, following Chris out the door. The two walked in sync in comfortable silence, as though they had known each other for years instead of just a week.

Laughing together they strolled in and out of the small eclectic shops on the square in Santa Fe and stopped occasionally to look at items sold by street vendors.

"Who would actually wear this?" Chris asked, running her fingers along the edges of one of the shaggy fur vests in a women's clothing store.

"My mom would have loved it," Raven said, letting out a laugh before abruptly shutting her mouth and looking away as if she had misspoken.

"Oh yeah?" Chris commented, determined to make the moment a breakthrough instead of another opportunity for Raven to put up an impenetrable wall. "Was she into the southwest flair?"

"Something like that," Raven said, walking back toward the ceramic section, where a local artisan had handcrafted everything from cowboy boot figurines to coyotes.

"What does she do?" said Chris, keeping her voice casual.

"I don't know," Raven said with a shrug. "Haven't known for quite some time."

Chris waited in silence, resisting the urge to pry. Raven gently ran her finger along the glass casing, intently interested in the little red and yellow ceramic boot in front of her.

"What do your parents do?" she finally asked, turning her attention back to Chris. Raven's forehead crinkled and she leaned closer to hear over the noise of a family of shoppers behind them.

"My father was successful," she said, her mind drifting back to how he would return home with his shirtsleeves rolled up and his tie loosened, looking every bit like he had just put in a hard day's work. "He was a commercial consultant and helped a bunch of people back in Texas grow their businesses. That's what he did right up until the year he passed away. He closed up shop when he was diagnosed with advanced heart disease. He passed two years ago and it's been a rough two years. It made me realize I had taken a lot of things for granted with him. I had always been pretty hard on him and thought he should have been more flexible and more understanding. He was the dad who tried too hard to fix my problems instead of just listening. He was the man who demanded perfection when I just wanted to live my life. He wanted me to be just like him and make the choices he'd made. At least, those are the things I thought he was.

"I was wrong in many ways. He was my biggest supporter, my most ardent cheerleader. He pushed me to be my best because of his solid belief and blind faith in me. He was my steady stream of life advice and the one who always sought out workable solutions. Most of the time he was right. He was a hard worker and a shrewd businessman. I always thought he worked too much. I felt like it took away from the time we had together but after he passed, I realized that he had done it all for me and for our little family. It was just the three of us—him, my mom and me—but he provided for us like it was his only job. Those long hours, the times he went without vacations, all of it. It was all to teach me about hard work and provide me with the best life possible.

"He was a good man and it's been a little hard figuring out how to go about life without him. A million times in my own career over the past couple of years, I've wished that I could pick up the phone and ask him for advice—even if just to listen to him try to fix it again. His passing left me pretty lost, and that's probably why I'm here now. I dove right into work and pushed it aside for a while but that gave me a lot of experience. Enough experience to take on an assignment like this one on my own." She stopped and looked around, aware that she had just crossed a line into too much personal information. "But, that's the long answer I guess. Sorry for that."

Her words had spilled forth without any warning. She cleared her throat to make the onslaught stop. "My mother is a therapist," she added quickly.

"Sorry to hear about your dad," Raven said, biting her lip and looking somewhat uncomfortable with Chris's emotional display. "I imagine that has been really tough on you. Are you and your mom close?"

She hated that question, but decided it was easier to invite closer conversation if at least one of them was sharing. "Not really," she said with a shrug, wishing she could avert the focus from herself as Raven had just done. "She's in the business of fixing people and thinks that I need fixing. Where my father would have offered solutions, she thinks I'm the problem ninety percent of the time."

"Yeah?" Raven asked. "What part of you is so fucked up it needs fixing?"

"You name it and it probably needs to be fixed," she said with a laugh.

"Yeah, well name some of them," Raven challenged.

"I'm a lesbian. I'm too messy for her tastes. I'm single. I'm stubborn. I'm too much like my father and though they stayed together, they were never really a pair that meshed. She is all about confrontation and pointing out one's flaws. He averted conflicts and used humor to make situations more bearable. To her, that meant he wasn't taking situations seriously. They argued daily and since I'm his little 'carbon copy' as she calls me, she and I don't see eye to eye. I laugh about things she thinks I should see a shrink for. I work too many hours and I also avoid confrontation. But that's just the stuff that falls into personality traits. I also dye my prematurely-gray hair instead of embracing my aged wisdom. I view all sides of a situation and often change my mind as a result of it all rather than commit to an opinion." Chris ticked off her "offenses" one by one on her fingers, hoping she had given Raven enough of who she was to allow her to feel comfortable to share as well.

Chris felt at ease in revealing all of this to Raven. There was a natural companionship between the two of them, making this feel more comfortable than just another work assignment. As she finished, she smiled up at Raven. "I think the worst part for her is that I'm happy with who I am and don't want her to fix me. That's probably my biggest sin."

"Just like a therapist," Raven said, shaking her head and smiling. The gesture warmed Chris's heart. It had been too long since someone had listened so willingly and actually had a genuine response, aside from Brittany. Brittany definitely had ulterior motives. Brittany had been there when Chris was her most vulnerable. She made a point to provide everything Chris might need. Chris was never certain if that was a ploy to get closer to her, or if it was simply her nature to be so loving and giving. Regardless, it was what she had done after every breakup and certainly after the death of Chris's father. It was that tenderness, that willingness to be available at any hour—*that and a lot of alcohol*—that she had mistaken for romantic intimacy.

The interest and kindness displayed by Brittany led Chris to the drunken night they shared—and the confusing nights of lust that followed. That kind of interest had a way of getting her in trouble.

This felt different—interest from someone who didn't feel the need to listen in the off chance that Chris might go to bed with her later. After her father's death, she had lost so many friends because she had pushed them away, opting to work late hours and get lost in the world of climbing ladders instead of downing drinks at happy hours or attending birthday parties and barbecues. After a while, no one reached out anymore and she hadn't had a romantic relationship that mattered once he got sick, as if getting too close to anyone provided the opportunity to experience even more loss.

She was self-aware enough to know she was doing it but she had seen little from anyone to make it worth changing. At least until this moment. Now she felt herself opening up with very little reservation. Raven had picked the lock that had kept her sealed away from this type of interaction.

"Have much experience with therapists yourself?" Chris asked.

"From afar," Raven said, shaking her head again. "I've never seen one personally, but I was in plenty of rooms with them for a while."

Chris cocked her head to the side slightly, leaning in and nonverbally asking for more information.

"My parents' messy divorce, a little assault and battery, that whole shebang," she said, casually waving a hand through the air as if to dismiss it all. "I was the kid in the room who didn't have to answer too many questions. I heard a bunch though and at the end of it all, I realized that no one person can really fix the problems of another. That's kind of an inside job."

"Inside job," Chris repeated the words and nodded her head in agreement. "I like that. And you're absolutely right. I've learned that those who work to fix the problems of others often have plenty of their own. But I guess that gives them some insight at least."

"Is that why you do what you do?" Raven asked, a smile playing with the corners of her lips as she raised an eyebrow. "You're here to fix me up, right?"

"Stop it," Chris said, jokingly nudging her in the arm, only to stop at the jolt the contact sent through her body. She took a deep breath, composing herself. "You know that's not why I'm here. I thought we had established that."

"We have," Raven said, throwing her arm around Chris's neck and leading her out of the shop. "I'm just giving you a hard time. But really, why *do* you do what you do?"

"I'm good at it," Chris said frankly. "I am a crafty writer, a spin doctor and an eternal optimist. I see the good in others, so it's easier for me to bring that out." She paused for a moment, eyeing another good shop to keep the day alive. "What about you? Aside from being insanely talented, why do *you* do what you do?"

"Same reasons, I guess," Raven said, pointing with her free hand to an ice cream shop on the corner, never making a movement to remove her arm from its resting place around Chris's shoulder. Raven seeming so casually comfortable warmed Chris's heart. "I like to express myself, without having to bare it all, you know? I mean, it's like I can tell the world what I'm feeling and I can make it real for them, too, for whatever they may be going through. But I don't have to get so descriptive that it makes it seem less real for them or too real for me. It's a way of being able to be genuine without being weak and transparent."

"Do you think transparency and weakness are synonymous?"

"I think they can be," Raven pondered, looking upward as they walked. "They're not always intertwined, but I think that at the root of being overly transparent is being weak enough to *need* someone to see all of you—to need all of you and want all of you, regardless of how ugly some of the parts are. I think that we should all be strong enough to keep some of that to ourselves, to find a way to express it a little more vaguely and still be able to cope and realize that some people might not like us."

"I've never thought of it that way," Chris said, taking in the words and trying them on for size. "What about you do you consider ugly?"

"I have horrible morning breath," Raven said, winking and playing the question off coolly. "I mean, let's face it, we can't all be perfect."

They laughed with ease and eventually Raven cleared her throat. "I guess I consider the parts ugly that are the parts that keep you employed. You wouldn't be here if I was palatable to every taste."

"But those aren't fundamentally ugly parts of you," Chris argued gently. "Those are just parts of you."

"Exactly. The same way you accept your mother's judgments and dismiss them because you're good with so-called ugly parts, I'm good with the parts of me that not everyone likes. Those things are part of me though. They're who I am and what I do. Some people think those parts are unacceptable, and that's why you're here. I'm okay not being everyone's cup of tea, but if I'm going to continue to be in the public eye, I suppose I have to be a little more acceptable to some. That's where you come in, I guess. You make me a little less bristly so parents don't freak out when their kids come home listening to my music."

Chris listened in awe. Just a few days ago, this was the same woman who wanted nothing to do with her, the same woman who would have rather rotted in her own self-righteous anger than take any help from some PR person.

"How am I doing so far?" Chris asked.

"There you go with that need to please," Raven joked, her throaty laugh ringing through the air. "I'm kidding," she assured her. "You're doing fine as far as I'm concerned, but I've *always* liked me. I guess the real test would be to ask someone who doesn't think I'm the greatest thing since sliced bread."

"Who would that be?"

"Probably your mom," Raven shot back. "Judging from how harshly she throws down judgment on you, I'm pretty sure she'd think I was the devil's mistress. If you being a conflict-averting, stubborn lesbian puts you on the naughty list, I don't think there's a prayer for a wrong-side-of-the-tracks, smoking and drinking, rebel rocker girl like me who's more at home in a hazy basement, surrounded by empty beer bottles, bumping speakers and half-clad misfits just like me."

"She would actually probably like you more than me," Chris said, carefully eyeing Raven up and down. "You're a brunette with a sassy mouth. That always seemed to win out over the blondie with an opinion. She has this assistant, Colleen, who has never been afraid to sass my mom. The one time my mom tried to 'fix' her, she told my mom where she could shove her quick fix. I've actually heard my mom tell Colleen that she considers her a daughter. The fact that she's the daughter my mom wishes she had is the underlying message and we all know it. I assume you would tell her where to go and she'd love and hate you in equal measure for you. At the end of the day, she would like you though because you don't mind jumping into confrontation."

"Forget about your mother for a while," Raven said. "Let me buy you an ice cream to pay you for your babysitting duties and we'll chat about something happier than family dysfunction."

"You've got a deal," Chris said, smiling as Raven opened the door and ushered her inside.

Their conversation came to a lull as they stood in front of the window, a myriad of ice creams displayed behind an old-fashioned glass case. Chris took the moment to watch Raven. She delighted in the way Raven's eyes flitted from flavor to flavor, her dimple showing as her smile deepened and her forehead creasing as she considered her choice. The sunlight glinted through the window, lighting up the entire establishment. Raven wore a look of childlike joy.

"What flavor are you going to get?" Raven's voice was distracted and heavy with uncertainty. The sound reluctantly brought Chris out of her own thoughts and back into the moment.

"I haven't decided," she admitted, glancing quickly at the glass and the task at hand.

She cast a sideways glance at Raven, watching her bite the corner of her lip. Chris felt her body shudder inwardly, entirely undone in an instant by the subtle sexuality of the movement. Raven cleared her throat, stepping up to the counter to order. Chris had to force herself to make up her mind. Rocky road versus mint chip seemed to be such a trivial decision in light of all that she was feeling, but she nonetheless stepped up and rattled off her order like an obedient child.

"Mint chip in a waffle cone, please," she asked, prompting a nod of approval from Raven.

"Solid choice," she said, giving a wink as she laid a few dollar bills on the counter. "I would have pegged you for vanilla."

"Ouch," Chris said, her tone light and playful. "You really think I'm that boring?"

"It wasn't meant to be an insult," Raven said, holding up her hands quickly to avert the damage. "Vanilla is actually quite an interesting choice. You just have to see it clearly. It's not boring. It's just for people who can find adventure in the ordinary."

Chris knitted her brow and looked deeply into Raven's eyes. After giving it a moment for Raven's comment to resonate, she said, "I never know what to expect when you open your mouth. Sometimes you've got quippy comebacks. And then other times, you eloquently string together deep philosophic thoughts on life."

"Kind of like vanilla ice cream," Raven said, pursing her lips together and nodding matter-of-factly. "You never really know what you're going to get, even though it's a classic and you think you've got it figured out. Somehow, it still holds a little element of surprise."

"Did you just call yourself vanilla?" Chris asked, winking in Raven's direction.

"I'm anything but vanilla, honey," Raven said, returning the wink and then quickly directing her attention back to the woman at the counter.

Even with their eye contact now averted, Chris knew neither of them could deny the sparks that had just flown between them.

She grabbed her cone and they took a seat next to the window.

"By the way, it was really cool what you did for Ryland," Chris said. "I wanted to tell you that it really touched my heart."

"It's what anyone would have done," Raven said, shrugging off the compliment.

"No, it's not."

"Well, anyone who is half-decent." She turned her head, averting her attention out the window to signify that topic was closed.

"So what else do you want to know?" Raven asked, her guard raised once again, but now without the earlier combative air.

"Whatever you want to share with me," Chris said. "But this isn't a job interview or an interrogation. Certainly not a therapy session! I'm just enjoying getting to know you." She hoped that Raven could hear her sincerity. The truth was, if she could have chosen how to spend the day, this is what she would have done. It had been nothing short of perfection.

"Well," Raven said, taking a long lick of her ice cream cone and using her free hand to tap the table absentmindedly while she thought things through. "I love sports. Chicago Cubs fan, even though they break my heart—what's left of it, that is—every single season. I like strong drinks, strong women and even stronger coffee. My favorite color is red, although I will occasionally go with blue, just because it's a fun color. I grew up playing softball and I've always been pretty competitive. I guess that's part of why I check my rankings on charts, sales numbers and interactions with my fans on social media almost daily. I want to be the best but more than that, I want my fans to *think* I'm the best. But aside from that, I'm your ordinary, run-of-the-mill lesbian next door."

"Except for the fact that you write songs that win the hearts of millions and that everyone in the entire nation knows your name," Chris said with a laugh. "I'd hardly call that run-of-the-mill." She wondered how many times Raven had considered facts like that as revealing something "personal," but she was enjoying hearing this side of things, nonetheless.

"Of course there's that," Raven said, her smile lighting up her entire face. "But not everyone really *knows* me. They don't even know who I am."

"Or your real name," Chris said, raising an eyebrow. The question had been burning.

"Are you asking?" Raven asked, focusing her attention on her dripping ice cream cone for a moment, before turning back to look deep into Chris's eyes.

"Not necessarily, but I think I am as curious as the rest of the world," she said.

"A Google search should do the trick," Raven said, offering nothing more than a casual shrug.

"You and I both know that's not true," Chris said, narrowing her eyes across the table. "It seems like someone on the inside has done a good job of keeping that all as clear as mud. A few years ago when someone reported using what was believed to be your given name, there were rumors and clarifying reports and a slew of other speculation thrown around. You even tweeted about six different names—all of which we know weren't true. And you've gone to great lengths to seal records."

"Like I said, no one really knows me," she said with a shrug. "I guess I would kind of like to keep it that way. I am who I am in front of them and that's all they really need to know. Truth be told, I'm much the same girl behind the scenes as I am on stage. I'm pretty simplistic in a lot of ways. I get deep with my music. Other than that, I prefer to have fun and see the light side of life. I enjoy cutting up with the guys, laughing over drinks, dancing like crazy and getting caught up in the silly things. That's the side I guess people don't get to see. But they do get to see who I am through my music, through my shows. They get to see edgy and a little deep from time to time, and they like that. People enjoy Raven, even if they don't fully understand her. I'm not quite sure they'd enjoy the person *behind* the performance to the degree they love the girl in the lights and smoke."

"I thought you didn't care what they thought."

"I don't, but some things are better left in the past."

Chris's curiosity was now burning. "What things? What are you running from?" she asked.

Across the table, she saw Raven's eyes darken and grow distant. As her forehead creased, she stood. "I'm running from a past of bad sweaters like the fuzzy one we saw back in that shop, bad decisions and a road that would have led to nothing more than a bad future. I'm running from bad and I'm working like hell to make good in myself and in the world. Let's go find somewhere else to walk," she said firmly, moving toward the trash can with her ice cream. "It's hot in here," she added as she strode to the door.

Chris tried to absorb Raven's vague history. She could connect the dots. The woman had lived through a shitty childhood—just how shitty remained to be determined. The details would flow on their own at some point. There was no need to rush it.

"Thank you," Chris said, when she finally caught up to Raven and matched her stride as they walked back down the plaza.

"For what?" Raven asked, not turning to face her, focused instead on a street performer dancing along to a tribal tune. The attire of the milling crowd made it clear this was a tourist destination for the wealthy and retired, as well as the artsy, inspired and eclectic traveler.

"For not telling me to go to hell when I asked questions and for just being a genuinely cool person," Chris answered. "Also for the ice cream. It was delicious."

Raven laughed. "You're kind of like vanilla ice cream too," she said after a moment, raising an eyebrow in Chris's direction. "You keep me on my toes and usually surprise me with what comes out of your mouth. You're pretty cool too."

They laughed together and Raven reached over, looping her arm through Chris's in a clear sign that there were no hard feelings, regardless of how tense the situation might have become.

As the day turned into evening, Chris was sure of a few things. She was peeling back the layers that Raven liked to keep hidden and she genuinely liked the person she saw underneath.

They danced through the streets, enjoying the street performers, who ranged from folksy singer-songwriters to tribal drummers to jazz trios. Chris let herself enjoy it all. She stood back in awe as Raven signed autographs. Even clad in nothing more than a fitted green T-shirt, a pair of skinny jeans, Chucks and a pair of oversized sunglasses, it was hard to disguise her easily recognizable beauty. She marveled at how easily Raven meshed with her fans, never irritated and always approachable.

As an admirer would spot her, Raven would smile and joke with them while signing her autograph and posing for a selfie. Then, as if nothing out of the ordinary had happened, she would catch up, loop her arm around Chris and continue their stroll.

By dusk, Chris wanted to make the day linger in any way she could, but the clock was ticking down.

"Have you had a good day?" Chris asked, turning to face Raven.

"I have," she said, her genuine smile stretching from ear to ear. "I don't get to do this as often as I would like, honestly. I mean, I get to live the life I choose most days, but that often means I'm in the studio, in practices or sleeping off the night before. This feels so regular, but so extraordinary at the same time—like I imagine it would be for someone who has lived in a big city for their entire life, only to take one day to do all of the fun touristy things in the area."

"Hanging out with me is like a staycation?" Chris asked, her amusement showing in her raised eyebrow.

"In the best way possible," Raven said. She opened her mouth to speak again, but was silenced by Chris's cell phone.

Chris sighed, noting that whoever was calling had horrible timing. Yet she figured anyone who interrupted at *any* point today would have horrible timing. Everything else seemed intrusive to such a wonderful day. Glancing at the screen, she bit her lip in consideration. She hadn't talked to Brittany in days and she certainly needed to hear how things were going back home.

"I have to take this," she said to Raven.

"Go for it," Raven said. "I'll busy myself over here." Raven took a few steps away and lit up a cigarette.

"Hello?" Chris answered.

"Hey there." Brittany's voice filled the line, warming Chris's heart to hear someone familiar and loving. "How's my big, bad, famous best friend these days?"

"I'm doing well," Chris said. "How are you?"

"I'm good. Nothing really exciting happening here. What's new with you?"

"I'm just out exploring Santa Fe and enjoying some local New Mexico culture," Chris said, laughing at the thought that this was such a "normal" day in her agenda. There was no staying in one place. There was nothing consistent and it was expected to see and do so many things in the span of a week. "I've been just about everywhere you can imagine on their southwest tour. So far just Austin, Phoenix and Santa Fe for shows, but I've been on the road at every place in between."

"Are you having fun?"

"Yeah," Chris said, the answer coming easily. "It's been a blast, honestly."

"Is it hard work? I mean, has she made even an effort to step up her game?"

"It's not too hard," Chris said, lowering her voice slightly. "There were some difficulties, but I think we're on the path to making a change."

"What's she like?" Brittany asked. "Is she as hot as you thought she would be? Is she nice? Is she crazy? Does she do lines of blow off strippers' chests? Does she sleep with everyone she sees? Is she always toting around a guitar? I'm dying with curiosity back home."

Chris laughed at her friend's onslaught, knowing that she would be asking exactly the same questions had she been in Brittany's shoes, even though she would be asking out of simple curiosity. Often, Brittany's questions about other women who had Chris's attention came from a different place. She tried to read Brittany's tone. She wasn't sure if it was jealousy seeping through or simply fandom. It was hard to tell over the phone.

"I can't," Chris answered, hoping Brittany would understand her vagueness. "But all is great."

"Oh my god!" Brittany exclaimed, her voice rising an octave. "You're with her right now, aren't you?"

"Mmmhmm," Chris murmured.

"Oh my god," Brittany said again, taking a deep breath. "It makes sense, I suppose," she added, her words tumbling out quickly. "Of course you're with her. You're traveling with her. But it still seems so surreal. I can't wait to hear all about it.

I want to know the details—everything. When you fill me in, leave nothing out. If you know dirt or if she's incredibly sexy or if she's a bitch, I want to know it all."

"What if I call you right before the show tonight?" Chris offered. "I should be free around seven, if that works for you."

"Yes! That works. I'll be here by my phone, waiting like a pathetic middle schooler, just hoping you'll call. In fact, don't be surprised if I pick up on the first ring."

"You're not even going to try to play the game, are you?" Chris joked, suddenly realizing just how much she missed Brittany, even if it was awkward at times. Brittany was her best and dearest friend and although Brittany undeniably wanted their relationship to blossom more than Chris did, the connection they shared was unmatched. The flashbacks of the nights they had shared popped into her mind. While their trysts had been short-lived, they had held unbridled passion. Chris shivered and righted her thoughts. "You're just going to show all your cards at once."

"We both know I have no game," Brittany said. "My game is being desperate. It's always seemed to work well for me."

"It's how you snagged me," Chris said, playing into the joke and glancing out of the corner of her eye to see Raven watching her curiously, her eyebrow raised and her smile growing. As Brittany laughed nervously, Chris shook her head. She should be more careful with what she said to Brittany. She had considered letting down her guard and giving it a real shot. Chris was curious and Brittany had once drunkenly admitted she would love to take it further.

But Chris was worried it would end badly, and she would be left with just one more loss in her life. Lovers had come and gone. What remained of her family was nothing more than a shred of contact with her mother. Brittany's friendship was important, and she hesitated to jeopardize it. Chris had very few people with whom she was close. It had been a long ongoing dilemma, and was clearly no closer to resolution.

Raven danced to the beat of a street performer, winking at Chris before turning to sign another autograph. The simplicity of her joy made Chris smile and long to join in. She cleared her throat and focused her attention back to the call.

"It sure is," Brittany continued after a pause, oblivious to the interaction on the other side of the line. "Anyway, have fun with your rock star and I'll talk to you tonight."

"Before I let you go," Chris said, "how's my little guy?"

She glanced back in Raven's direction and saw the rocker was done signing autographs and had once again cast her attention in Chris's direction. The questions danced in her eyes. *No poker face*, Chris thought to herself, turning her attention back to Brittany.

"He's doing great. We went for a walk today and then to PetSmart. We've been all over the place running errands. He shredded his stuffed bear and now he's napping on my lap. Aside from giving me an irritated look every time I speak, he's doing wonderfully."

"I miss him…and you," Chris said, wanting just a day to go back and spend with them before coming back out to continue here. "Thank you for loving him and taking such good care of him."

"It's what we do for each other," Brittany said, dismissing it casually. "Besides, you'd do the same for me. Go have fun and I'll talk to you later."

"Okay," Chris said. "Love you."

"Love you too. Bye."

She weighed the exchange. Before they slept together she had never questioned expressing her love to Brittany. But so much had changed since that fateful night just three months earlier. She took a moment to remember it in full, something she had refused to do for too long.

Chris had been down in the dumps. Her work week had been stressful and her mother had been terse. To top it off, it was her father's birthday. As always, Brittany was the one to step to the plate. What had started off as a night to blow off steam—one of their typical girls'-night-in celebrations—had turned into taking shot after shot and reliving college drinking games. Brittany had been smooth, turning a 'truth or dare' moment into an opportunity to share a kiss with Chris. With inhibitions lowered, there was little to stop her from enjoying Brittany's soft lips. And when they tumbled on top of each other, tearing at each other's clothes, their bodies fitting together like puzzle pieces, she hadn't stopped to think what the aftermath might be. She had been too lost in how it felt to touch Brittany's body, to have Brittany take control. She shivered, remembering the magic Brittany's tongue had worked, savoring the sight of those blue eyes. From between Chris's legs, Brittany had looked up, making eye contact and winking as Chris came. Chris's body tensed at the memory. It had been hot that night. And with the lines already blurred and both of them hungry for good sex, the nights that followed had been lost in waves of passion.

For almost a week, they went to work, came home, and fucked the night away, spooning together once it was over. Yet it had been too strange and too many lines were crossed. After a quick talk about going back to normal, it had never been verbally addressed again. Sometimes she noticed Brittany biting her lip or giving her a longing stare but it was a topic they didn't bring up. She had hoped this time away from home would clear her thoughts and make the situation easier to understand, but it wasn't working yet.

Chris walked back over to Raven, amused by just how engrossed the rock star had been in her conversation. Deciding to be as enigmatic as a vanilla-flavored person could be, Chris changed the subject. "Want to head back to the bus, so you can get ready for tonight?"

"I do," Raven said slowly. "But first, I want to grab a turkey leg from that street vendor over there. It's been calling my name for the past half hour and I know I just need to do it."

"It's destiny," Chris said, laughing at how serious Raven was about food choices. "Go get one and then we'll go back."

Raven nodded and put her arm around Chris, ensuring that they'd walk together over to the little stand. While they waited, Raven chewed the inside of her cheek, clearly wanting to say something but trying with all of her might to resist.

She finally turned to Chris. "Wife and kid? Girlfriend and kid? Or what?" she asked, her forced smile a plain attempt to appear casual and aloof.

Chris laughed, unable to hold it back. She wished Raven could see how transparent she was. Gone was the badass woman in control of everything. When she didn't answer immediately, Raven's brow lines deepened, her unspoken questions screaming at Chris.

"You have a wife, don't you? Even though you don't wear a ring, you have someone you left behind and hit the road," Raven said, this time making it a statement instead of a question. Raven shook her head. "They worry when you're out on the road doing god knows what with god knows who. It's not an easy life when you're connected to someone."

Chris let her continue, amused by the train of Raven's thoughts.

As Raven's eyes bored into her own, Chris laughed again. When Raven's eyes widened, she finally shook her head. "Roommate and dog," she said.

"*Roommate*?" Raven asked, her dimple showing her mischief.

"Roommate."

"Female?"

Chris nodded, wishing Raven would drop the subject.

"Our team?"

"What are you really asking?" Chris stopped walking and put her hands on her hips.

"Clearly it's a touchy subject," Raven said, her laughter growing. "I'm asking if she's a romantic interest."

"She's my best friend," Chris said. She let out a sigh, knowing she was blushing and that it was of no use to lie. "We hooked up a few times. I was in a rough place, and vodka helped start it. It was comfortable and safe."

"Was it good?" Raven asked, nudging Chris's arm.

"Dammit," Chris said, letting out an exaggerated sigh. "I don't want to talk about it or even think about it. It was amazing. It's a strong connection when you already love someone for the role they play in your life. But you add in sex and it gets complicated. That's the real answer. But that was a while back and now she's just my roommate. That is all. I think..."

"Oh..." Raven said, dragging out the word as she nodded. Her brow furrowed. "That makes sense I guess. I had to wonder why you hadn't ever mentioned having a kid or significant other before. But she sounds pretty important to you. I wonder why she hasn't come up."

"Maybe I'm just mysterious," Chris offered with a shrug. "As mysterious as you, even."

Raven laughed and shook her head. "You're mysterious, but not near mysterious enough to hide away a kid. And not mysterious enough to keep your true feelings about this roommate of yours hidden for very long."

"I guess you're probably right about the kid part but the roommate thing is settled."

"What kind of dog do you have?" Raven asked, turning to continue their walk.

"He's a Chihuahua."

Raven's smile grew and Chris breathed a sigh of relief that the subject had changed. "I love dogs," she said, her voice taking on an almost whimsical quality. "I always wanted one."

"You never had a dog?"

Raven shook her head, her eyes filling with sadness, before looking away. "No," she said quietly.

"Why not?"

"Didn't really work with timing and such when I was growing up," she said, casually waving her hand through the air, as if to ward off any emotion. "And it isn't really conducive to my current schedule."

"You could have a band dog," Chris said, her heart hurting for the girl who had clearly gone through a great deal. "It could be like the mascot and you could all take turns caring for it."

Raven looked at Chris, her expression torn between wanting to dream about the possibility of having something so playful and full of love and knowing it would never work. "One day maybe," she said. "When I'm a little more settled and the world doesn't move at the speed of light."

"Yeah," Chris said, working to move the conversation back to a more pleasant space. "One day."

They walked in silence until Raven asked, "What's his name?"

"Paco," Chris answered, laughing slightly to herself about the silliness of the dog's name. "He was named when I rescued him and I kept the name. I've had him for eight years. He's a good dog. He can get a little hyper and a little too attached to me. But he's a lot of fun."

"You'll have to bring him with you sometime if you stick with us on our way back through Houston in a couple of months," Raven said. "I'd like to meet him."

"Okay," Chris agreed, even though she wasn't quite sure how long it would be necessary for her to stay on the road.

"So have you given any thought to what it is you're going to do to work some magic for me?" Raven asked, abruptly changing the subject, as if she could read Chris's thoughts. "You've been here over a week and we haven't really dug into the meat of it yet."

"Yes," Chris answered, knowing that this would be the moment of truth. "If you don't like what I have in mind, remember that we can always work on something else—something that you're comfortable with."

Raven nodded, urging her to continue.

"I think we let this last episode with the underage girl blow over," she said. "It was bad, yes. But the media seems to already be talking about other things. We've waited too long to make a statement. If pressed, I have one drafted that you'll just have to sign off on—but I don't think we'll need it. It would only draw attention back to an unfavorable situation. We'll work to paint you in a positive light by getting you involved with a charity. You make some appearances and prove that you can—and want to—do good for the community."

"Okay," Raven said, her tone hesitant, but she wasn't shutting Chris down entirely. "What kind of charity?"

"Whatever you'd like," Chris said. "I think we can find something that you'll enjoy, something that you feel passionate about, something that needs help…your help."

"Okay," Raven said, nodding and seeming satisfied with the plan. "So what's the statement if it comes up again?"

"We reiterate what you've already said," Chris said. "We can't backtrack on that. I know you were telling the truth, and we'll want to remain consistent so that it doesn't appear that we're changing our story. We let them know that you had no idea the girl was underage, that she was only nineteen. She wasn't served alcohol on your bus—she had her own. You did not have any sort of relationship or relations with the girl and you were unaware of the Snapchat video being taken. We'll offer the reiteration of the story, even though they all know it—in gory detail. And then we will apologize and ensure that every effort is being made to make sure that all after-party attendees are of legal drinking age. We'll leave it at that and then we'll do the rest of the image polishing with your charity work."

"What about the drugs?"

Chris winced. She had forgotten the video highlight of a pipe in the corner. "I think it's best if we don't even address that. Basically, if we don't acknowledge it, we don't give it legitimacy. Anyone who has seen the video can tell that there are a ton of people at your after-party. It could belong to any of them. We don't even address it, so that we don't give their claims a leg to stand on."

"It was mine though," Raven said, her eyes clouding.

"They don't need to know that."

"Okay," Raven said, nodding her head. "Let's move forward. I like you, by the way. I'm good with you being here."

"Thank you," Chris said, genuinely touched by the compliment. "I like being here too."

When they finally made their way back to the bus, Chris glanced at her watch. An hour and a half until showtime.

"Before we all get ready, do you want to have a pregame drink?" Raven asked as they stood in front of the bus.

"I probably should go clean up a bit and let you rest."

Raven nodded and was about to speak as the door swung open behind her.

"So glad to see you finally made it back," a busty blonde, dressed in a crop top and miniskirt said from the doorway. "I've been waiting and we both know I'm not good at that."

"Tanya," Raven said, a playful smile edging up the sides of her lips. "When did you get here? I didn't know you were coming."

"I wouldn't miss it, baby," she said, winking at Raven before turning and looking at Chris. "Who's she?"

Chris felt out of place. Nonetheless, she stepped forward. "I'm Christina. I do public relations for Raven."

Tanya looked her up and down before nodding. "Okay, well have a good night," she said, waving her away.

Raven looked back, as if she wanted to stop Chris and ask her to stay, but Chris shook her head. "Go have fun and have a great show," she said, ignoring the way her heart fell as she watched Tanya throw her arms around Raven's neck and plant a huge kiss on her lips.

"I'll see you at the after-party?" Raven asked, pulling away from the kiss.

Chris nodded. "Of course," she said. "After all, I live here." Her words were nothing but a whisper as she turned away so she didn't have to see as Raven was pulled inside the bus by a clearly very excited Tanya. She walked quickly, unsure of where she was going. Her stuff, her current life, everything aside from her home back in Houston sat inside that bus, where Raven was no doubt being ravaged by a skanky groupie—or girlfriend. Whatever she was, her message had been clear.

Chris was unwelcome.

CHAPTER SEVEN

Sitting on the couch, Paul watched Raven slip into her room with Tanya. The two of them were up to no good. He knew that much. Anytime Tanya came around, it was bad news. But that's how Raven coped.

He let out a sigh and scratched his head, wondering if he should alert Frank. They had an unspoken rule about letting one another know when something was amiss that might tilt the axis of the regular schedule. He weighed his options, picked up his phone and set it back down. Until he knew more or saw a sign of disturbance, he wasn't going to rock the boat.

After all they had been through, he owed Raven the benefit of the doubt. Leaning back against the soft, worn cushions, he replayed their history.

Together, they had seen it all. Childhood friends who lived next door to each other, torn apart when she was taken from her mother, they had met again by fate in their high school years. He had never been so happy to see someone again. She was his fellow adventurer, his kindred spirit. In the early years, it had been fort building and camping out in each other's backyards. As time progressed, the days and nights got rougher. Her crazed environment had brought self-doubt, fear, uncertainty and much pain. Yet, she had stood strong against it all. He had been her safe space, her confidante, her one constant friend.

When it got too bad at her house, she had sought refuge at his. Even as a kid, she had insisted his parents not know she was there. She would sneak in at night, sleep on his bedroom floor and be gone before morning. He had been the only one she told about her mother's boyfriends' abusive rages, the syringes, the fridge full of alcohol but no food.

Her insistence to keep her struggles secret had kept his hands tied. While she would confide in him and show him her bruises, she never wanted his parents or anyone in authority to know.

Not that his parents were around enough to know. They had provided him a home and had never raised a hand to him. But they had been absent. He couldn't have told them if he wanted to. Still he felt the guilt for not knowing how to help. When she was finally taken away, he had lost his best friend.

Raven had been placed in many foster homes. Some were little better than where she had come from, and others were good, but short-lived. They were fifteen when they reconnected. She was living at Home Again, the home for older teenage foster kids until their eighteenth birthday, when they were tossed out into the real world ill-equipped and left to their own devices.

They shared a common love of music and had formed a band. They'd hang out after school, drinking cheap beer they had convinced people to buy for them, playing with guitars and a drum set he got from a pawnshop.

She told him about the men who had taken their touches too far, the times that—even in a home dedicated to child care—she still went hungry or found herself not missed when she wasn't around. He'd shudder as he listened, hug her tighter and remind himself that, even if his parents didn't care enough to ask how his day was or even notice if he didn't come home, he was still comparatively fortunate.

He had always been fortunate enough to have a roof over his head, food in the fridge and freedom to explore life. As long as he had that, he could get the love of a family from his little sister. Even if she wasn't blood, she would always be his sister—the only thing he knew of family and the only one with whom making music had been more than a passing hobby. It was a way of life. For the two of them, it was survival and it was the one thing that made sense in the world.

He smiled, his trip down memory lane holding more fond memories than dark ones. Whatever the road would bring, he would stay by her side and would fight for her through it all—even if that meant putting up with another visit from Tanya and the havoc she brought.

* * *

Pacing outside, Chris smiled as she dialed her boss for one of her twice-a-week check-ins. Susan had always been somewhat of a mother figure to her, and she missed her.

"Good afternoon," Susan answered.

"Hey! Good afternoon to you. I just wanted to touch base."

"How are things on the battlefield?" Susan's laughter filled the line. They had both agreed this would be the challenge of her career, and Susan enjoyed reminding Chris that she had a tendency to take on the world.

"Going well today. We're kicking off the campaign we brainstormed last week. How are things back home?"

"Crazy as ever," Susan answered and Chris could hear the clicking of a keyboard in the distance. True to form, Susan was multitasking.

"Anything exciting?"

"It's always exciting. You know that...Anyway don't worry about any of this stuff. You've got your hands full as is. Any press booked for the morning?"

"I've got someone lined up to cover the photo shoot. I think it'll be a good event and will serve its purpose in rebranding her image little by little."

"Mmmhmmm. Good. Good."

Chris wanted to prolong the conversation but time wasn't on her side. As usual, Susan didn't have time for chitchat. "You take care and let me know what you think when you see the coverage," Chris said and let out a sigh.

"You take care too," Susan said as she cleared her throat. Chris smiled at the gesture. She recalled the throat clearing mechanism Susan employed often to rein in her focus. "And know that we miss you around here."

"I miss you all too." As she hung up, Chris recounted the many times Susan had reminded her that Chris was special to her. While Susan loved all of her employees, Chris knew she reminded Susan of a younger version of herself—of what she could have had if she had taken the time to have a family instead of building an empire.

The thought made Chris's smile droop. Even though she was having fun, she needed to make a trip home soon to see Susan, to change out her wardrobe and to get her life back in check before jet-setting again. Her clothing options were limited and she was beginning to feel frumpy.

She looked down at her street clothes and decided they would be good enough for the show tonight. Although she had wanted to look special and don her new black leather pants, she shoved the shopping bag into her purse. There was no reason to dress up.

Picking up her phone, she took the opportunity to call Brittany back.

"Hey, stranger," she teased. "Have you found time to talk to your long lost roomie yet?"

Chris laughed, Brittany's excitement and silliness putting her at ease. "Yeah, just got booted from the bus by a lover of the rock star, so I think I'm all yours for a while."

"Lover, huh?" Brittany's voice practically squealed. "Spill it. I want to know the gossip."

"You know that my job is to counteract the gossip, right?" she said with a laugh. "I'm supposed to say that all of that stuff is nonsense and that the real story is somewhere in the music."

"Yeah, save me the PR spiel," she said quickly. "Tell me what she's *really* like."

"She's a tough case," Chris admitted, walking farther to make sure she couldn't be overheard. Her best friend held the key to the vault of her own life secrets, so she spoke freely. "She is one of the coolest people I've ever met, without a doubt. But she's stubborn. She's guarded and unyielding in some areas."

"So she still won't sleep with you?" Brittany teased. When Chris didn't respond right away, Brittany laughed. "Ill-timed joke. I'm sorry. Continue."

"It has nothing to do with whether or not she'd take me to bed," Chris explained. Brittany gasped and Chris wished again for the ease with which they had once talked about lovers or potential lovers. She pressed on with the conversation, determined to make this about something other than what *could be* between her and Brittany. "It's just that she bounces between the real version of herself and the jaded version, like if anything gets too real, it's just too much for her to handle. And once she's done that, it's hell trying to bring her back. If she would just let down her guard for a while and let people see who she really is, I wouldn't have to fight so hard to get her positive publicity, but she goes back and forth between genuine and amazing to jaundiced and crazy. I'm afraid that at any minute, she's going to go off the deep end, or come to a show fucked up, or overdose."

"Damn," Brittany said. "I'm sorry. I thought you would be having more fun than that."

"It's not that I'm not having fun," Chris said, letting out a long breath. "That's the problem. When I'm with her, I'm having the best time ever. It's just that I packed up my life for this. I've left behind Susan and you and everyone who feels like family. I've left the rest of my clients to others at the firm to help someone who, half the time, seems content going on with her wild lifestyle, consequences be damned. And the other half of the time, she only wants to be helped on her terms and only if I'm partying right beside her. I can't help but feel like my work might be compromised and like she's going to walk into another landmine at some point. But I can't change it. It's like

I'm operating with my hands tied. And I haven't slept anywhere that doesn't have wheels in over a week.

"I have traveled across state lines and through several cities. She's played three shows but the process of show to show is crazy. There are rehearsals, shoots for videos, trainers, choreographers and then the hair and makeup team trying out new looks. It's a constant cycle when we're on the road between shows. And then we spend the days checking out local areas whenever we stop. I've tinkered around in gift shops, been to more rock shows in the past week than I have in my entire life and I'm partying like a college kid. I feel like I've somehow gone off to another reality and I'm not sure how I'm going to adjust once this is all over."

"Any idea how long you'll be gone?" Brittany asked.

Chris sighed. It had been left so open-ended when she left town and she still had no more to go on. "I have no idea. I know that I'm going to try to garner a bunch of interviews, photo shoots and some publicity stops, all as part of a spearheaded campaign to drive up her positive press. I'm not sure how long that will take or if she'll fire me before I finish the job. She's kind of a hothead."

"Sounds like it," Brittany said and Chris could just imagine her shaking her head, giving Chris the "stay away from that" look Brittany often wore at bars whenever a girl tried to give Chris her number. "After all, nothing sounds fun about a masochistic child hell-bent on self-destruction."

Her choice of words made Chris laugh loudly. "I needed this," she said. "Sorry to vent. I just needed to get that all out."

"Anytime," Brittany said, her voice serious and sincere. "You know that's what I'm here for. We're best friends. You've talked me off the ledge a time or two, and talked me out of blowing up a girl's house a time or two."

Her words trailed off for a moment, and Chris recalled the times Brittany referenced. They had always teetered on the edge of more than friends, but Brittany was right. They *were* best friends.

"We've gone through tough times, breakups, new starts and more. We listen to each other. We're there for each other and I want you to remember that, even while you're out there on the road, okay?"

"Okay," Chris promised. "Thank you."

As the conversation went on, Chris felt better. They chatted about Brittany's job, about Paco and about life. By the time they hung up, Chris felt more relaxed—but tired. She wished she had a place to go lie down for a little while and just let some of the craziness fade away. She let out a long sigh and headed for the arena, missing her stable life back home.

Inside the hall, hundreds waited already. She felt lost in the sea of people—adrift among a crowd of smiling faces. All she wanted to do was find a hole to disappear into.

A clearly intoxicated teenage girl bumped into her as she took her seat next to Chris. "Sorry," she mumbled, her words easily slurring together. "Are you excited about the show?"

Chris nodded, not wanting to dull the shine in the young girl's eyes.

"Raven is my favorite singer of all time," the girl babbled. Chris called upon everything in her power to offer up a smile, before turning her attention to the empty stage. She wondered who was checking IDs or if this girl had been drinking before the show. She didn't care and tried to block out her constant commentary.

Chris listened to the music, watched Raven move on stage and tried to remember that this was a woman she was beginning to respect, to enjoy on a personal level. Even so, pettiness crept up within her, making her feel every bit like a jealous lover. She scanned the crowd for Tanya.

Her heart pounded, and she grimaced at the thought of the trashy woman, the way she had excluded Chris. She tried to tell herself that her immediate and intense dislike was aimed solely at her rudeness. But she knew herself too well to think that was really the case. It was jealousy, plain and simple, and it was ugly. Her mind flashed to the way Tanya had so crassly put her hands all over Raven's body, all while giving Chris a "go to hell" look.

Thankful when she couldn't find her in the crowd, Chris tried to focus on the music. She just wasn't feeling it tonight.

She didn't want to sit in a concert hall full of hot, sweaty people, much less tolerate the drunk teenager next to her yelling, cheering and generally making an ass of herself. I'm getting old, Chris thought to herself, realizing that she once would have been doing exactly the same. Now though, she was tired. She was tired of so many things—mostly of trying so hard, just to get tossed to the side like a pair of dirty socks.

As the show came to an end, Chris wanted nothing more than to disappear into the sea of people and then be back at her house in her Jacuzzi bubble bath. She sighed, realizing those creature comforts were too far away. She looked longingly at the crowd, wanting to follow one of them home instead of having to trek back to her home on wheels and party it up with complete strangers all night.

"It's no wonder you weren't a rock star," she muttered to herself, deciding that she wanted out of there as soon as possible. She needed to breathe. She made a beeline for the long hallways of dressing rooms, bolting through the back exit and inhaling fresh air.

She threw her hands out by her side, looking up to a full moon and the mountains of New Mexico illuminated in the distance. Forcing herself to breathe deeply, she worked on calming herself back down.

She reminded herself that this was temporary and she was going to get to go home eventually. She briefly felt some sadness for Raven's gypsy life, but just as quickly as it came, she pushed it away. She needed to prioritize her job, feelings and concerns about being liked be damned.

"This is work," she whispered to herself. "It's nothing more." Sure, she might be getting a behind-the-scenes look at a life she had always wondered about and she might be getting to spend every day with a woman who had been her celebrity crush for years, but this was *work*. It was an assignment, nothing more than another challenge at which she was going to succeed.

Once her heart rate had returned to normal, she turned on her heel and walked back to the bus. Thankful that none of the crew had returned she went straight to her "room" and shut the door behind her. Closing her eyes, she relished the softness of the pillows. In an instant, her tired body gave way, letting her finally rest.

Exuberant shouting just outside her window startled her. Slightly disoriented, she glanced at the clock. Only ten minutes had passed, but it felt like she had been asleep for hours. Blinking, she tried to force herself awake.

"Let's do shots," she heard Tanya's high-pitched and irritating voice as the door of the bus flew open. She could hear people rummaging through cabinets and then rushing back outside.

She wanted to scream. She reminded herself of her pep talk. She was going to paint on a smile and handle this like she would any unpleasant work situation.

"She's a client," Chris said under her breath, before taking a quick look in the mirror. She touched up her makeup and smiled at her reflection. For just a moment, she looked at the eyes staring back at her, remembering the same strong and somewhat wild green eyes of her father. She looked at her smile and remembered that she was beautiful. Regardless of what the night might hold, or how catty Tanya might be, Chris was determined to make the best of it.

With her head held high, she emerged out in front of the bus, and followed the noise. There was a party already. Chris fought to keep her expression neutral. She had never seen it quite like this. On the pavement in front of the bus, people were scurrying to set up speakers and a makeshift dancing area. Nearby, two scantily clad women were lurking. It appeared that the party people had arrived.

"There you are," a husky voice shouted from behind her, causing her to turn and face a glassy-eyed Raven whose head was bopping along a little too freely with the music. "I've been watching for you."

Chris nodded. "I was inside," she said, trying to catch her breath, suddenly taken back to feeling completely out of place. "I was just stepping outside to smoke."

"I'll come with you," Raven offered.

As she caught Tanya's narrow-eyed stare, she considered dismissing Raven's offer, but she shrugged and nodded instead, turning to lead the way away from the crowd. Once in an open space, she gulped in fresh air, silently willing this night to turn around—even though she still couldn't quite pinpoint what had her so jumbled.

"What's wrong?" Raven asked, sidling up beside her and lighting a cigarette in one fluid motion.

"Nothing," Chris lied.

"Ah, come on," Raven urged, putting an arm around Chris's shoulders. "I spent all day with you and this isn't how you were acting earlier."

Chris felt an odd sensation, as if she was being watched. Turning around quickly, she saw Tanya peeking out of the bus window, her eyes flashing with anger. Her long, red fingernails tapping on the edge of the windowsill seemed to scream at Chris.

"I think it's safe to say your girlfriend isn't too pleased about you coming out here," Chris said, lighting her own cigarette and taking a deep drag.

Raven laughed, amusement spreading as quickly as her grin grew. "She's not my girlfriend," she said with a shrug. "She can get upset about whatever she wants."

"What is she then?" Chris asked, giving into her curiosity and deciding that if Raven was going to discuss things freely, so would she. "A groupie?"

Raven's laugh grew, until it sounded hearty and she wordlessly shook her head. Once she had regained her composure, she faced Chris with a raised eyebrow. "I like that you think I have groupies."

"Don't you?"

"No," Raven said. "Fans that I fuck, on occasion. Groupies, no. And Tanya is neither. She's my New Mexico road stop for items out of the ordinary."

Chris nodded in understanding. "I suppose that's your nice way of saying she's a dealer."

"It's all in the wording," Raven said, a half grin lifting the right corner of her mouth.

"You should be doing my job then," Chris said, taking a long drag and opting for a subject change under Tanya's hostile glare out the window. "What I do is all about positive messaging. Smoking and drinking are not vices—they're hobbies. PMS does not make women moody—it gives them versatility to figure out how they feel about a certain situation. I'm not indecisive—I'm simply weighing my options and giving my situation the attention that it deserves."

Raven laughed and shook her head. "Are you going to do some of that voodoo on me?"

"We're already doing it," she said. "There's been nothing but positive stories on you for the last three weeks. As you'll recall, even before I hit the ground, we were working in partnership with Frank to issue statements and set up partnerships. The results have been great. We're going to keep doing that and we'll distract from the bad. In addition to the charity partnership we've agreed to, I've got a slew of press junkets lined up for the next couple of weeks. We have a stop in Fresno at a youth center on our way through. We've planned backstage visits with some Make-A-Wish kids. You have your interview with Ellen coming up when we're in Los Angeles, and we're going to continue to release positive statements, monitor social media use and drive home the message that you care about things other than the party-hard lifestyle. It'll be a strenuous couple of months, but I have it all lined up with the concert schedule."

"Thank you," Raven said, her dark eyes filling with a direct look of sincerity. "I really do appreciate what you're doing."

While Raven's words had calmed Chris to some extent, the intensity of Raven's eye contact made her heart speed up again.

"You're welcome," Chris said. "Thanks for giving me a shot—"

She was about to finish her thought, when Raven leaned in, maintaining eye contact. Inches from Chris's lips, she stopped, causing Chris's heart to pound even more. At the last moment, Raven offered a smile and leaned the rest of the way in to wrap Chris up in a warm embrace.

With her body pressed tightly up against Raven's, Chris could smell her hair, could feel the way their bodies fit together. She felt herself tense, but returned the hug, enjoying the feeling of being so close.

"This is nice," Raven murmured into Chris's neck.

"It is," Chris agreed before reluctantly pulling back to stop the embrace. She glanced to the window and saw the curtain swing quickly back over it. Message received. Tanya was not happy. "Does your dealer know she's just your dealer?" she asked, turning back to face Raven.

"Yes. She does, but she's a little crazy," Raven said, looking back to the bus. "Truth be told, she's just jealous because you're hot."

"I'm hot?" Chris asked, raising an eyebrow.

"I know we have mirrors in the bathroom," Raven said, nonchalantly stomping out her cigarette on the ground. "You have to know just how good you look."

"Thank you," Chris said, cocking her head to the side as she replayed the compliment in her head.

"Don't doubt me," Raven said. "This is my bus and my party and I said you're hot. Go with it. Rock it. Go in there and make those other girls jealous. And if you want to make it fun, we'll play it up a little for them. I'm in the mood to be a little silly tonight, so let's go have some fun."

Chris laughed. She hadn't engaged in jealousy games since junior high and it wasn't really her style. Regardless, it would prove interesting and fun to mess with Tanya just a bit. "What the hell?" she said, her grin growing. "Let's do it."

"All right, 'atta girl," Raven said, looping her arm in Chris's as they walked back onto the bus.

She watched as Raven fist-bumped people on her way to the couch in the corner, making small talk as she went, but never removing her arm from Chris's side. She nodded at Tanya, who glared pointedly at her rival. Raven immediately lost herself in head banging to the beat of the music, letting her long, dark hair flow freely through the air in mesmerizing fashion. Chris stared in awe, wanting to define this woman's charisma. All eyes were glued to Raven, the revelers seemingly fueled by her energy. Like a skilled conductor, she owned the room, causing everyone to amp up their own tempo and reach her level.

The night progressed with girls providing near striptease dances outside the bus, and shots downed like it was a rave.

Even as her head started to spin from the alcohol, she noted the way Raven's attention to her never faltered. She had to remind herself that it was all an act on Raven's part, but the sincerity in Raven's gaze was very convincing.

When Raven took her hand and led her to the dance floor as old-school R & B pumped through the speakers, she couldn't resist. Wanting nothing more than to get lost in the pure sexuality of dancing with Raven again, she followed eagerly. Raven quickly straddled Chris's legs and began moving with the beat. Transfixed, Chris watched the display of visual lust in front of her, her body burning as though she had stepped into a bonfire. As much as she wanted to watch the gyration of Raven's hips, she couldn't pull herself away from Raven's face.

She's on multiple substances, Chris reminded herself silently. Even so, there was a beauty in how easily she moved and how her eyes no longer held even a hint of being drug fucked. Still, Chris was cautious. Raven was gasoline. No good would come of lighting a match.

She took a few steadying breaths, attempting to move to the beat, but there was no denying how distracted she felt, or just how hard she was fighting to keep her composure. Her body pounded from the electricity in Raven's every touch, every grind against her thigh. When Raven winked and moved in close to brush the hair from her dance partner's neck, Chris thought she might explode.

"Are you having fun yet?" Raven's sultry whisper cascaded against Chris's ears and made her knees weaken. Her entire body tensed with desire as Raven, less than an inch from Chris's skin, trailed her lips all the way down to the base of her neck. She ran her full lips gently over Chris's neck, causing Chris to gasp in pleasure. "I'll take that as a yes," Raven whispered again, pressing the length of her body against Chris's and continuing to move to the music.

She pulled back without warning, leaving Chris wanting more. When she gazed deep into Raven's dark eyes, Chris could see clarity, full awareness of the situation shining in their depths. In one fluid movement, Raven brushed the hair out of Chris's eyes and leaned in for the softest kiss Chris had ever experienced. When their lips met, Chris felt her own breath catch, just as she felt Raven's small gasp. Raven's full lips engulfed her own, setting a fire across every part of her. As their tongues danced, she knew there was no turning back. Lost in desire, she threw her arms around Raven's neck, pulling her closer and not caring who saw—or if anyone else was even there. Nothing more mattered aside from the feel of soft lips against hers.

There was a loud, low whistle in the background, but Chris ignored it, wrapped up in what was happening between the two of them. Intertwining her fingers in Raven's hair, she could feel the passion mounting within her, culminating in wetness between her thighs.

"I think everyone is calling it a night," Pete's voice called. "We'll leave you two alone."

Chris moved back reluctantly, but suddenly all too aware of how many sets of eyes were on them. Near the door, a woman was trying to push her husband out the door, but he stood staring, slack-jawed and completely immobile. Tanya sat stoically on the couch without averting her gaze.

Raven cleared her throat and offered a huge smile to everyone. "I think we're all going to call it a night," she said, walking over to the bar and grabbing her drink to raise it into the air. "Thank you all for hanging out and for making New Mexico one of my favorite stops. We'll see you all again soon."

With that, she took a big sip, set her drink back on the bar and grabbed Chris's hand. Chris smiled as she was led out of the main room. Without questioning motives or intentions, without caring what would happen next, she knew she had reached a point of no longer caring. She needed sex. She needed it badly and she had never felt so strongly aroused by anyone. Whatever may come, she was going to fuck Raven.

Raven closed her bedroom door behind them and offered a sideways grin as she looked Chris up and down. "You're so sexy," Raven said, leaning in to kiss her softly. "Do you want to sleep in here?"

"I wouldn't have followed if I didn't," Chris said, laughing. "This is far from my first rodeo."

Raven winked, the gesture so commonplace, yet undoing Chris completely. No longer waiting for orders, Chris stepped forward boldly, throwing Raven against the wall and kissing her with unapologetic fury. She looped her fingers through the hem of Raven's shirt and expertly pulled it off with one smooth movement. Fueled by her lust, she unclasped Raven's bra and let it fall to the floor. She quickly removed Raven's pants, not taking her mouth from those delicious lips, until Raven stood naked in front of her.

Pulling back briefly, she assessed the sight in front of her, taking in every curve, every angle of Raven's body. Her full breasts displayed hardened nipples. Chris couldn't resist the urge to have them. She wrapped her lips around one of them and used her tongue to tease the tip, eliciting a series of low moans from Raven. Encouraged by the response, Chris sucked gently and let her teeth glide over the tip.

Clearly wanting to be in control, Raven moved to pull Chris's face back up to hers, but Chris wasn't about to let that happen. Reaching up, she used one hand to secure Raven's hands and press them up against the wall and the other to reach down and slide inside Raven.

Raven let out a loud gasp as Chris slid in with ease. Pumping her fingers in and out, she brought her lips back to Raven's and kissed her deeply. As she picked up the pace, Raven groaned loudly, grinding her hips and letting Chris get even deeper. When Chris could feel Raven tighten against her fingers, she slowed and pulled out, teasing and making the experience last longer.

"Please," Raven begged, breathlessly. "Don't stop. Please don't fucking stop."

"Beg for it," Chris said, grinning.

"Please fuck me," she begged. "Please I need it."

Needing no further invitation, Chris plunged back inside Raven's wet vagina, enjoying taking complete control. She picked up the pace and expertly pounded her until Raven screamed and arched her back, finishing with a shudder. Panting open-mouthed, Raven looked Chris in the eye, a mix of wonder and amazement dancing in her half-closed eyes. "Where did that come from?" Raven asked, trying to settle her breathing back to normal.

"From wanting to fuck you since the day I first met you," Chris said, pressing her lips against Raven's once more.

"This is far from over," Raven said, picking Chris up and throwing her on the bed. She stood over her and smiled. With her blond hair streaming across the blankets and her eyes sparkling despite the dull lighting, she winked at Raven. Raven's breath caught in her throat and her hands trembled, even though she had been in this very spot with plenty of women before. This was different. She climbed on the bed, straddling Chris and leaned in for another kiss, before pulling at the hem of Chris's shirt. She worked it up Chris's body, kissing every inch as she exposed bare skin.

She knew she was playing with fire, her movements far more intimate and slow-moving than usual, but she didn't care. Too absorbed in the beautiful sound of Chris's moans to pull away, she traced her fingertips along Chris's bare body.

When she pulled back, Raven could see the questions in Chris's eyes.

"Don't worry," she whispered. "I'm just taking my time, savoring every second." Her words were raw. She needed to savor the moments, her desire growing with each passing second. Chris arched her back and raised an eyebrow, seductively inviting Raven closer. When Raven didn't comply immediately, Chris's eyes twinkled with mischief.

"I'll get started without you then," she said. Without wasting another second, Chris slid her hand inside her own jeans and undid the button to pleasure herself.

Raven's jaw dropped open and her eyes widened. She sat propped up on one elbow, lost in the incredible display of lust unfolding before her eyes. As Chris moaned, Raven's body convulsed, overrun with passion. She moved back in front of

Chris, slid her jeans to the floor and dropped to her knees in between Chris's legs.

Engaging in what she deemed the most intimate act possible between two people, Raven dove in and tasted Chris's wetness, teasing Chris with her tongue. Chris threw her head back and grabbed the back of Raven's head. Encouraged by Chris's increased moans, Raven sped up, working her tongue into overdrive.

Chris tangled her fingers in the sheets and her body tensed. "Oh god!" she shouted as Raven gave her what appeared to be an earth-shattering orgasm.

When Chris's body stopped convulsing, Raven pulled her in closer for a kiss, letting her taste the remnants of what had just occurred. Breathless, the two collapsed back onto the bed.

"How do you like the new job now?" Raven asked, nudging Chris with her arm and leaning over to kiss the top of her head.

"Best fucking job I've ever had," Chris answered honestly, feeling at ease in Raven's embrace.

They shared a laugh before Raven turned to face Chris. "Thank you," she said, her voice lighter than usual.

"What for?"

"For this," Raven said, running her fingers through Chris's hair. "For everything. For making me open up, even if just slightly, and for making me feel comfortable. It might come as a shock to you but you have seen more of the real me than a lot of people have. I'm in the spotlight all the time and typically only show people what I want them to see. You are different somehow. I can't nail it down but you're different. You make me feel like I can show you some of the other parts of me. Thank you for that." She paused for a moment. "And also for getting me off so well," she added with a grin.

"You're welcome," Chris said, reaching up to trace the outline of Raven's breasts. "Thank *you* too."

"It's Erin, by the way," Raven said softly.

"What?" Chris asked, leaning in closer, with her head on Raven's chest.

"My name," she said, looking away briefly before bringing her full attention back to Chris. "My name is Erin. You asked earlier, and if anyone deserves to know, it's you. I prefer Raven. It's who I am. Erin is an old identity and she's long gone. I don't identify as that girl any longer. I haven't in a long time. To me, I'm Raven. To everyone else, I'm Raven. Raven is who I am, who I've become. I no longer respond to Erin and even those who know it, know better than to call me by that name. It's irrelevant to me. That's why I keep it so under wraps, so hidden, but I wanted you to know."

Touched by the tenderness of the statement, Chris wrapped her arms around Raven and kissed her once more. "Thank you," she said, nestling closer as they drifted off to sleep.

CHAPTER EIGHT

"Why the long face?" The question from one of her staff pulled Susan from her morning tasks.

She looked up over the rim of her glasses and shook her head. "Just a busy morning."

"Do you need help with anything?" Brynlee, her youngest employee, stood in her doorway, smiling and exuding an enviable eagerness.

For a second, she considered the thought. The girl was an untested assistant who hadn't been in the industry long enough to help with most of the tasks on Susan's plate. She shook her head. "Check with one of the account managers. I can handle my projects. But thank you."

Though the words had clearly been a dismissal, Brynlee didn't budge.

"Are you okay?" It was a good-natured question but she wasn't in the mood for small talk. Nor did she make a habit of opening up to new employees.

"It's not a good time for chitchat, Bryn," she said.

Quietly Brynlee nodded and walked away. Frustrated, Susan removed her glasses, relaxed her eyes and massaged her temples. "Too much to do," she whispered, spinning in her chair to face away from her computer for a moment.

It wasn't necessarily the workload. It was because she had been operating without her right hand for a month now. She had lost her confidante. Letting out a heavy sigh, she turned back to her computer and readjusted her glasses. She typed out a quick email to touch base with Chris. After she hit the send button, she caught sight of her niece's photo on her desk. A slow smile spread over her face. Her sister was the lucky one—so much love surrounding her every day. Susan surveyed her office. Her sister had all the love in the world, and Susan had this. She tried to take a deep breath but the air felt heavy in her lungs. Standing, she pushed away from her desk.

Desperately needing fresh air or a fresh start…or something, anything, she called out to her staff. "I'll be back in a while." No one batted an eye as she strode out the front door. Perks of owning your own business, she thought as she got into her car.

Turning up her radio, she rolled down the windows and let the wind and music calm her.

It wasn't that she was worried about Chris doing her job. Quite the opposite in fact. There was no one more capable of tackling the task at hand than Chris. The young woman was her protégée, her most gifted employee and more of a daughter figure than Susan wanted to admit.

She let her mind drift back to a time when she thought she would have a life and family of her own. She had the perfect man, her Marcus—or at least the one perfect for her. But try as they might, those two pink lines on the test never came. And eventually nothing came but hurt and disappointment. Fighting the reality at home, she had filled the gap and built her corporate empire at the expense of her personal life. She couldn't shake the memory of Marcus walking out the door of their home, never to return again.

She parked the car in front of Starbucks and steadied herself. Looking around the parking lot, she smiled despite her pain. If nothing else, she had this place and with it the many memories of her long talks with Chris. She had a successful business and she had her own version of a family—even if her *family* was away for the time being.

She ordered her non-fat soy latte and caught sight of a middle-aged woman sitting at the table across from a young woman who was obviously related.

"The best part of summers are days like these," the older woman said.

"I like these days too, Mom," the young woman said, reaching across the table and patting her mother on the hand. They continued in trite conversation—classes, whether or not the girl's car was in good condition to go back to school in the fall and whether or not the girl's boyfriend treated her well. When the barista called her name, Susan snapped back to attention. Grabbing her coffee, she made a beeline for the door.

She could feel the sting of hot tears. How was it that she wound up alone? The black hole of despair was never far away. Shaking her head at the harsh slap of reality, she took a sip of her coffee, only to burn her tongue.

"Shit!" she called out as her anger and frustration boiled. She glanced across the parking lot and took in the sight of her shiny BMW and thought back to the office. She had things. She had a business. And she was being ridiculous. Straightening her shoulders and holding her head high, she vowed that this would no longer affect her this way.

* * *

The California sun beamed and Raven could feel the heat permeating her body. Sweat dripped down her face and her legs burned with each step. Even so, she rounded the corner of the street, encouraged by the sound of her footsteps pounding on the pavement.

Morning runs were her time, and she had been neglecting them. Refreshed by the time she stopped in front of the bus, she snagged the water bottle she had left by the tire and took a long drink.

She took her time stretching, enjoying a final moment of solitude for the day. While she was having a good time, it was all a little too confusing. She had started to develop a genuine connection with Chris, and the mere concept of letting someone in was terrifying. But she was helpless to fight it.

Closing her eyes and taking a deep breath, she stretched her neck from side to side and steadied her shoulders. Like she did with most situations, she was going to wing it. Whatever happened was going to happen anyway. In the back of her mind, she considered that it might be stupidity or irresponsibility. But those were just semantics. After going through possibilities of what could or could not happen between the two of them, she focused her attention. With her *Ellen* interview coming up the following morning, she had to mentally prepare.

With her back to the door, she gave her legs one final stretch, hearing a low whistle behind her.

"Looking good," Chris called out from the doorway.

"You are aware that catcalls are insulting, correct?" Raven asked, feigning annoyance as she turned to face Chris.

"I'm aware," Chris said with a wink. "I just thought you should know I appreciate the view."

Chris's laughter filled the air and made Raven laugh as well. "You're something else," she said, closing the distance between the two of them. Her hair was swept to the side in a messy ponytail and she wore no makeup. Clad in nothing but a tank top and yoga pants, Chris looked like a model. Her eyes lit up as Raven stepped close enough to kiss her softly.

"Yeah. I've heard that a time or two." Chris shrugged. "But you're the one sleeping with me. I guess you might just be something else too."

"You might be right," Raven answered, leaning down and planting a kiss on Chris's head as she walked onto the bus. "After I shower, what do you say to a smoothie and watching something mindless on my iPad?"

"That sounds like a plan," Chris said still suggestively eyeing Raven.

"I'm covered in sweat. What has you so worked up?" she asked, raising an eyebrow.

"Like I said, you look good. And I'm looking forward to getting a little one-on-one time this morning. I'll whip up that smoothie and see you when you're done."

Raven laughed and shook her head. This woman made her life happier, regardless of the confusion. "I'll be back," she called, shutting the door behind her.

After her shower, Raven beckoned Chris to follow her into her room. Smoothie in hand, Chris heeded without speaking. Raven dropped her towel once they were both in the room, embracing the intimacy of the moment. Gratefully, she accepted the drink and crawled next to Chris on the bed. She got out her iPad and pulled up Netflix. Relinquishing control as she so uncharacteristically did in Chris's presence, she handed over the device.

"Pick whatever you want," she said, taking a sip. "This is delicious by the way."

"Glad you like it." Chris smiled and turned her attention to selecting a movie. After a few minutes of comfortable silence, she sat the iPad on the bed. "I have a different idea."

"Yeah?" Raven asked, raising an eyebrow.

"Not *that*. At least not yet. Let's just talk."

"Novel idea, Ms. Villanova," Raven said, her smirk growing. She laughed, marveling at how Chris made her feel so peaceful. "What did you want to talk about?"

"Everything. To start, why don't you fly everywhere? Why take a bus?"

Raven shifted, turning to face Chris. "I like it."

Chris nudged her playfully. "Come on. Real answers."

"Fine." Raven let out a mock sigh. "I like it because it feels authentic. It seems more genuine to me. It also gives me the chance to see parts of the country I'd fly over otherwise. I take flights when my schedule warrants it, but this works just as well most of the time. Aside from that, it keeps me close to the guys. It gives me that family feeling."

Chris nodded. "I can see that. What about any other family?"

Raven took a deep breath and her body tensed. "No," she said after a pause.

Chris furrowed her brow in question.

"I don't know where my father is. And I haven't spoken to my mom in years. I'm fairly certain you overheard everything I discussed with my friend before Ryland's visit. After my parents finally divorced, child support payments stopped. That was really my mom's only reason to keep me around. I had seen too much for a kid that age, and all in all, it was pretty dreadful. I ran away at ten—only to be returned. After that, she got into some trouble and I got stuck in a series of foster homes, mainly with people who didn't give a damn whether I was there or not, and some who knew I was there and physically reminded me I shouldn't be. There really isn't anyone to write home to. What else do you want to know?"

"That sucks," Chris said, reaching out to run her fingertips up and down Raven's right arm. "At least you have the guys."

"Thanks." Raven nodded, thankful Chris hadn't offered an apology or some sort of ill-directed sympathy. "It is good to have them. They're my brothers. Paul especially. He was there during the really rough years of my early childhood. Even though he had a steady upbringing, it was one devoid of real affection, so we bonded quickly. He was my best friend and we met again when we wound up at the same high school. He's the best thing that has ever happened in my life, the one constant.

"And then there's Joe. He joined up with Paul and me right out of high school and made our little band a trio. We toured around small areas that would let us play our songs. Once we were well known enough in Detroit to start getting paid gigs, we needed to expand. He hit the road with us and never looked back. He's the guy who will always offer sound insight and joke around with me but who takes music more seriously than anything else. We need him to keep us grounded.

"Then, Pete is a good guy too. He's like the annoying, pesky little brother I never had. I'm sure you've picked up on his lighthearted jabs and silliness. He's our prankster, but he's also very protective of me. When he took over for our previous bassist, he completed our family. We're a successful team and we have a good thing going. I love those guys."

Her smile grew and she let out a contented sigh. “Next,” she called out in a playful tone. She wanted the mood to stay light.

“Let’s see,” Chris said. She looked off into the distance and jokingly stroked her chin as if she was contemplating the secrets of the universe. “Superman or Batman?”

“Superman…speaking of superheroes, I called to check on Ryland this morning. He’s in his first round of treatments. He sounded tired but he’s upbeat. I just thought you’d want to know.”

“Of course I do,” Chris said. She reached over and ran her fingers through Raven’s hair. “Keep me posted on how he’s doing.”

“Absolutely,” Raven said, nodding. “Next question.”

“Any past lovers who are going to show up at one of the stops and beat me up?”

“No.” Raven laughed. “They’re all long gone by now.”

“Yeah?”

“They don’t stick around very long,” she said, waving her hand in dismissal. “Something about the time I spend on the road destroying *what we had.*”

“Any other reasons for them running off?”

“What is this?” Raven joked, leaning down to kiss Chris and make the questions stop for a moment while she searched for an answer. “I’m probably the reason for the latest ones—not hard to imagine why. Then there was my first girlfriend, Staci. She was something else. We were buddies in high school and then more as we got older. She was a looker and just *got* me, you know?” Raven shook her head, clearing the dust off the old memories. “Anyway…we lasted about two years. It was bliss—just the most amazing connection. Everything was great right up until the day she showed up at my apartment and told me that what we had was wrong and gross. Now she’s married with two kids in the suburbs of northern Michigan.”

“That first heartache is brutal,” Chris said. “I know mine was.”

“Yeah? Let’s hear it.”

"Well there are two for me," Chris said, sitting up and straightening her shoulders. "The first was my junior prom. My date, Brent, was my best friend. We ran around together, I let him drag race in my car, we watched sports, the whole nine yards. Neither of us had dates, so we went together. That was great. It was a blast. I really thought I felt something for the guy. It all goes back to that connection thing. But he hooked up with one of my good friends at the after-party. I drank a bottle of rum with another sad guy whose date had dumped him mid-prom. Then I went home, drunk and alone. Looking back, I think it was my pride that shattered that night. But it still stung."

"I want the real one now," Raven said. "That was weak."

Chris laughed and nodded. "You'll get it. Her name was Renee. I met her when I was twenty. She was six years older. That's a hell of an age gap when you're in college. But I was mature and thought I could handle it. I fell hard and fast. She said she did too. I guess I'll never know if that statement was true or not. We were inseparable, and she gave me my first true experience with love. She also handed me my first genuine heartbreak five years later when she cheated on me." Chris paused and crossed her arms over her chest. The move made Raven want to move in closer and protect her. But she waited silently, giving Chris the emotional space to finish her story. "I kicked her out, threw the ring she had put on my finger at her and never heard from her again until my father died a year later. She reached out to me. I never called her back."

"Damn," Raven said. "Women can be the worst."

"They can be. I haven't really connected with anyone since then. After my father's passing, I closed myself off a bit. I got busy at work and liked it that way. I do my own thing, and the dishonest women of the world can do theirs—with someone else."

"Agreed," Raven said, reaching below her bed to grab the stashed bottle of whiskey. "Cheers to leaving the dishonest women of the world behind and embracing the here and now."

"Cheers," Chris said, taking a swig.

"You're pretty hot when you drink it straight from the bottle like that."

"You like that?" Chris asked, winking and taking another drink.

"Mmmhmm." Raven's response came as more of a growl than words.

"So tell me more," Raven said, composing herself. "What is it you dream of?"

Chris's eyes glazed over and she bit her lip. While the move would have typically made Raven crazy with desire, she waited. Chris's caution was evident. "Typical dreams," she said, nodding and taking another drink.

"Like what?"

"I want to have a strong career and to make a difference."

"That's cliché and not true. I can tell by the way you've shifted. You're holding back. Lay it on me."

Pain evident in her eyes, Chris took a deep breath. "I want that same connection that we've both talked about. But I want it without the heartache. I want kids and a family. I want love."

"I hope you find it," Raven said, replaying Chris's words. What must it be like to think those were attainable dreams? She knew they were for some people. But to her, they seemed so foreign. Rock stars didn't settle. People who didn't give love didn't get love. That wasn't a future she could envision for herself, but she wished it for Chris—if that's what she wanted.

"Thank you," Chris said. "And what is it you dream of?"

"Selling albums, rocking out to crowds, watching you press that bottle to your lips again and then getting to taste the remnants of whiskey from your lips."

Chris raised an eyebrow. Raven was thankful Chris didn't take offense. She lifted the bottle to her lips and ran her tongue around the rim.

"Sexy," Raven commented. "Let's see what else you can do with those lips."

"Come and see for yourself." Chris shimmied her body on her side of the bed and set the bottle down.

"Oh I will."

This felt normal. It felt right. She smiled as she crossed the distance, needing to feel Chris's body against her own.

Before their lips met, she pulled back briefly. "I like the way we mesh, by the way," Raven said, her smile growing. Not giving her a chance to respond, she pressed her lips to Chris's, giving into living life in the moment.

CHAPTER NINE

Overstuffed couches and abstract art filled the plush room and overhead an obscenely pretentious chandelier lit the room. Chris looked around, taking it all in. She had been in her share of fancy places, but this room screamed of money. It was *Rolling Stone* magazine after all.

New York hadn't been on the schedule but since Raven had been asked to play at a tribute concert for an ailing bassist whose music had influenced her life, schedules had been off-kilter this week. Regardless of circumstance, she was taking advantage of every PR opportunity—and that's what brought them here today. After watching how well the *Ellen* interview had gone back in LA, Chris was certain this one would be a winner as well.

Across from her on the couch, she watched Raven, poised and at ease. She smiled, noting that this was nothing out of the ordinary for either of them. National media was commonplace, given their work.

Clad in a black tank top, ripped jeans and a fedora, Raven looked every bit the part of a rocker, yet she somehow managed to make the look seem elegant. On the other side of the coffee table, the young reporter shifted in his seat, ready to start the interview. Much like Raven, he looked his part. He was an up-and-coming reporter. His slicked-back black hair and his thick-rimmed hipster glassed paired perfectly with his sleek, gray button-down shirt. The only indication that he worked for *Rolling Stone* and not the *New York Times* were his jeans instead of slacks and the Def Leppard tattoo on his right hand. She smiled at the thought, hoping the distinctions made Raven feel more at ease for the interview. He was one of her kind, a lover of rock 'n' roll and a young person paying his dues.

"I'm Geoff Thomas," he said, shaking hands. Chris had exchanged emails with him for the past two weeks. "Thanks for making time for me today," he said, looking nervous "You look great."

"Well, thank you very much," Raven said, smiling warmly at him. "And it's my pleasure. Thank you for reaching out. I'm Raven, by the way."

Chris watched as the young man returned her smile, relaxing in her presence. Chris had realized over the past month and a half that Raven had that effect. It was a gift.

"Can you tell me a little about how you got started in the industry?" he asked, not taking his eyes off the star. Her beauty emanated throughout the room.

"It's what I always loved," Raven said. "I loved music as a little kid. I'd hang out at home in the basement with an old record player. I got my start on a dusty, out-of-tune guitar that had been in storage for years. I'd jam out to Zeppelin, Janis Joplin and Jimi Hendrix, and I'd just get lost in it all. It was my escape. Eventually, basement playing ceased to be an option but in those days I'd entertain anyone who would listen. It was my form of expression, my outlet for anything I felt or thought. By the time I was a preteen, I was writing my own lyrics and branching out. Childhood comes with its fair share of life challenges and everything seems bigger when you're a kid, so I needed a place to just be me and express everything going on in the world around me. Music was that for me and it still is—after all this time."

"You mentioned your childhood," he noted. "What was that time like?"

"It was the eighties," she said, offering a smile. "So, pretty much what you'd expect. Good music, big hair, lots of bike riding, lots of MTV."

He nodded, taking notes. Chris admired the way she was able to give people enough of an answer to keep them satisfied without baring her soul. It was a trick she had tried to teach many of her clients, but Raven was a natural.

"You've got a tough image," he noted. "People regard you as the goddess of rock. How does that feel and is that an image you, too, feel you have?"

"Wow, a goddess?" she asked, her tone conveying genuine gratitude.

"Not a goddess," he corrected. "THE goddess."

"Well, thank you," she said, grinning largely enough to let her dimple show. "I don't consider myself a goddess, but it's flattering to hear that some may believe that. I'm just your ordinary rebel kid who loved music enough to make it my life's work. That's all. I worked my ass off, playing in every bar that would let me in the door. From my first gig, it's been the same motivational factor. I don't care about the charts or the sales. I just want to make music, to be heard for standing up for those of us who are a little different, those of us who don't fit the norm, those who don't do the nine-to-five in a suit thing and those who maybe have felt a little too much pressure to fit the mold."

Pausing dramatically, she took a drink from her water bottle. "We're all told who we're supposed to be. Sometimes it's spoken blatantly. Other times, it's subtle. But everyone has an idea of who everyone else *should* be and I'm a big fan of saying 'fuck what everyone thinks.' I want to be known for encouraging everyone to follow their own dream and for making some of the outcasts like me feel a little more at home with who they are. If you're weird, own it. That's what I'll always stand for and I'll always be making music. So, if that makes me a goddess, I'll claim the title, but no, that's not how I see myself."

Chris silently cheered at the answer—modest, yet uplifting. And she noticed the spark in Raven's brown eyes. They were not just simple words. They were the truth and that's the part of Raven she wanted people to see. This was genuine. This was legitimate feeling from the girl who was more typically bottled up and closed off, unless she was pouring her heart out in song.

The reporter smiled and nodded with every word, taking notes, looking up only when she had finished speaking. "I think that's a great way to look at it," he said, nodding again. "What kinds of things are you working on lately? Anything new in the works?"

"There's always something new in the works, Geoff," she answered, her raspy voice deep with excitement. "That's the beauty of life on the road. I'm always with my guys. We have a lot of fun and sometimes that means we just sit around and create. I wrote a new song a while back for the album that I'm working on. Right now, I'm doing a little at a time, to let it all flow. As the songs come, I'll share them. I've got one I just started writing this morning, though, and I think it's going to be a hit. It falls in line with my life philosophy. It's all about being who you are—whoever that may be—and kicking society's rules to the curb."

"The bad girl of rock 'n' roll," he commented. "I like it. Care to share the name of the song?"

"It's not really named yet," she said. "It's not quite finished, but I'll give you a call for an exclusive listen when I have it finished."

"You've got a deal," he said gratefully. "Now can you tell me a little about the charity work you're starting?"

"Absolutely," she said, her face lighting up again like a child. Chris smiled to herself, thankful she had chosen something that Raven was passionate enough about to exude this level of excitement. "I'm working with a nationwide rescue group, Pawsitive Projects. They are focused on rehoming pets. I'm not sure if you've heard their new jingle or seen the commercials, but I'm currently serving as their spokeswoman. I wrote and recorded the song, and will be performing at events throughout the summer to raise money. I'll match every dollar raised at the shows and will continue to serve as a proponent of their no-kill policies and their advocacy in placing pets with responsible pet owners." She paused long enough to smile, adding depth and sincerity to her words. "I've always loved dogs in particular, and I think they all deserve great, loving homes, where they will be cherished for the treasures that they are."

"Very cool," he said. "Do you have any pets of your own?"

"I don't," she said, not faltering. "My life on the road doesn't quite allow for that at this point, but I will one day."

"And what about your life back home, when you're not on the road?" he asked. "Is there anyone special in your life?"

"I've got my home in San Diego and, of course, my place in Boston. I like the coast to coast option. I think that we have far too many beautiful places here in the US to stay in just one. I don't see my places regularly but I'm told they're still standing. And there are a lot of special people in my life," Raven commented, brushing her hand through the air. "I have wonderful friends, a great band and a strong support team. They're all special enough for me right now."

The reporter raised an eyebrow. "You should be a politician," he said, laughing. "But I'll let it slide for now. Maybe you can tell me more when I listen to your new song."

"Maybe so," she said, winking and placing her hands back in her lap.

"In the meantime, I do have a couple more questions," he said, good-naturedly moving on to another subject. "You seem to be one of those people who stays below the radar of the paparazzi and who is out of the public eye most of the time. I mean, we've all seen glimpses—and there were a couple of unflattering stories a while back, but no one really seems to know you. Who would you say is closest to you?"

"Tricky way of asking that," she said, laughing even though it was clear that she was a little less than impressed with his tactics. "I would say that first and foremost, it's Frank Karnes, my manager. He's the best thing that's ever happened to my life. He's always there, always stable, always has good advice and truly always has my best interest at heart. He's a good guy and he's like a family member to me. I couldn't do this without him.

"Next, it's my band guys, Peter, Paul and Joe. I guess you could say they're *my* version of Peter, Paul and Mary." Geoff and Raven both laughed at her silly pun. "Paul Warner, my drummer, is my rock and a lifelong friend. I credit him not only for his musical talents, but also for his ability to see me through any situation. I also have Pete Riley, who plays bass for the band and offers much-needed comic relief, well-timed pranks and moral support. And Joe Easton on guitar. He's our wise one, always fun but wise beyond his years. They're all crazy talented and make a rock show look like as easy as setting up a lemonade stand. More than that, they're like brothers. We see each other at our best and our worst, we challenge each other, we make each other better and of course we bicker and joke like family as well. Beyond that, I think it changes from time to time. Currently, I've got some new team members who really go above and beyond to make my days great and make this whole thing so much fun."

He opened his mouth to speak, but Raven continued. "Christina Villanova here," she said, pointing in Chris's direction. "She's new to my team this tour and she's been an incredible asset. She's got great energy, enthusiasm and is always an encourager. It's people like that who work so closely with us that they almost become a part of who we are. Those are the people who are the closest to me and those are the people who see the true me, behind all the lights, behind the music."

"Behind the music," he laughed. "MTV to VH1."

"And on every radio station between, hopefully," she joked. "What other questions do you have?"

"I'll get to those, but you seem to be a young woman wise beyond her years and with enough talent to really make a change in the world—and that seems to be something you really want. So, I'd like you to tell me what you'd like to tell the world."

Raven didn't flinch at the open-ended question. She leaned forward, her elbows on her knees. Looking him in the eye, she pondered his question for a second before speaking. "I want everyone—especially all of the girls out there—to think about who they want to be. We've made a lot of progress as a society, but the fact remains that there are still so many preconceived notions about women. I want everyone to challenge those norms, to be who they want to be—unapologetically so. I want people to step outside the box and be those rebellious girls who make things happen and make a difference."

"Very nice," he commented, making a couple of notes. "What about those women who believe their worth is found in finding someone to love?"

"I'd say that we *all* want to be loved," she answered with ease. "I think that love is wonderful. It truly is, but it shouldn't define who we are. And it shouldn't stop you doing what you want with your life—it shouldn't be an either or. We are great. We are beautiful. We are fierce—with or without someone."

"On the topic of love, what are your views on finding love on the road?"

The questions were coming at rapid pace now, as if he was aiming for something other than just another fluff piece.

"I believe that love happens when it does," Raven said, her voice taking on a nostalgic softness. "Love is beautiful. It's the most powerful, most frustrating force on the planet. But you either find it or you don't. You keep it or you don't. There are a lot of factors outside our control, so I think chasing love will always be futile. I believe in the power of love, but I also believe in the freedom of having fun, living life and chasing dreams."

Chris hung on every word, wanting to understand as badly as the reporter did. Despite the past six weeks, she had little idea of how Raven viewed love—or if she considered the concept at all in the same way as Chris did. All Chris knew was that Raven had experienced love and heartache before. And that they "meshed." Raven had admitted as much too, but what it meant to Raven was still a mystery.

"Anything you'd like to add?" Geoff asked.

"Depending on when you go to print, I'd like to invite everyone to come out tonight to the tribute to Jonathan Liss. He is a good friend of mine, an incredible bassist and a legend in the music world. He deserves every bit of honor coming his way at tonight's show, and I'm fortunate to have had the chance to fly back here with Chris and the band for the show. I'm proud to be a part of it. Other than that, I'll be back in Los Angeles in a week to continue my southwest tour. And I'll do my best to keep LA interesting."

As she finished with the pleasantries and the interview came to a close, Chris knew that this was going to be a solid article, positive press that Raven really needed to get the ball rolling on her new image. She mentally patted herself on the back, but she knew that the credit really did have to go to Raven.

As they left the reporter, Chris placed her hand on Raven's shoulder. "Good work," she said.

"Yeah?" Raven asked, raising an eyebrow as she grinned. "Did you like that?"

Chris bit her lip, knowing where that teasing grin led. "Not here," she said, pointing her finger at Raven. "Also, thanks for the shout-out. I'm glad I make your days better."

"You're welcome," Raven said, letting her eyes trail down to the opening of Chris's blouse. "And you certainly do. I probably shouldn't have said the 'fuck' word, but I don't care. He won't print it. If he does, he will use those goofy little stars."

"I like when you say the 'fuck' word," Chris said with a smirk, watching Raven's eyes once again settle on her breasts.

"I said not here," Chris said with a laugh, putting her hand up to cover her cleavage.

"How about here?" Raven asked as the doors to the elevator closed. Pressing Chris up against the wall, she kissed her passionately. When the elevator dinged open, they pulled apart and made space between them before walking out into the lobby of the hotel. "It's not my fault that I can't keep my hands off you, you know?" Raven whispered as they walked. "If you weren't so sexy, it would be easier."

Chris laughed and shook her head. "I think it's all you. After all, you're THE goddess, remember?"

They laughed in playful banter and made their way back to the waiting car. "And back to normal," Raven commented as she opened the door for Chris.

Normal. Chris let the word play again and again in her head, as if on repeat. There was little semblance in her life of anything she had once considered normal. She was sleeping with a rock star, touring the nation on a bus and pretending that nothing was out of the ordinary. Normal did not exist.

The driver took them back to the hotel. The coast-to-coast flight had been last minute, and Chris was still unsure how she felt about the whole situation. They were both exhausted. But it didn't really matter. If nothing else, Raven was teaching her to live in the moment and to enjoy every possible aspect of it while it lasted.

Chris retired to her room. She needed a nap and to unwind a bit after all the stress of the interview. Raven proved today that Chris had nothing to worry about. It was highly unlikely that a journalist would get inappropriate information out of her. Not even her band mates seemed to be able to get anything much out of her, even if their efforts came in the form of good-natured ribbing. Raven was coy at all costs, never giving more than she was required to—and sometimes even less.

Anytime one of the guys gave her a hard time about hooking up with the "PR lady," as they liked to call her when they thought she wasn't listening, she never confirmed or denied the allegations. No one—especially not a reporter—would get her to budge on her private life.

She could hear the chatter and laughter of the band in the room next door. She chuckled silently to herself, noting that these sounds—things that would have seemed so foreign just weeks ago—merely served as a sort of white noise lulling her to sleep.

A knock on her door shook her awake. Glancing at her clock, she realized she had been out for well over two hours. "Come in," she mumbled, not wanting to move. Accustomed to life on the bus, she waited for the only person who would actually venture into her room to open the door.

"I can't. I don't have a key" she heard Raven call from behind the closed door.

Blinking, she remembered the change in location and reluctantly rose from her hotel bed to open the door.

"Hey there," Raven said when she threw open the door. The sound rolled over her skin like soothing balm. "Mind if I join you?"

"Are you all done playing with the boys?" Chris asked sleepily.

"I am," she said, a sultry smile toying with the corners of her lips. "And now I'd like to play with you, if that's okay."

"Mmmhmm," Chris said, returning to the bed and wiggling slightly to invite Raven to join her. Raven climbed into bed behind her, wrapping her arms around Chris and looping her long legs around her body. "Just like that," Chris urged, leaning back into the embrace to receive a soft kiss to her neck.

Behind her, Raven let out a yawn and Chris nodded her head. "Let's just nap," she said, settling into the comfort of their position.

"Yeah," Raven agreed, her voice barely a whisper.

"Before you fall asleep, I have a question," Chris asked, feeling Raven's body stiffen behind her. She wanted to laugh at the response. It wasn't like she was going to ask the woman to marry her. Brushing her amusement aside, she continued. "Does the reporter guy really get the first, exclusive listen to your new song?"

Raven's body relaxed and she let out the breath she had clearly been holding. "No," she said, kissing Chris on the back of the head. "I'll play it for you tonight, after the show, after I fuck you."

The words alone were enough to make Chris's entire body tingle, but she resisted the urge to give into desire right now, when Raven needed to rest. *You care*, the words played through her head. Pushing them to the back of her mind, she closed her eyes, willing her growing feelings to stop. *Live in the moment*, she reminded herself, stopping any more thoughts about what any of this meant.

Behind her, Raven's breathing deepened as she drifted off to sleep. Try as she might, Chris couldn't do the same. She lay there, wrapped up in the embrace, wishing she could have stopped this before it started. But she also knew that, given the chance to rewrite the past month and a half, she wouldn't have done a single thing differently.

It had been a blur of making out, different cities, going to the shows, partying, fucking, cuddling and flirting. It had been fun and it had been a whirlwind of not thinking about consequences. Sure, it popped up in her mind from time to time, but she had been so tired, so busy and so out of her element, that she had been able to put them on the back burner. Here though, in this moment, things were different.

She had professional concerns. This was a breach in any office protocol and wasn't something to be taken lightly. If this ever got out, she would be in trouble. She thought back to Susan. Chris had rushed her off the phone the past few times they had talked, afraid to let anything suspicious show in her voice. She was in a mess.

On top of that, she had to consider matters of the heart. It was becoming apparent that, as much as they both fought it, this was more than just a hookup along the way, even though there was little to no possibility that anything real could ever happen between the two of them. Life with Raven wasn't reality. It couldn't be. Chris wanted to settle down. She wanted to start a family one day. She longed for stability, whereas Raven was happy flitting around from town to town, doing whatever felt right in the moment. There was no future in all this.

Future. Home. She played the words over in her mind. There was a place where she could have both. She thought back to the way Brittany's arms had felt around her, the softness with which she yielded all of her being. There were no emotional walls. There was unconditional love and the possibility of a future. Whether she wanted that future or not was still up in the air, but it remained a steadier foundation.

She watched Raven sleep, wishing the tables could have been turned. She knew the depth of feeling she was developing for the singer. There was no second-guessing how her heart was connecting to Raven, just as it had with Brittany. Brittany wanted her—plain and simple. If Raven proved even half as steady as the love she knew she could have with Brittany, she would have jumped headfirst. It was dangerous though, and she knew it. Her thoughts swirled as she contemplated the heartbreak ahead and the future she could have if she stopped this in its tracks and went back home.

She cared about both women and was attracted to both of them, but this seemed deeper. Tears of confusion pooled in her eyes, but she willed them away. For over an hour as Raven slept peacefully, she lay still, waging war with herself, her feelings and her logic. Finally, when Raven stirred behind her, Chris seized the opportunity to take her mind off her dilemma.

Sliding down to the bottom of the bed, she slid her fingers below the waistband of Raven's jeans, unbuttoning them. She gained a sleepy smile from Raven, who said nothing, but nodded and tilted her hips up, an open invitation for Chris to proceed as she pleased.

Chris removed Raven's pants and slowly, gently feasted on her body. She traced her tongue along the inside of Raven's thighs, before finally setting in on the prize. Licking and sucking like she had no cares, subsumed in all that Raven had to offer. If this was it, she would take it gladly. When Raven's body exploded in a powerful orgasm, Chris lingered for a moment before coming back up to kiss Raven gently.

"That was my way of wishing you good luck this evening," she said between kisses.

"Best send-off possible," Raven said, laying her head back on the pillow, and glowing with plain ecstasy. "Thank you."

"My pleasure," Chris said coyly.

"Not yet," Raven said, smiling. "But it will be after the show. My goal for the night is to have you screaming and losing control, so loudly that you don't care if anyone else in this hotel hears. I want you that lost in how good it feels to let go and have fun."

"Don't threaten me with a good time," Chris said. As Raven dressed, Chris watched, glued to the scene playing out before her. Raven's long legs stretched one at a time to wiggle back into her tight, skinny jeans and she walked over, towering over Chris. She lay helpless to do anything but drink in Raven's curves. Reaching down still topless, Raven trailed her finger across Chris's face, before leaning down to give her a long, lingering kiss.

"See you out there," she said, standing back up and putting on her shirt, still holding her bra in her hand. "I'll put it back on before I hit the stage," she said with a wink as Chris looked longingly at the material clinging tightly to her still-hard nipples.

"Go kick ass," Chris said, smiling as she laid her head against the pillow.

"I'm off to my nightly makeover," she said, heading for the door. "I'll sing something sexy for you tonight. We'll think of it as foreplay."

Although she was no less confused, she was certainly turned on. She waved as Raven exited the doorway, her feelings a mix of anticipation and fear of what would become of her heart, not to mention her career.

* * *

Paul watched from the hallway as Raven stepped from Chris's room, her eyes hazed in pleasure. He sighed and walked out of the hotel. He needed some fresh air. He needed to clear his mind and hopefully shake off some of his overly protective big brother ways.

Lighting a cigarette, he walked along the sidewalk. Looking at his reflection in the puddle across the parking lot, he figured he didn't have much room to judge her behavior, but he was definitely worried. Yet his tall, lanky frame seemed to mock, reminding him that he was just a scruffy drummer with little else to offer. He owed it all to Raven for bringing him along for the ride. Had she not been so loyal, chances are he'd still be playing in smoke-shrouded basements in between his shifts at the factory. That would have been his fate had she not insisted he be a part of her fame. If it hadn't been for her, he would still be back in Detroit, living paycheck to paycheck, breaking his back all day at work and spending evenings lounging on a couch with a bunch of other kids who refused to grow up, waiting on his 'big break.'

He reflected on his friends and family members back home—each of them too stubborn to take his financial help but struggling under the burden of everyday life in the lower class. *That could be me*, he thought. Even so, he felt protective and knew what had to be done. When he saw Frank approaching in the distance, he took a deep breath. It was now or never.

"Hey man," Frank called out, waving as he walked closer.

"Hey Frank," Paul said, reaching out to accept the fist bump. He had learned long ago not to question the fist bump. Frank was a genius, a little weird at times, but a genius in the business nonetheless. "Can I talk to you for a minute?"

Frank glanced at his watch, then toward the hotel entrance. "I've got ten minutes and then I have to have her loaded up and ready to be made up and prepped for the night."

Paul nodded, pursing his lips as he chose his words carefully.

"What is it?" Frank asked.

"I'm worried," Paul admitted. "I'm worried about her and I guess I need you to tell me that my fears are unfounded," he continued, opting to speak straight from his heart. "We have all seen her get like this a time or two and as soon as she gets close to happiness, she tosses it all away, hell-bent on self-destruction."

"Are you talking about the situation that seems to be developing romantically?" As always Frank's voice was even, showing no hint of surprise or concern.

Paul nodded, hoping the nicotine would calm him. "Think about it," he said, reflecting for a moment. "We can look down the row of women who have earned their way into a special place for her. None of them lasted and it's not because *they* didn't want to. It's because she goes on a destructive path, killing anything that gets too close to her and taking part of herself in the process."

Frank frowned, but said nothing.

"Before we started on the road, there was Staci, who broke Raven in so many ways. Since you've been around, there was Emily," Paul continued when Frank didn't interject. "She was amazing and I thought she might be the one. The minute she got a little too close to our beloved prickly cactus, she was done and Raven spiraled out of control. That was PR nightmare number one, which is far less important than the fact that she almost overdosed that night. Then later we had Dani, the sweet little Midwestern princess, who fit so well with our lifestyle, a chameleon. When she didn't work out, Raven started a bar fight in Denver. More bad headlines and a few stitches on her arm from a cleverly placed broken bottle. There were quite a few others. But we all know what happens."

"So are you saying we should fire Christina?" Frank asked, leveling his gaze at Paul. He held an even nonpatronizing tone. "What can we do at this point? You said it yourself—she's hell-bent on destruction. It's who she is."

"I guess maybe that's more the issue," Paul said, shrugging and giving voice to the worries that had plagued his mind not just now but for years. "She is like a sister to me. She is to all of us. I care, dammit. I wish I didn't some days. It would make her so much easier to brush off and ignore, but when we all know it's coming, I feel like we have to do something. I know she has a good heart and that she doesn't want to hurt anyone. In fact, when she gets like that, she's more into hurting herself than throwing anyone else under that bus. But I can't stand to see her hurt herself again, not how she's done before.

"She's happy, and I'm happy for her. I just want this happiness to last, even though we all know it's not going to. I want to believe that there's room for personal growth and change, that this time could be the time she turns it all around. She may be happy now, but it's just a matter of when the hammer drops and the crazy train takes off. Maybe, we should try to talk to her and get her some help."

"We've been through this before. You can't help those unwilling to help themselves," Frank said, shaking his head as his eyes darkened with sadness. "She doesn't think she needs help and it's the last thing she wants. When she changes that attitude, she'll actually let someone in. Until that point, there's little we can do. I've talked to her and I'm sure you have too, but it's of little consequence when she is still running."

Running. The word tripped a slew of memories for Paul. Unlike the rest of them, he had seen it. He was there when she ran away from her mother, when she tried to run away from the foster homes in high school, and when she had successfully run away from everyone over the years who tried to get too close. He closed his eyes, willing the memories to fade, but they wouldn't. Instead, he was plagued by the vivid recollection of how it had felt to hold her while she cried all those years ago.

"You're right," Paul finally answered. "But I'll try again. And I won't stop trying until she listens to me. I don't care if she hates me for a bit, or even forever. I know she's stubborn. It's that stubbornness that brought us all here—maybe not you but certainly all of us guys. We were all stubbornly refusing something—whether that be refusing the cookie-cutter nine-to-five lifestyle or refusing to give up on a dream. I'm here because I'm too stubborn to believe I'd be fulfilled doing anything other than making music I love. Joe is here because he was too stubborn to give up on the same dream. Pete was too stubborn to believe that drinking on the job was frowned upon."

He laughed to lighten the mood. "I'm kidding. Pete's here because he's too stubborn to settle for less than his absolute best—which fortunately happens to be making killer music. You are here because this is the world you were made for. You would have been here anyway, because you're just that damn good. The rest of us, though, we're her band of misfits. We're her people, her people whom she pulled from the same depths of hell where she was, and brought us here. For that and for what she means to me, I'll keep trying."

"What do you think is best in this situation?" Frank asked, stuffing his hands in his pockets, no doubt stifling an urge to look at his watch.

"Christina is good for her, honestly," he said, after a brief pause. "She is level-headed and she has Raven's best interests at heart. That's something that we can't say for everyone in this fame-chasing world. And who knows, what's going on between them may be nothing more than a fling. But the way they look at each other is more. It's deeper. I've seen her look at a lot of girls, but this one is different somehow. So, I hope she stays. I hope Raven doesn't fuck it up in her own fucked-up way that she's so skilled at, and I hope she learns to be—to be who she is, to embrace who she was and to be with another."

Looking away momentarily, Frank exhaled deeply. When he turned back, he placed his hand on Paul's shoulder. "She's lucky to have you. You're a good one."

"Thanks," Paul said, shaking his head as Frank walked away. He knew Frank cared. In fact, he knew that anyone who cared any less would have walked away years ago. Raven was a handful—not for the band guys. For them, she was fun. She was lively and spirited. She brought spunk to their group that couldn't be matched and she brought so much happiness into their lives.

But to Frank—and to others—she seemed to have a knack for figuring out what would piss them off the most and doing it. She had bratty teenage syndrome, delayed by a decade or more. She was prickly. Yet she was soft on the inside, warm and loving and always ready with a quick wit to make any mood better. Over the past weeks, he had delighted in watching Christina sift through the bullshit of the façade with ease.

At the end of the day, no matter what had come between them or what might be eating at them, they all had the music in common—as did the crowd. Everyone wanted to get lost in the music, to feel alive, to feel something, to be something other than themselves, even if only momentarily.

And tonight in New York City, that's just what Paul was going to do. Later, he promised himself, he would have a talk with her. Later, he would figure out a way to broach the subject casually without having her run like a wild animal at the sound of gunfire. Later, he would do his best to help his little sister navigate her way through a world that had always brought her someplace just shy of satisfaction and contentment.

CHAPTER TEN

She couldn't put her finger on it, but something felt off. As Raven lay awake in bed, she felt Chris stir beside her. Glancing down, she was relieved to find her still breathing deeply, still sleeping. Rising quietly, she threw on an old T-shirt and a pair of boxers from the bedside drawer.

Looking around the room, nothing was different. They were back on the bus after playing San Francisco. Things had settled into a normal rhythm after their jaunt to New York. Sure, the guys had seemed a little odd after the show tonight and Paul had been insistent on trying to get her alone to "talk" for a few minutes. She had brushed it off, assuming he was just on one of his pot-fueled philosophy rants, wanting to discuss the meaning of the universe, what really made a family and what their dreams and goals were. She crept from the room, careful not to let the door make a sound as it closed.

Stumbling through the darkness, she was grateful that she knew this place better than any she had ever called home. She wound her way expertly around the guitar cases and couches, straight to the kitchen area. She grabbed a glass of water and a bag of Cheetos and took a seat on the couch. Apart from wanting a late night snack and to reflect on the great sex she and Chris had just had, she was bothered by how strange everyone was acting.

Move by move, she went through her memory of the show. All had gone well and they had put on a concert second to none. Sure, there had been those funny moments that seemed to occur every night, the banter onstage, sultry eye contact with fans, the joking. But that was normal. Everyone had complimented her on a spectacular night, but their words had been clipped and short—Frank's especially. Her mind swirled with possibilities.

If he was going to suggest rehab again, that was a definite no from her. They had discussed it and when she needed to, she laid low for a while and gave her body a break. She wasn't going to sit around a campfire and sing "Kumbaya" with a bunch of loser alcoholics and druggies.

If he was going to come at her with a new publicity stunt or something to soften her image, she was out. Chris was doing a damn good job and the *Rolling Stone* article had been a hit. She had more fans now than ever and that didn't seem to be at risk of changing. She had a PR person and she didn't need Frank to concern himself with that.

If it was about the way she dressed or how she should try to look more like a pop star, she was going to tell him to shove it.

As she ate Cheetos angrily, she tried to place what could have been so wrong that he'd been walking on eggshells for days.

She glanced back to the bedroom doorway and let out a sigh. Who was she kidding? She knew what he was upset about. They all got weird whenever she spent more than one night with *any* girl—let alone one who happened to be on staff.

It had been weird enough for her to have someone around constantly, but she had to admit that she was enjoying it. Even so, it would probably be best to cut Chris loose soon, so that things didn't get any more complicated than they already were.

Shoving a handful of the crispy chips into her mouth, she shook her head. One of these days she would learn to keep people at an arm's length. She would learn that letting them come any closer would only wreak havoc on the system she had so carefully worked to establish.

She closed her eyes, trying to think of how she could end this with grace. Technically, there was nothing to end. They hadn't discussed what it all meant and what would warrant a parting of ways, but the fact that Chris also lived on the bus and was doing a great job of handling Raven's PR was a complication. Every scenario had Chris hating her. Normally that wouldn't be an issue. Girls across the globe hated her and with good reason. She was an ass when it was necessary and she put an end to things when they needed to be finished.

The thought of never seeing those green eyes, of never again feeling that soft touch or seeing that smile that held the power to light up an entire room made her heart feel empty and she wanted to cry. For the first time in years, she wanted to cry over saying goodbye to someone. She let that thought resonate, but only for a minute. Pushing it away, she recalled what Paul had told her over and over throughout the years.

"At some point, you have to let somebody love you."

"You have to let someone in—someone other than me."

"You have to trust. Not all people are bad."

"Stop running so damn hard."

"Just let go, Rave, just let go."

His words made no more sense to her tonight than they ever had. Everyone had the capacity to detach, to abuse and hurt, to ruin her—and that was the last thing she was ever going to let happen again, consequences be damned.

Her mind slipped back to another time, a place she never let her thoughts venture.

"Why don't you just get the hell out of here?" Angry shouts woke her. Glass breaking.

Ten-year-old Erin trembled in her room, wishing she could drown out the noise, but knowing it would only get worse. Far too accustomed to this, she looked around the tiny room, looking for someplace to go, someplace she would feel safer. As quietly as she could manage, she slipped from her covers and hid behind the door, knowing it was only a matter of time until the attention turned to her instead of her mother.

He would find her. He always did, but at least this way, she could have some sort of cover. She hoped tonight would be one of the nights he passed out early, in the middle of his rage—not one of the nights when his outbursts went for hours, a raging, living nightmare.

"Where do you want me to go?" her mom's voice slurred. The unmistakable sound of a fist crashing into flesh.

"Anywhere but here," he spat out. Another shattering sound. "You're nothing but a whore. Who did you use today, while I was out?"

"I was making a sale," she said, her voice solid, no trace of regret.

Erin's hands shook as she listened.

"It doesn't matter." Another crash, followed by a yelp from her mother. "It doesn't matter at all. You're no good at making sales. You're no good at anything. You're a fucking awful mother, a nothing girlfriend and a shitty business partner. You don't deserve to stay here. You and that little brat of yours can hit the streets."

Hot tears stung her cheeks.

"You're a monster," her mother shouted back defiantly, her voice shrill.

The sound of his fists whaling against her mother's body and her screams. Erin looked around for an escape and considered the window. It was too risky at this point. She'd be heard and it was too late. She knew what was coming next.

"What did you need the money for?" he shouted. "What was it for?"

"She needs school supplies." Her words were ragged now as she gasped for air. For the millionth time, she wished her mother would learn—or care—that whenever her daughter was mentioned, they both knew what was coming next. Her mother knew all right. She just didn't care. After the divorce three years ago, she jumped from boyfriend to boyfriend and needle to needle. Somewhere along the way, she had stopped caring. Her crazy logic accepted that it was better that Erin take the beating than her.

In control more than a child should have to be, Erin dismissed the hurt and focused instead on survival. If nothing else, she would be a fighter. She would take whatever was coming and she would leave this place as soon as she was able.

Silence from the living room—a warning the impending storm. Heavy footsteps filled the hallway…

Shaking her head violently to end the flashback, Raven tried to slow her breathing. In the darkness of the bus, she cried silently for all she had seen, all she had lost and all she would never experience because of who she was—what she had gone through. Placing her hand over her heart, she felt the beat, strong and steady, reminding herself that she was not a tenderhearted being, nor would she ever be. The delicate flower had grown into a fully fledged warrior, ready for anything and ready to pick up the sword first, before another had a chance to arm themselves. The minute that she stopped being a valuable asset, she would be nothing. Everyone could and would, hurt her, given the chance. She wasn't going to give anyone that opportunity.

"Never again," she whispered to herself. "Never."

No one had raised a hand to her in years, but that wasn't the only way someone could come in and tear her down. There were plenty of other ways, and people were good at finding them if you gave them an opening. Her mother had proven as much. The woman never raised a hand to her, but destroyed her all the same.

Chris was a loving soul, but everyone was capable of selfishness, self-preservation, jealousy, weakness and mistrust. Everyone had the capacity to hurt someone—whether intentionally or unintentionally, and it was never worth the risk. She let out a sigh, wishing there was another way.

She stood, crumpling the empty bag in her hand and taking it to the trash can. She realized she was getting ahead of herself. No one had said anything and Chris had given no indication that she had feelings for her. Perhaps it was still fine.

Unsettled and standing in the middle of the darkened kitchen, she made a commitment to herself that she would let things go for the time being. When and if she needed to act, she wouldn't look back. She had never been weakened by love, tainted by a too-soft heart and she wasn't about to start now. She would handle this swiftly and decisively. For now, she would enjoy the gorgeous blonde in her bed.

Wiping her fingers off on a paper towel, she let her thoughts clear and channeled nothing but animalistic lust. When she made her way back into the bedroom, she stood momentarily, gazing at the beauty in her bed. Covered by a sheet, Chris looked at peace, with her blond hair tumbling over the pillow and her chest rising and falling evenly. Her full lips were turned up at one corner, a lazy smile that spoke volumes about the ecstasy and passion they had shared just hours before.

Chris's relaxed natural beauty completely erased everything negative from Raven's mind. Her doubts, her fears, her strategy, her demons, her worries all faded in an instant and she wanted nothing more than to feel the closeness of Chris's skin. She glanced in the wall mirror, wiping away any smeared mascara and shed her clothes again, needing to feel the warmth of a naked embrace. As quietly as possible, she climbed into bed beside Chris and wrapped her arms around her.

"Mmm," Chris let out a satisfied moan and wiggled back, closer into the embrace. Raven leaned forward, bringing her lips against her soft skin and kissing her neck, while she ran her fingers up and down Chris's arms. She breathed in deeply, taking in the sweet scent of the beautiful woman beside her and let out a contented sigh.

She matched her breathing with Chris's and continued to trail her hands over her body, the epitome of perfection. She kissed her way across Chris's shoulders, smiling as she thought of how quick-witted and sassy she could be, how funny, smart and professional she was. Admirable traits that had magnetized Raven from the beginning, even more so than her incredible body with its enchanting curves, her boisterous laugh and piercing green eyes. Somehow, she had landed this incredible woman. She reminded herself that she had only landed her in her bed. Nothing more had been defined or discussed.

Fleeting, though it might be, it was magical. Raven reassured herself that, even if they had softened, her defenses were still intact. Raven wanted nothing but to get lost in the moment, to absorb every bit of Chris's magic.

* * *

Frank paced outside Raven's room, wishing he could barge in and tell her to get dressed and focus. Paul's worries that had surfaced three days earlier in New York still plagued him, making it hard for him to sleep and even harder for him to turn a blind eye. There was little doubt that Paul, the one who knew her best, was right. In fact, his insights were spot-on and Frank knew it.

He shuddered thinking about how it would affect them all if she was left to her own devices in whatever was unfolding. Giggling and hushed whispers leaked through the doorway and he balled up his fist. Christina seemed to be a smart girl, but a smart girl would never have put herself into this position—knowing full well what Raven was capable of.

She had read the press. She had seen the headlines and gone through the files cover to cover. Frank knew she had, because they had discussed them in depth. Still, she had been stupid enough to jump at the attentions of a rock star and fall into bed with her. Particularly when she was her client.

The whole situation made him want to scream. This was supposed to be the move that saved Raven's image. He glanced at Paul whipping up a smoothie in the kitchen. Paul raised an eyebrow in his direction and shrugged. Frank could almost hear his silent "I told you so."

"What *is* that?" Frank asked. Its bright green color made his stomach churn, yet Paul whistled along as it whirred around the cup.

"Greens," Paul said, offering a smug, chipper smile.

"Are you gloating?" Frank asked, narrowing his eyes at the scruffy hippie and marveling at all the sides of this kid. He was a rough-around-the-edges drummer who just happened to have a big heart. He was the one who was perfectly okay with chowing down on a greasy burger, yet consumed vile-looking green smoothies each morning. He was the ultimate contradiction, all wrapped into one insanely talented package, clad in a wife-beater and ripped jeans.

"Not at all," he said, taking a big gulp of the pulpy mixture. "I wouldn't gloat about something I worry about. Quite the opposite, in fact. I'm just glad that you can finally see that my worries are warranted. I'm happy that, maybe, I'll have someone else standing in my corner for this round of the fight."

"I'm always in the corner that's fighting for her," Frank said, careful to keep his voice stern but low. "Don't insinuate that I don't care."

"I didn't insinuate anything," Paul said, shrugging. "I just like knowing that you see it."

"And how do you know that?"

"Your face gives you away, Frank," he said, his voice nonchalant. "Maybe not to everyone. I've heard people say you're hard to read, but I can see it. I can see the wrinkles in your forehead when you're thinking and I can see the worry cloud your eyes, turning them darker. I can see you fidget when you know that we're in a rough situation. I can read it and I am just happy that you finally see it all."

Frank wanted to pop the kid on the chin. Paul was right and he was proving, once again, that he was far more nuanced than anyone gave him credit for. Frank had wanted to ignore what was happening, hoping it would fizzle out on its own. But nothing fizzled where Raven was concerned. Nothing was a half commitment. Either she was in, or she was out, and the results of getting out were always explosive. It was who she was. Sighing, he watched Paul drink his smoothie.

He wanted Paul's insights on how to get through to her. None of them knew how to talk her out of what was coming. Even Paul who knew her so well had no ability to break through her obstinacy. Discussing it with her would only drive her deeper into the usual cataclysmic pattern. As Paul took the last few gulps, he shot Frank a sideways grin.

"Whatever you come up with, I'll be there fighting with you, champ," he said, placing a hand on Frank's shoulder before heading out the front door.

Frustrated, Frank slapped his palm against the counter. "It's my job to manage this fucking band not be a therapist," he said, his voice a low, hissing whisper. In the back of his mind, he knew that therapist had always been part of his role.

He thought back to when Raven had first signed with him. She was a punk in her early twenties, thin as a wisp and ready to fight—for or against anyone or anything and at any odds. Having split from her previous manager after three years on the scene, he knew he was taking a risk. But he had a hunch she was a chance worth taking. He had admired the fire in her eyes, but he had since come to realize that it came with a temper and an ability to dismiss people mercilessly. It came with a raging past of bad memories and trauma and it came with a troubled future.

She was and had always been, in a word, hell-bent. Hell-bent on success. Hell-bent on making a change in the course of her life—from rags to riches. Hell-bent on expressing herself. Hell-bent on speaking out in anger. Hell-bent on living as she pleased. Hell-bent on being on her own. Hell-bent on fun. Hell-bent on sex, drugs and rock 'n' roll, just like the greats who came before her. Hell-bent on making history. Hell-bent on needing no one. And unfortunately, hell-bent on destruction.

The door creaked behind him and he turned slowly. He saw Chris standing in the hallway, disheveled and looking like a teenager caught missing a curfew, and he cursed himself for invading her privacy.

"Uh," she stammered, her cheeks blushing crimson. "Good morning."

"Morning," he said, nodding his head and turning back to face the wall. Even though he knew her professional line had already been crossed, he felt their working relationship had just changed.

He reminded himself that boundaries were nothing in this business. If he had a nickel for every time he had seen a team member in a compromised state, he would never need to work again. He breathed a sigh of relief when he heard another door close behind him, knowing that Chris had disappeared.

Moments later, he heard a door throw open forcefully, hurried steps and Christina's voice.

"What are you talking about?" she said agitatedly, her words running together. He resisted the urge to turn around, but after he heard, bus door open, he walked closer to the window.

"When?" he could hear her voice rising. "When did it hit? Is it bad?"

His heart rate rose, as he listened in on what had to be a negative call. When she shook her head, his stomach fell.

* * *

Chris's heart pounded as she listened to her boss. Seeing Susan's name pop up on her screen had warmed her heart and she wanted to touch base and see how her other clients were doing. Yet the mood had quickly changed.

"Looks like you're having a blast out there on the road," her boss had said, her tone only slightly amused, but nonetheless stern.

"What do you mean?" Chris had asked, trying to keep things conversational, all the while running through the list of no-no's she had committed while on the road. Partying, smoking pot and sleeping with clients were all against the rules, although they had never been spelled out as such. It was just common sense that those things were not ethical or professional.

"Saw you on the cover of a tabloid this morning," Susan said after a brief pause.

"What?" Chris had felt her nervousness rise.

"Yeah," she said, "you two look like you're getting really close."

"What do you mean?"

"You're making out on the cover of *People*," her boss said, her tone still level, but concerned. "You two are trending on Facebook. It's all over the web. I'm not quite sure what to think."

Wanting privacy, Chris had fled the bus to take this call. For a while, she had been in her own little cocoon, thinking no one else had a clue of what was happening behind the scenes. She now knew she had been stupid. There was only so much time you could spend with a public figure with such a high value to the paparazzi without being dragged into it yourself.

"We just clicked," Chris said, deciding it best to not try to lie it away. "I don't really know how it happened, but it did. I'm still doing my job. I'm still taking care of things. Other things just came up as well."

"Your personal life is your personal life," her boss said, softening. "I want you to be happy. We all know you work too much. You and I have talked about our personal lives. I know it's been a while since you've had that connection with anyone. I care about you. You know that."

Chris could hear the sincerity and reflected on how many times Susan had asked about her dating life, only to be let down that Chris had little interest. "I didn't mean for it to get out like this," Chris said, her breathing quickening as she realized what a mess she was in. "I wanted to tell you. It's just so unprofessional."

"Yes. It is," Susan said. Chris imagined her shaking her head and strumming her fingers on the desk like she often did when trying to process difficult information. "Like I said, I'm not sure what to do just yet. I'm trying to put out my own fires over this. And yours is just getting started, I'm afraid. I'm calling for three reasons. I am calling to let you know that I'm figuring out how to proceed. I also want to make sure that it's not interfering with why we sent you on the road. And I'm calling so you know that this mess is *yours* to clean up. You're good at what you do. I'm going to need you to show me that on this case. This is not to interfere with our business back home—or with the work you're doing on the road."

"Not at all," Chris said, confident in her answer. "I'm a professional, first and foremost. Well, I usually am...I just got caught up in how good it felt to be around her."

She was careful not to make an apology. While she knew that it wasn't the best light in which to be painted, she wasn't sorry for anything. She had already accepted the consequences and she was—for the first time in a long while—just living.

"Okay," her boss said. "You take care of the PR if a statement needs to be made. I'm going to trust your judgment here. This is your brief. I just don't want this to get carried away and hurt your career down the road or to damage what I've worked so hard to build. We're both aware that the press typically follows up on stories this dynamic. I'm sure it won't take long for them to find out exactly who you are and what your role is *supposed* to be with Raven. And every one of our clients knows what you look like, so it won't be a mystery for any of them. It could look very bad for us. And while I will handle talking to the clients, I am relying on you to fix this publicly or make sure it's not a hindrance."

The underlying threat was clear. Fix it or deal with the fallout. Chris agreed quickly and moved the conversation on, catching up on her other clients and how things were back home.

She felt more at ease, but only momentarily. Sitting on the ground outside the bus, she realized that she was going to have to be the one to break the news to everyone, unless that was the reason for Frank's early morning visit. Her hands were shaking and she couldn't breathe. This was a worst-case scenario. She should have been more prepared for it. You can't sleep with a rock star for two months and expect that no one will find out. She chided herself, shaking her head and breathing out through tight lips.

Susan was too good to her. Any other boss would have fired her on the spot. Though she knew that would leave Susan in a bind, she also knew that she was more than lucky to have received a slap on the wrist and a "deal with it" message. She should have been overjoyed. Instead, she felt like she had let Susan down.

Hanging her head, she reminded herself of the task at hand and the busy morning ahead. She found the story on her phone. Reading it as if it were her own eulogy, she looked for anything negative. Thankfully, no one identified her. She was the nameless, faceless woman splashed against the cover photo, the eye candy of the queen, THE goddess of rock. Thankful for the anonymity, she knew that it still wouldn't matter to Raven. It was emotional exposure. A sign of weakness. It was her being seen connected to someone, instead of standing proudly alone. And she knew Susan was right. There would be investigative stories—who she was, where she worked and more.

She skimmed through the articles again, noting that she had been called "incredibly beautiful," and that together, they were deemed a "hot couple." The word "couple" jumped off the page at her, threatening to ruin all she had built in two months and wondered if this was the end of the road. If this was the moment Raven decided that promoting a positive image no longer mattered if it breached her privacy and enigmatic image.

Her stomach churning, she stood, steadying herself against the nightmare coming down on top of her. Gripping the wheel well, she played through what she was going to say to the others, Raven in particular. She knew this was going to come back with a "this has to stop" ruling, but the other part of her wished against all the odds that it could continue, even if only for a while. Whatever the fate of this fast-paced romance might be, she would deal with it and she would do so professionally. Grimly, she climbed the steps and reentered the bus.

Frank and Raven stopped talking and looked at her quizzically.

"What's wrong?" Raven asked, looking her up and down. "You look like you've seen a ghost."

"Not a ghost," Chris said, taking a seat next to her on the couch. Frank sat opposite on a barstool. "I just got off the phone with my boss. Has anyone seen the cover of today's *People?*"

She watched their faces fall in an instant. Her phone buzzed again in her pocket and she quickly read the text from Brittany.

"Damn. Get it, girl! You both look amazing and that looks like one hot kiss. Call me and tell me all about it soon!"

She sighed, shoving it back into her pocket and wishing that she could feel the excitement. Of course Brittany would be one of the first to know. It related to Chris's love life. She had other things to deal with right now rather than feeding Brittany's curiosity. She felt helpless, anticipating Raven's wrath.

"So what is it?" Raven asked, pulling her phone out.

"It's not a smear story," she answered, holding up her hand. "Don't worry about that. Actually, I think it's probably worse for me than it is for you."

Raven raised an eyebrow, and Frank cleared his throat.

"I was afraid of this," he said in a gravelly, almost fatherly tone. "I don't care what the two of you do behind closed doors, or if you want to make it public. But I think it's time that you talk about it and make a decision about it."

"What is it a picture of?" Raven asked impatiently.

"It's a picture of us kissing. A picture from dinner last week in Fresno in that sushi restaurant. A damning picture, with a headline about your new main squeeze," she said, hating what she had said, knowing that it would only serve to usher Raven out of her life more quickly than she wanted.

Raven stiffened, reacting as though she had been slapped in the face. "I guess it is news to them," she said, clipping her words. "It's been years since I was photographed with anyone the press regards as more than a one-off fling."

"Is there anything negative in the story?" Frank asked, bringing them both back to the meat of the problem from the standpoint of the band—not their romantic interests.

"Nothing negative. It mainly just poses questions, like 'who is she' and 'is the queen of rock settling down?' But there's nothing in the story that smears. In fact, they write that it's nice to see a bit of a more personal look into Raven's life. It was all very positive, just more than we want."

With each word, she could feel an increasing chill from Raven, as if any indication of a commitment between the two of them—even if it wasn't Chris's doing—was grounds for immediate termination of their business agreement.

"I see," Frank said, standing from his stool. "Then, you two figure out if a response is needed, or if we just ignore it and let it stand as the gossip that it is. I'm going to leave you two to figure out next steps. You're the public relations expert, Christina, so I will let you handle this. However, I think it's time for you both to consider the fact that, if this is to continue, the public *will* find out. You need to decide if that's what you both want."

"What do you think?" Raven asked, turning to face only Frank.

"It doesn't really matter what I think," he said softly. "It's your life. Everyone already knows you're a lesbian. That's no shocker. Everyone already knows that you can pull beautiful eye candy." Chris cringed at his use of the word "pull," but let him continue. "The only thing that remains for you to decide is if this is something you want made public. If it is, go ahead, post a picture on social media of the two of you together. If this is something that you both deem better to keep behind closed doors, then do that but stop kissing in public places. Paparazzi are everywhere. Everyone can be paparazzi—or at least get paid for their photos.

"I will say that it wouldn't hurt to have a little more of you shown to the public. They've never photographed you with a woman of interest before. It may actually help your image. It would help to make you more relatable. However, since this is your personal life, I won't recommend that you make dating decisions based upon what is best for your career."

He turned to walk toward the door, stopping only before he grabbed the handle. "Good luck kid," he said, nodding in Raven's direction. You know I'll support you whatever you decide. I always have."

Frank walked out of the bus, leaving the two of them alone, sitting in silence, their fate hanging. Chris glanced over, attempting to make the first eye contact with Raven. Raven sat, motionless, eyes staring blankly at the wall.

CHAPTER ELEVEN

Taking a deep breath, Chris didn't care that it was only ten o'clock in the morning. She needed a drink. Making her way to the kitchen, she mixed two tequila sunrises and walked back to the couch, setting one in front of Raven.

"Something to clear your mind a little," she said, hoping her playful tone would shake Raven out of whatever funk into which she had disappeared.

"Thanks," she said, her voice barely a whisper.

"Look," Chris said, sitting down next to her and positioning her body so that Raven had to look at her. "We don't have to talk about this right now. We can keep doing what we're doing for now and we can play it by ear. There's nothing saying that everything has to be black and white by the time we walk out of here today."

"What is it *you* want?" Raven asked after a moment. "What is it that you think will be best?"

"For your image? For you? Or for me?"

"All of the above," she said, averting her gaze once more and setting her jaw as if she was ready for a blow.

"I think that your image is off the charts right now," she said. "I think that nothing written today took a toll on any of that and I think that the work we're doing together is really making a difference. Hell, most of what has been printed lately has you in pictures with puppies. They are mostly fluff stories talking about what a badass you are—a badass with a huge heart. That's awesome. What we're doing is working. This image campaign is fine, regardless of whether or not you and I are sleeping together. As far as what's good for *you*, only you can decide that. Frank said it's not his place to give advice and it's not mine either. That's all you.

"As for me and my career, I'm just fine. My boss said as long as it doesn't impact negatively on me or the firm, she's fine with it. I'm fine with it. Does it blur a line? Probably. Actually, yes, it does. But at the end of the day, I'm an adult and I wanted to fuck you. I've wanted to fuck you every time I've gone to bed with you, so I got myself into this and I'll keep fucking you as long as that's what you want and as long as it's what I want. I'm an adult and I make my choices."

"What about the rest of what they said? They called you my girlfriend. They said that you were the one who could change me. After all, look what you've done to my image in your time with me. They said it looked as if I had finally changed my ways and decided to settle down." The words were heavy and Raven's darkened eyes spoke volumes. If she was looking for a fight, she was going to find it with Chris. She seemed to want a reason to push Chris away.

"Fuck what they said," Chris answered, waving her hand through the air dismissively. "These are the rags that report alien sightings and stuff like that. There's no weight in what they say—especially when it comes to someone's personal life. They should have no influence over any of your actions. As long as they don't have pictures of you in compromising positions—say snorting coke off a stripper's chest or something, I think we're fine."

"So, we don't need to talk about it?"

Chris watched Raven carefully. She wasn't sure if she was more relieved or disappointed to not be put on the spot and having this all-important chat about their relationship, the definition of "couple" and exclusivity.

"No," Chris answered, shrugging her shoulders. "As far as I'm concerned, they can write what they want. If there are follow-up stories, we will deal with those like we're dealing with this one. We can talk about it then. And if *you're* fine with it, I'm going to fuck you now and stop having this conversation."

She watched as Raven's lips turned up in a half smile, once again making eye contact. Her deep brown eyes sparkled with a mixture of confusion and lust as she cocked her head to the side with unspoken questions.

"That's right," Chris said, lowering her voice and reaching down to slide her hand into the neckline of Raven's shirt. She walked over and locked the door. "Since the guys are out hiking and exploring the beauties of Colorado dispensaries, I'm going to fuck you until you forget about anything that's stressing you out right now and then I'm going to fuck you more until nothing else matters but you giving into pleasure."

Raven bit her lip and Chris could hear her breathing change. Needing no further invitation, she slid closer and moved to straddle Raven on the couch. Bringing her lips crashing down against Raven's, she let out a moan, pent-up frustration and stress leaving her body in an instant, knowing that she wouldn't feel complete until she ravaged Raven's magnificent body.

Tangling her fingers in Raven's long, dark hair she kissed her with reckless abandon, no longer caring where this might lead. Like a hungry animal, she ripped at Raven's clothing, pulling her shirt off as quickly as her fingers would allow and set to work teasing Raven's nipples with her tongue.

Smiling to herself, she knew what was needed in this situation. Raven was so used to being in control of everything—standing completely alone. She needed to let loose. Pulling back from their embrace, Chris stood.

"What are you doing?" Raven asked, her voice thick, clouded with lust.

"I'll be right back," she answered with a wink. "Until then, I want you to sit right there, and don't move."

She looked like she might protest so Chris shot her a stern look. "Stay," she said, motioning for Raven to remain where she sat. Raven bit her lip, a mixture of confusion, desire and awe dancing in her eyes.

Quickly, Chris made her way into her bedroom and grabbed a scarf before returning to the main room, walking slowly and deliberately. She leaned down to kiss Raven once more, before positioning her in the middle of the couch.

"Might as well go ahead and make sure you let go of everything," Chris said, tying Raven's hands together and putting them behind her head. "I want you to let go, completely and just be pleased."

Chris positioned herself over Raven's lap, straddling her legs and grinding against her body. Pulling off her own shirt, she let her bare breasts fall in front of Raven's face.

Knowing that Raven would want to take control and touch her, Chris grinned. Massaging her hard nipples with her own hands, she continued the tease. She could feel Raven's hips grind and writhe beneath her, silently begging for more.

"Are you ready?" she asked, looking down, pleased to see such raw desire in Raven's eyes.

"Yes please," Raven said, through ragged breaths.

"Beg for it," Chris said, feeling her own body tighten at the thought.

"Please, I need you to take me." Her words came out as a moan as her hips continued to gyrate.

"Good," she said in reply, standing up. "Spread your legs for me."

She grabbed Raven's legs and spread them for her, stretching her body out across the couch. She quickly unbuttoned Raven's jeans and pulled them off, tossing them on the floor.

"God you're sexy," she said, stopping for a moment to look at Raven's naked body, her lust showing in the ragged breathing and in her open legs. She knelt down and slid deep inside in one fluid motion, while Raven moaned in response.

"You like it?" Chris coaxed, needing to hear from Raven just how much she wanted it.

"I love it," Raven shouted. "Harder, faster, however you want."

As Chris took full control, Raven arched her back, biting her lip and moaning for more. When she came, she let out a loud scream. Chris reached up to untie the scarf and give her a kiss on the forehead. Raven stared at Chris with wide eyes.

"What?...Where?...What did you do to me?" Her words came out breathlessly as she regained control of her still-trembling body.

"I showed you that you don't always have to be in control," she answered, helping Raven sit up and sliding onto the couch beside her and kissing her lips gently. "I wanted you to feel nothing but pleasure, without any thought to anything else."

"Holy fuck," Raven said. "You certainly did that."

"What do you say we go enjoy a day on the town and just goof off until time for practice this evening?"

Raven looked around the room, eyeing the pile of her clothes and nodded. "I'd like that," she agreed. "But first, I have something I'd like to share with you."

"What's that?" she asked, wondering what else was left to share after that experience.

"I want to show you the new song," she said, a smile spreading across her face, causing her dimple to show distinctly.

"I'd love that," Chris said, giving Raven a hand up.

"I'm still a little unsteady, clearly," she said, laughing as she gripped the side of the couch. "Good game."

Chris laughed in response. "I didn't even get an ass smack with that 'good game' remark?"

"My bad," Raven said, reaching back and planting an open palm against Chris's backside. "Good game."

They both laughed as they made their way back to Raven's room. To Chris's surprise, Raven didn't dress. Facing Chris, she picked up her guitar and took a seat on her bed.

"It's a little raw still and it needs some finessing, but I promised you that you'd be the first to hear it. I want to give you that—especially after what you just gave me," she said, raising an eyebrow, an unmistakable dirty smile playing across her face.

Chris blushed at the compliment and nodded, urging Raven to continue.

"Here it goes," she said as she strummed her guitar.

Instead of the fast-paced rhythm that Chris had come to expect, this was a softer, slower, ballad-style tune.

"Turn out the lights," she sang, her voice low and tender, but exuding power with each word. "Turn off the haze, turn off the glitz and glamour, just hear what I need to say."

Chris watched as her eyes locked with Raven's. Her lover's expression displayed more rawness, more authenticity than ever before.

"Words I never heard," she belted, sincerity ringing in every line. "Words for all of you, words to build up, oh these words of endless truth."

Watching her sing, Chris wanted to reach out and place a hand on her shoulder. For the first time, she felt like she was seeing the exposed parts of Raven, the parts no one got to see. She waited, needing to hear more of the secrets being spilled out for her, for her alone.

"You're different and you're unique, but so are we all," she sang, closing her eyes as the words flowed. "So just be you, be you boldly.

"With our different battles," she sang, as the pace picked up. "Our changing scars, our dreams and our fears, our battered hearts; they say, 'be this,' 'be that,' 'be like them all,' but fuck what they say, you just stand proud and tall."

Mesmerized, Chris couldn't take her eyes off the woman. Raven, speaking through the one medium in which she bared her soul, was showing Chris a version of who she was—what she had been through. She had given glimpses. But this one was precious and unfiltered.

"No one can define it; they don't have the right to say anything to you, so just be you today." As she continued and sang the chorus again, Chris felt goose bumps rise on her arms.

"Some will leave, few will stay and all will say things that hurt, but pay them no mind today," she sang the bridge with such depth that Chris could feel her pain. Nothing could have prepared her for the tear she saw slide down Raven's cheek as she sung out what could have possibly been the truest words she'd ever sung.

"Words I never heard," she sang, each word leaving a haunting presence in the air. Caught so off guard by Raven's reaction to the song, Chris felt tears sting the corners of her own eyes. She blinked them away quickly once Raven made eye contact with her.

"What do you think?" she asked, looking up at Chris, her voice still thick with emotion.

"I think it's the most beautiful thing I've ever heard," she said. "Honestly, it's incredible."

"Thank you," Raven said, putting her guitar back in its case.

"No," Chris said, shaking her hands and stepping forward to embrace Raven's naked body. "Thank *you*."

They stood in silence, clinging to each other, neither one needing to expand upon what had been unspoken between the two of them. If only one thing was clear after all of the morning's confusion, it was the fact that they both understood what the other needed in the moment.

Right now, that was really all that mattered.

* * *

Paul paced outside the door. He had come back early while the rest of the guys had chosen to continue their daytime party. He could hear them and wished it would stop. He was angry that he couldn't get in, yet relieved that they had been smart enough to lock the door. There was no way he wanted to walk in on them, but he still felt his blood boil, knowing that they could have been courteous enough to have sex in a bedroom. Hell, they each had one. Sighing, he felt his key in his pocket and thought about using it. If worse came to worse and they didn't emerge before he really needed to get to work, he would use it. Until then, he would let them have their fun.

He took a seat on the ground and pulled out his phone. No doubt, they had seen the article of the day, showing them embracing warmly and kissing. They were either in there fighting or making up. Regardless, but didn't want to be a part of it.

After debating, he knocked forcefully. When no one answered, he knocked again and then sat on the steps to wait.

Finally, he heard the door lock click open and Raven threw open the door. Within seconds, he was up and inside. Raven looked dazed. He eyed her curiously and she smiled at him.

"What's up?" she asked, her voice lingering on each word, as if she was stoned.

"Not much," he said, hoping his expression alone asked his question.

"Lots of sex," she mouthed the words, pointing her finger to the bathroom, where he figured Christina must be.

He gave her a thumbs-up and sat next to her. "Are you high?" he whispered.

"No," she said, shaking her head and letting out a low laugh. "Just satisfied…like a lot."

He laughed. "Good," he said. "Are you happy?" he asked, careful to keep his voice low and out of earshot of the bathroom.

She nodded and then cocked her head to the side, as if considering his question in more depth. After a second, she nodded again. "I am," she said. "I don't know how or why, or where anything is headed, but I'm happy."

"Okay," he said, accepting it at face value. It wasn't often that she admitted to happiness, so he would take that for what it was worth. "If that ever changes, you know I'm here, right?"

She nodded again and laid her head on his shoulder. "You always have been," she said, keeping her voice low. "I know I don't say it often enough, but thank you."

"Thank you too," he said. "For everything. And my offer still stands. If you ever want to talk about things, I'm around. Hell, I'm right down the hall."

She laughed. "I know," she said, playfully smacking him on the arm. "I can never get rid of you. But honestly, I wouldn't want to. I wouldn't know what to do without you. You're my family."

He smiled down at her. In this moment, she wasn't guarded or jaded. She wasn't running. She was just here and for the most part, that's all he ever wanted for her. Right now, she was soft and she was real. She was present—not dealing with the past or ignoring the future, just present. He threw his arm around her, knowing that if Christina truly did make her this happy, maybe there was hope.

Stroking her hair, he thought about what they'd been through together, and for the first time in a while, he thought about all that was ahead. The future could contain anything, but as he watched her sweet smile, he thought that, maybe, the future was going to be a little brighter than it had been in times past.

CHAPTER TWELVE

"Did you see it?"

"Oh my god. It's scandalous."

"I wonder if she will get away with it."

"Do you think she'll get fired?"

The whispers had wafted through the office all day, accompanied by the circulation of the tabloid featuring Chris's now-infamous kiss. It had provided a tiresome soundtrack to Susan's day. Like mischievous children, every staff member had been seen holding the copy of *People Magazine*.

Now at home, Susan's head was still spinning. Though she had spoken with Chris earlier in the day, little had been resolved on her end. Was she supposed to punish Chris? Fire her? Was she supposed to let it slide this one time and focus on Chris's continued loyalty to the company? She had been at war all day, trying to figure out her plan of action.

She had deliberately left it vague with Chris. She needed time to process it all and sort out an appropriate solution. Everyone knew she ran a tight ship. There were no slipups or missteps. But they also knew how valuable Chris was to her. Hell, they used Chris as a liaison to speak with Susan when there was a problem.

Until this morning, it had only been a matter of time before she was going to name Chris her business partner. Now she wasn't sure what she should, or even wanted to do. She craned her head side to side, hoping her neck would pop, relieving some of the tension. She had called an afternoon staff meeting and told them to all butt out and let both Chris and Susan do their jobs without the gossip.

She just needed to buy a little time. She filled the bathtub with steaming water and lavender bubble bath. She shook her head as the water rose, willing her turmoil to even out and make peace with itself. Glancing once more at the tabloid before slipping into the hot water, she noted Chris's look of sheer and utter bliss. It was a look Susan hadn't experienced—or even imagined—in years. It was the same look she had once worn, long before the pain of a failing, childless marriage. She closed her eyes, seeing nothing but that bliss. Chris was happy. She longed for that feeling. And she wanted it for Chris. That's what made life enjoyable, instead of merely bearable.

Sighing heavily, Susan slid down into the water until it was just below her chin and closed her eyes, breathing in the lavender. Giving in to the relaxation, she let her mind drift back to the past.

Lively jazz filled the precinct as two young lovers drifted down the streets of New Orleans. A mix of smells lingered in the heavy swamp air—some pleasant, some not so much—but somehow wafting the scent of possibility and freedom.

"Isn't it lovely?" she asked, turning to look at Marcus. His dark skin glowing, no doubt a result of the incredible humidity, his dark eyes sparkling with the flashing signs all around them.

"It certainly is," he said, grabbing her hand. Her body tingled with excitement and pulsated with electricity in their connection. He spun her in a quick circle to the rhythm of the saxophone playing in the bar behind them, only to swing her back into his arms for a lingering warm kiss. Walking hand in hand she knew she was done for. This was

her first vacation in years and there was no one she wanted more to share it with than the wonderful man by her side.

"I love you," he spoke the words aloud for the first time, his voice confident and unwavering.

Each word replayed in her mind, echoing her unspoken question. "How did I get so lucky?"

"I love you too," she responded.

Side by side and arm in arm, they journeyed through the city, taking in all of the sights, but mostly falling more in love.

Susan sat up in her tub, her heart pounding from just how real and vivid the memory had been. Instead of going down into the depths of the course their love had taken—the proposal, the wedding, the years trying to get pregnant, throwing herself into her work to avoid the pain, and finally the messy, brutal and heartbreaking divorce—Susan reminded herself again that it was over. She winced, replaying his last words in her memory. *"We just burned out. There's nothing more left."*

As she had come to realize, it had been worth every moment—even the ones that hurt. Just to feel that strongly in love, that connected to someone, that lost in insane, fiery passion had been worth every tear—and every sleepless night. It had been worth waking up in a panic, searching the sheets for someone on the right side of the bed. It had been worth every moment of self-doubt and despair in the aftermath.

Though it had been fleeting, as love too often was, she would do it all over again. And truthfully, she could have tried to find someone else, had she not buried herself in work. She had seen that Chris was determined to go down the same path—working too many hours and losing herself to it alone. For that reason—for the hope of Chris's happiness and for how amazing it was to see Chris's joy in the picture—Susan knew she didn't have the heart to punish her. Much as she figured a mother would feel, all she could focus on was Chris's bliss. Of course she wished it had happened differently. But Chris was happy. That's what mattered.

Chris was being a twenty-something. She was giving love a chance—wild, unrestricted, uninhibited love like Susan was pretty sure was only a possibility in one's twenties. She was happy and Susan was happy for her. Maybe Chris would be smarter somehow—smarter than she had been and smart enough to make it last.

Her loneliness was tangible, and she slid back into her bathwater, listening to the echo of the water droplets falling from the faucet into the tub. She reflected upon her empire and deemed it worthless. It wasn't lasting. It wasn't substantial. And it certainly didn't keep her warm at night. She ducked her head under the water, holding her breath and considering what it would be like to have it all end…

She gasped for air, letting it fill her lungs. She promised herself to live vicariously through Chris's happiness and work on finding her own. For tonight, she would hold on to that. She had nothing else anyway. Tears slid down her cheeks and she covered her face, wondering how it all came to this.

One of them deserved not to have to feel this way every night.

CHAPTER THIRTEEN

Smiling with an adorable pit bull on her lap, Raven glanced from camera to camera flashing as people chattered on about angles and lighting. The Denver branch of Pawsitive Projects had asked her to stop in and she had been thrilled to oblige. She looked to the crowd, smiling to see Chris, thankful to have her here. After more than two months, she still hadn't tired of having Chris around. It baffled her. The dog licked her and she crinkled her nose, turning her attention back to his chocolate-brown eyes.

Glancing down, she smiled at her flannel shirt and jeans. She looked every bit the part of the good old lesbian next door. This campaign was proving to be an eye-opener, one that she wouldn't have admitted she loved had she not been so over-the-top excited about it. With her help, shelters around the nation had found homes for hundreds of rescue dogs. It gave her a sense of fulfillment she hadn't had in years and it made her heart sing.

She stifled a yawn, forcing a smile in its place. Though she wouldn't have traded it for anything, the month since Chris had suggested the charity campaign seemed to be a blur of photo shoots, interviews, rehearsals and fucking. She had hit a point where the after-parties got shorter and shorter, because all she had wanted to do was to spend time enjoying Chris.

Everyone had noticed her lowered alcohol and substance intake. She played off the boys' jabs, but every time she thought about snorting or smoking something, she could hear glass smashing in the back of her mind. It was a triggered reminder of all that she could become if she wasn't careful. That, combined with how good Chris was in bed, had made it quite easy to walk away from the parties, to say her greetings, have a drink or two and disappear into a back room where nothing else mattered but pleasure.

"That's a wrap," she heard the lead photographer shout.

"Good boy," she said, patting Charlie, the pit bull, on the head. "Thank you all," she said, waving as she walked over to Chris and Frank.

"How did it look?" she asked.

"Looked great," Chris said, her smile stretching from ear to ear. "You looked like a natural."

"You did good kid," Frank said, patting her on the shoulder.

"You really should consider getting a dog," Chris said. "You're a natural with them."

"You really should consider bringing Paco on the road," Raven said, feeling her nose crinkle as she smiled, thinking of the little dog whose pictures always made her smile. "He could be our band mascot and travel the road with us and then we could kill two birds with one stone."

"Probably not the best time to use that analogy," Chris said, laughing with ease. "This is about saving animals, not killing them."

They both laughed and Frank shook his head. In the two weeks since the kissing photo had gone viral, he had seemed aloof, as if he wasn't going to be a party to any of the fun the two of them were having. As Raven had become accustomed to doing, she brushed off his coldness, wanting to live in the moment. She and Chris had decided that's how they'd proceed.

No labels. No talk. No pressure. No rules. No anything until they *had* to deal with it. It was the way she preferred, even though she knew it was making Frank—and the rest of the band—crazy. But for once, she truly did not care. That was their business. This was her life and she was going to live it.

"You need to go sign a couple of autographs for the photographer's kids," Chris said. "Over there at the booth, he's got photos for you to sign."

"I'll wait outside," Frank said, nodding at them both before taking off.

"Is it just me, or has he gotten weirder?" Chris asked.

Raven shook her head. "He's Frank. He's always a little off, I suppose, and I'm sure I don't make his job any easier, but he's always going to be weird about something. He's got to have something to obsess over, to control, and if I don't give him that, he feels restless."

"Okay," Chris said, her brow furrowing. "What control have you taken from him?"

"Right now, I'm doing the best I've ever done—with my music, my career, my own happiness and my publicity," she said, cocking her head to the side, remembering all of the scrapes he had extricated her from. "How well I'm doing has little to do with him so he can't control it, since it's not something he set up. I honestly don't think he can handle that, but that's his deal. Because, this is awesome and I'm loving it."

"Yeah?" Chris asked, raising an eyebrow, wearing that sideways grin that drove Raven wild. "You enjoy working with me, do you?"

Caught up in the moment and knowing no one could overhear them, Raven leaned close to Chris's ear. "I like working inside you," she said, grinning as she pulled away. She watched as Chris's body shivered at her words and delighted in being able to undo her so completely in just a matter of seconds. "Be back soon," she said, winking as she walked away to the signing table. After a personalized message for each, she turned back, smiling at the sight of Chris waiting patiently. There was nowhere she wanted to be more than right beside Chris. Walking over, she looped her arm through Chris's not caring who saw, or if anyone else cared. This, she decided, was what happiness felt like.

They walked out into the sunlight and she flipped on her aviator sunglasses, basking in the glow of sunlight and joy. She removed her arm, only for a moment to roll up the sleeves of her shirt and let her skin feel the heat of the sun. Then, she placed it back inside the place where it felt most comfortable, wound through Chris's.

"I'm glad we opted to walk back, as it's great to get some fresh air and sunshine," Raven said. "We need every ounce of alone time we can get."

Chris nodded in Frank's direction, easily already twenty yards ahead of them, careful not to look back at their public display of affection. "Not really alone or private," she whispered.

Raven laughed. "It's private enough to do this," she said, kissing Chris lightly as they stepped to the backside of a tall building.

"I guess you're right. He still doesn't seem happy."

"He would have preferred we call the car, I'm sure. But this is what *I* wanted. It's good to enjoy time outdoors. We're only half a mile away from the bus anyway."

Stepping around the building and back on course, Raven could sense Frank's disdain up ahead. She had been around him for too many years to not see it. He was clenching his jaw, forcing himself into silence, when he really wanted to say something.

She could hear the words in her head.

"Everything you do is public, Raven."

She knew he was right, but she didn't care. Humming carefreely, she caressed Chris's hand as they walked.

"Did you enjoy this morning?" Chris asked, breaking the silence.

Raven could see Frank turn his head back slightly, as if waiting for an answer as well, but he said nothing.

"I did," she answered honestly. "Thank you for setting this up. I think it's the best idea we've had so far and I'm really enjoying it. It's fun and it creates positive stories. It's a win-win scenario really."

"Did you ever get the *Entertainment Tonight* interview set up?" Frank asked, still steadfastly facing forward, his stance rigid and cold.

"Yes, I did," Chris answered in a poised, chipper tone. Raven admiringly made a mental note of her "work voice." "It's next Thursday. We'll go through some of the things they'll want to talk about and the three of us can sit down over lunch and knock out some answers, so that we're all prepped for the show."

"What if I get stage fright?" Raven asked, grinning as she nudged Chris in the arm, giving her a seductive wink, well out of Frank's peripheral vision.

Chris opened her mouth, but Frank answered first. "I'm sure your girl there will be right by your side before and after to calm you down."

She watched as Chris's cheeks turned red. The whole thing made her laugh. "*Will* you be there?" she asked, giving Chris a sidelong glance and her best "come get me" stare.

"I'll be there, like he said," she said, still bright red. "Before and after."

Raven reached over, placing her hand on the small of Chris's back and rubbing it in a circular motion. She wanted to play, to get lost in each other just a bit and she didn't care who was watching. Chris shot her a warning look and raised an eyebrow, nodding her head in Frank's direction.

Raven shrugged in response, smiling at the silliness of their wordless flirting. The two of them continued as they walked along the street, before ducking into a tea shop for a quick refresher. Once inside, Chris made her way to the restroom, leaving Raven and Frank alone for the first time in days.

"What is going on between the two of you?" he asked, while they waited in line. "Looks like it's getting more serious."

It was an observation, nothing more, Raven tried to remind herself, but even so, the words made her anxious. "It's not serious," she said, shrugging it off. "I enjoy spending time with her. If you haven't noticed, she's kind of amazing. Funny, sweet, caring, smart as hell and hot. She's doing her job—and helping with my happiness levels too."

"I know." Frank nodded, keeping his expression neutral. She knew there was more that he wanted to say, but he was waiting, a tactic she understood. If he left the silence hanging, he knew she would fill it.

"It's just fun right now," she added, hating herself a little for giving in, but knowing that he wouldn't continue the conversation until she did so. "I'm not going to stress about putting things into a box for right now. I'm not going to push her away, just because I may or may not feel something. I made that decision a while ago and it wasn't easy. But for once, I'm going to let something run its natural course."

She watched as he turned slowly to face her, looking surprised.

"What?" she asked.

He shook his head slowly. "My little girl is growing up," he said, a slow smile forming at the corner of his lips. "That's all. You usually wouldn't admit that you push others away."

"It's a fault of mine," she confessed. "I know it is. You know it too. Anyone who has hung around long enough knows it. It's what I do, but I'm tired of denying myself happiness because of it. I'm trying. That's all I can say. I'm doing the best I can and we'll see what comes of it."

"Okay," Frank said, nodding in agreement. "But of course, it's nothing serious." His tone was wry, but she dismissed it, uncertain of how she could respond. There was little argument that Chris had, indeed, changed her. She had helped her to grow up a bit, just as Frank had stated.

Frank stared at the menu, but his smile was unmistakable. It made Raven smile too. Whatever came later on didn't matter. Right now, things were good.

Back at the bus, Raven wanted nothing more than to get lost in Chris's presence. Following her to her room, Raven couldn't wait anymore. She closed the door behind them quickly and turned to face Chris. The morning of flirting had heightened her desire to kiss Chris's lips, to feel their bodies pressed tight against each other. Chris raised an eyebrow at Raven and bit her lip.

"You seem a little excited," she said, her voice light and teasing. "What are you so excited about?"

Raven smiled, moving closer and pushing Chris up against the wall. After kissing her deeply, she pulled back. "I'm excited about this," she said, running her fingers up and down Chris's body. "I'm excited about giving into all I've wanted all day and then I'm excited about taking you out on the town tonight after the show. I've had enough of these tight-knit, close-quartered parties for a while. Let's say, I release every bit of tension in your body and then tonight, we go out and see what this place has to offer. What do you think?"

Chris smiled, her eyes sparkling. "I think that sounds amazing," she said, giving Raven a light kiss on the lips. "We don't go out nearly as often as we should."

The word "we" made Raven's heart beat faster. Unsure if she was more excited or scared, she pushed the notion aside, deciding that it would be better to figure it out later. "I know," she said, kissing Chris deeply, letting her tongue dance inside Chris's mouth.

When she pulled back, she winked. "You know it's mainly because of the way people get weird. They want to hang out and buy us drinks, but then they decide that it's not enough to just party with us. Suddenly, we have crazed fans who won't take a hint, and I even got a stalker once after a night out in New Jersey. But I want to take you out. I think it'll be a blast. Aside from all of that, if we don't mix it up, this just becomes the same old party every night. And Denver is a blast. I'd love to show you around. So let's go meet some locals, stalkers be damned."

"I'll protect you," Chris said, playfully flexing her arms. Raven raised her eyebrow, taking in just how cut and fit Chris's arms were.

"That's hot," she said, pushing Chris onto the bed and straddling her. "Sexy girl with guns. What a beast."

They laughed as they tumbled around the bed, kissing each other and continuing their teasing. "It's from my hardcore Pilates."

"Pilates got you those arms?"

"No," Chris admitted. "CrossFit got me these arms. But since I've been bunking here, Pilates has had to do the maintenance."

Raven's laughter filled the air as she poked Chris's arms and felt the firmness.

"I like laughing with you," Chris said, her legs tangled around Raven's body.

"I like it too," Raven admitted before lying down beside Chris. Chris wrapped her arms around Raven's body and Raven smiled to herself. She had always said that laughing in bed was one of her favorite hobbies. Sex should be fun, and connection—no matter what type—should be based on the ability to laugh with one another. She toyed with the word "connection," trying to decide what it really meant to her. As Chris drifted off to sleep for a quick nap before the concert, she felt her anxiety rise. Alone with her thoughts, she couldn't quite push away all that she had been pushing away for so long. Whatever this was, it was getting real and it was happening really fast.

CHAPTER FOURTEEN

The music shook her to her core tonight, but it paled in comparison to the rough-around-the-edges beauty performing it. As always, Chris was mesmerized. The people around her wore the same adoring gaze.

Sure, there was this public side—the side that everyone loved. There was the cover-ready, insanely talented girl who couldn't give a damn what anyone thought of her style or her lyrics. Everyone could get on board with loving a girl like that. But Raven was more—so much more. She was the one who, guarded as she was, looked at the world with such rawness and purity—seeing beauty in everyone, no matter what their differences. She was the chaser of her dreams, encouraging others to chase theirs as well. She was fire and she was willing to share that with the world. Watching her move across the stage, Chris felt the familiar stir, this time not in her lust, but in her heart.

She closed her eyes, bidding her feelings to stay at bay, but knew they couldn't. She was too far gone, despite her many attempts to suppress them.

"It's just sex." She had said the words at least twenty times when Brittany called for details, wanting to know how her *girlfriend* was doing. The words had come easily every time, but she now knew they would never again truthfully pass her lips. She might still tell Brittany that for the time being—at least until she had to face her in person. It would be hard for her to understand that whatever they might have, or have had, was over. *It's just sex.* It wasn't true.

She was in trouble. She was in love.

As the concert came to a close, she hurried backstage, wanting nothing more than to press her lips against Raven's. As she had become so accustomed to doing, she flashed her Staff pass at the bouncer by the backstage door. Thanks to Raven's propensity to making out before the show—after her makeup and hair artists had finished with her—and of course after the show, she had been given clearance to all secure areas. She made her way back to the dressing room, only to come crashing into Frank.

"You made good time," he said, looking her up and down, his criticism all too evident.

"I just wanted to…" she started to explain herself, but let her voice trail off. "Yeah," she said after a moment, moving past him.

With the dressing room door shut behind her, she settled onto the couch. Letting her mind drift back to the show. Imagining Raven onstage dancing and singing, her lust built. Hiking her skirt up higher, she positioned herself so that she was lounged across the couch in a "come and get me" pose.

She heard the door open, but didn't turn, wanting to play it cool.

"Some show, huh?" she heard Raven's voice and then the pause filled the room. She turned her head, suddenly afraid maybe Raven wasn't alone.

Raven raised an eyebrow, nodding in approval and letting out a low whistle.

"Damn," she said, staring open-mouthed for a minute, seemingly unable to move in Chris's direction.

In any other circumstance, Chris would have felt insecure and exposed, but right now, she felt sexier than she had ever been. She smiled slyly, winking and nodding at Raven.

Raven let out several heavy breaths, nodding in unison with Chris, before straddling her on the couch in a wave of pure lust.

After they had enjoyed each other's bodies, Raven sat up on the couch, looking deep into Chris's eyes. Chris felt her cheeks blush crimson, her earlier thoughts discovered—forbidden thoughts about connection and *love*. She averted her gaze, but Raven put her hand softly on Chris's face, directing her gaze back into her eyes.

"What?" Chris asked, feeling awkward under Raven's scrutiny, no matter how gentle and sweet.

"I just want to look at you and enjoy this," Raven said, her voice low and hoarse, as though the words were difficult to express. "It's tender and for me, that's rare. It's pretty fucking awesome, honestly."

Chris's heart beat faster, hearing the underlying meaning. "What's rare about it?" she asked, hoping she wasn't prodding too far.

"You," Raven answered, her voice barely above a whisper. "You are rare and the way you make me feel whole is rare. I'm enjoying every single minute of it."

"Me too," Chris said, simultaneously both touched and undone by the simplicity in Raven's words.

"You know I wouldn't admit it if it wasn't true," Raven said, bringing her lips to softly touch Chris's forehead. "I really do enjoy my time with you." She paused for a moment, leaving them both in silence. "I care," she added after a minute, but stiffened as soon as the words escaped.

Chris wanted to let the conversation unravel, but she knew if she did, the moment would pass. "Me too," she said. "And I guess you're not so bad yourself," she added with a playful giggle, thankful when Raven broke the silence with a laugh.

Leaning in to tangle herself up in Raven's kisses and embrace once more, she let the serious moment fade, hanging on to the fact that Raven was on the same roller coaster as she was—even if Raven couldn't or wouldn't name it.

* * *

Out on the town for a change, a steak dinner followed by a visit to a local Colorado brewery set the perfect atmosphere for a laid-back night out. And Chris relished every minute. She let the mountain air and altitude of the Mile-High City take her to another place and time, a place with no stipulations on what she should and shouldn't feel. Instead, she focused on the effect of the beers swimming in her brain and the feeling of Raven's hand intertwined with her own, knowing that, at least for now, everything felt wonderful.

The final stop of the night was a small locally owned hole-in-the-wall called McDaniel's. Though Chris had eyed the place skeptically with its clientele of burly men and tough women, it lived up to Raven's description. It was quaint and lively. And it was a one-eighty from their lifestyle. In the corner on a makeshift stage a local band played country music and their lead singer belted out honky-tonk tunes. It was a hoedown, but Chris didn't care.

"It's kind of nice, isn't it?" Raven asked, leaning in, her breath cascading across Chris's ears and igniting a fire across every inch of her body.

"It is," Chris said, knowing exactly what she meant. "The change of atmosphere is a little refreshing."

They laughed and watched as locals sang along and two-stepped across the floor. The scene was lively and it was impossible not to let their own excitement build. Raven tugged on her hand as the band started to play a Garth Brooks cover.

"Dance with me," she said, enjoyment bubbling with every word.

Chris glanced over at the lovely woman holding her hand and caught her contagious smile.

"I don't know how to dance to this," she said, protesting slightly, but when Raven raised an eyebrow and tugged on her hand again, she knew she was done. There was no resisting. "I'll give it a shot," she said, letting Raven drag her across the room to the dance floor.

Taking notes from other couples, they positioned their hands and began to move to the music. Chris breathed in deep, enjoying the closeness and lingering in Raven's sweet scent. Halfway through the song, she felt more than heard the watchful eyes and cameras clicking around them, causing her steps to falter and then stop altogether.

"What's wrong?" Raven asked, cocking her head to the side in concern.

"Don't you care what they'll say?" she asked, recalling Frank's words about being careful.

Raven shook her head, smiling wider and again placing her hand on the small of Chris's back. "Let them say what they want. Let them sell the pictures. Let them do whatever. We're having fun and we're allowed to do exactly that."

Chris smiled, taking Raven's words to heart and resuming her dancing. Even if Raven wasn't comfortable voicing all she seemed to feel, her actions defied her normal shroud of secrecy and spoke them loudly enough for all to hear.

Chris was right where she belonged—happily in Raven's arms. She felt the sweaty man bump into her backside before she saw it.

"Excuse me," she said turning around, suddenly eye to eye with a shaggy, blond-headed man, whose bloodshot eyes were as off-putting as was his whiskey-soaked breath.

"No excuse needed for a hot broad like yourself," he slurred, stumbling backward before forward. "What do you say I make it so that you don't have to dance with another woman? You can dance with a real man instead."

"No thank you," Chris said, leaning closer into Raven's arms.

Not taking "no" for answer, he stepped closer, grabbing her hand and pulling her in his direction. Chris stiffened and tightened her arm, holding her ground.

"I believe I made myself clear," she said, maintaining a smile, but wanting to punch him in the face.

"You just don't know what you're missing," he said, smiling at her like a cartoon villain. "Trust me. I've got moves she's never even dreamed of. I'll make you happy."

"I'm gay," she said, shaking her head and yanking her arm back to her side.

"That just means you haven't found the right man yet."

"Enough," Raven said, stepping around Chris to stand in between the two of them. "Leave her alone."

"I wasn't talking to you," he said, grabbing Raven's shoulder to push her out of the way. Raven grabbed his hand before it could connect with her skin and shoved it back downward to the floor. "Don't touch me and don't touch her."

"Your girlfriend is a bitch," he sneered, looking around Raven to look at Chris one more time, nodding his head and winking in her direction.

"Go to the bar, grab another drink and then maybe we'll talk," Chris said, pointing in the direction of the bartender.

"No," he said, "you're what I want right now."

"Too damn bad."

"You're stubborn," he said, his grin growing as he raised his eyebrows. "I like that in a lady. It shows they've got enough fight to be good in the sack."

"She's *my* girl," Raven said, giving no further warning and throwing a quick right hook to the man's face. "Let's go," she said, turning back to face Chris as the man stumbled back into the wall.

Everyone stood staring. Chris froze until Raven took her hand, rapidly leading her out of the bar. "We're getting the hell out of here in case that creep has buddies or something."

"Okay," Chris agreed, keeping pace with Raven's quick steps. She tried to wrap her mind around all that had transpired, but the only thing she could focus on were Raven's words. *"My girl."*

CHAPTER FIFTEEN

"Oklahoma City, I'm about to share something special with you all tonight and we're going to end the show with a bang," Raven shouted onstage, gaining the cheers of thousands. Chris stood proud, watching as Raven unearthed the deepest parts of herself for the crowd. Chris knew that she now had better control of her emotions during the new song, so that she could give a heartfelt performance without being overcome. That was the last thing Raven wanted and she had perfected walking the fine line. "It's a bit of a love song," she added. "A love song to yourself."

An eerie silence fell among the crowd as she strummed the opening note.

"ERIN!" a voice from the crowd called out loudly. "I'll always love you!"

Raven looked up, bewilderment written across her face.

Chris's heart sped up and she watched helplessly, wanting to come to Raven's rescue. Someone knew. She wanted to scan the crowd to see who had called out the name but the crowd seemed unfazed. Not wanting to cause a stir, she remained still, her eyes never leaving Raven. To her surprise, Raven closed her eyes and continued to play, perhaps needing to get these words out in the open now more than ever. Chris's head was spinning, but around her all was calm and she breathed a sigh of relief.

Raven performed beautifully, maintaining her composure despite the outburst from someone who knew her true identity. She sang the words with grit, focusing on a place just above the heads of the audience. Leveling her gaze to the back of the crowd from where the voice had come, Raven sang with gusto the last haunting words, "...words I never heard."

As she left the stage, Chris felt pride again swell within her. Raven had handled the truly awful situation like a champion, never letting on that she was bothered. Chris knew otherwise, though, and knew she would need to unwind after the show. Leaving her seat, she walked quickly to the dressing room backstage.

She paced around the room until she heard Raven. Nervously, she took a deep breath. Uncertain how Raven would handle the situation, she knew she was going to have to be the strong one and help her get through this.

"Hey," she called as Raven entered the room. "Want to go back to the bus, and I'll make you a drink?"

Raven's eyes flashed with fire as she looked around the room. "No, thank you," she said curtly. Making her way to the counter, she grabbed a bottle of tequila, popped off the lid and took three big gulps.

"Can I do anything?" Chris asked, walking over to put a hand on Raven's shoulder.

Raven shook her head, pursed her lips and attempted to breathe normally. They were still standing in awkward silence when the door opened behind them, causing Raven to jump as though she had heard a gunshot.

It was just the guys from the band and Paul came up behind her. "I called off anyone coming to join us for an after-party tonight. Are you good with that?"

She nodded and let him pull her into a hug. “Thank you,” she said, her voice just above a whisper. “I do want some people to come over, though. I know who I want. I’ll call them.”

Without another word, she disappeared out of the dressing room, leaving the three guys and Chris standing around the table, all wordlessly staring wide-eyed, unsure what to do.

“What now?” Chris asked, looking at Paul.

He raised an eyebrow, as if to ask Chris silently if she knew the significance of what had happened out there. She nodded in response, causing him to take a deep breath. Clearly, it was not a secret Raven handed out to many.

“This has never happened before,” Paul said. “So, I’m going to be by her side and let her do her thing. If she has partygoers she wants to have at the bus, I’m going to support it. If she wants alone time, I’ll give that to her. If she wants to go out, I’ll go with her and not leave her side. She’s vulnerable right now, but I will let her make her own decisions.”

Chris nodded as she felt her phone buzz in her pocket. Looking down, she saw Brittany’s picture flash across the screen. It was late and she knew it must be something important, but she put it back in her pocket. She had to deal with this first. Not only was the woman she cared about hurting, but this was also a situation that could blow up badly, making things worse professionally.

On her walk back to the bus, her phone buzzed with a text message. She pulled it out and read the text from Brittany. “I know you’re probably busy, but this is important. Please call as soon as you can.”

“I have to take care of this,” Chris said, pointing to her phone. “It won’t take long. I’ll be back.” She didn’t want to leave, but she knew that Brittany wouldn’t have said it was important if it wasn’t.

Brittany answered after one ring.

“Hey,” she said, sounding out of breath.

“Hey, what’s wrong?”

“It’s Paco,” Brittany said and Chris could hear a distraught sob.

She felt her body tense. "What's happened?"

"He was hit by a car," Brittany said, now crying freely.

Chris felt like someone had knocked the air out of her lungs. Sliding down the side of the bus to a sitting position, she wailed. She heard very little else Brittany said and Chris assured her that it wasn't her fault. It was Chris's fault. She was the one who had ditched her dog and her best friend for months on the road. She was the one who had taken his happy loving home and turned it upside down. She thought of the way he was always right by her side.

She listened to the details. Brittany had been out. Paco had busted through his dog door and dug out of the backyard during a thunderstorm. Not used to being off leash, and running hysterically, he had made it several blocks before being hit. Someone had found him and called the local vet who called Brittany. They were too late.

Comforting Brittany, she promised to call her the next day. Chris should have been there, she thought. She should have done *something* differently. Overcome by grief and guilt, she hung her head.

Letting her phone slip from her hands, she buried her head into her knees and cried, remembering all of the times he had been there to pick her up when she was sad—the way he had snuggled close to her side on each of the lonely nights after Renee left, how he'd lick her gently on the hand and provide a quiet presence when she cried, the way he had been her little heart healer when her father had died.

The call from her mother had sent her into shock. Unable to do anything other than stare at the wall in disbelief and cry for hours, Paco had stayed by her side, never wavering or moving even to go outside. When she didn't want to see anyone for weeks, he provided her with the companionship she needed. When she had a bad day at work or felt the stress of never meeting her mother's expectations, he was there—always there. There was no love like the unconditional love of a dog. Her tears fell and she wished more than anything, he could be there to crawl up in her lap and lick her cheek one last time.

She let the memories roll, from the day she brought him home to the day she had left on this assignment. Clutching her chest, she was pretty sure she could feel her heart actually break in two. A few people passed by her and entered the bus. She felt as if she had been beaten and she couldn't take on anyone else's pain at the moment. She was engulfed by grief and loss. Paco was her family. He was her loyal companion. She couldn't imagine him gone, especially knowing how he had gone.

Finally, she stood, drying her face, knowing that she had to go inside. Breathing deeply, she leaned against the side of the bus once more to steady herself. Somehow hours had passed. She hadn't been missed.

The guys were gathered around the couch. When they looked up at her, their conversation hushed.

"Are you okay?" Paul asked, noting her streaked mascara.

She just shook her head "Where's Raven?" she asked.

The guys looked at each other, transparent in their hesitation. They didn't have to say anything. She wasn't sure how many people had come inside, or if they were male or female, but whatever was happening, Raven was with them. Was she using or fucking…or both?

She felt the sting, but her heart couldn't actually absorb any more pain. Shaking her head, she walked away from them. "Have a good night," she called out as she walked to her room. She looked at Raven's door as she passed, wanting to ask what was going on, but she resisted, too defeated by the day's events to care too much.

She threw open her bedroom door, wanting to fall into her bed and cry herself to sleep. Her jaw dropped and her heart plummeted. She stood transfixed, unable to look away.

Her entrance had done nothing to still the three writhing bodies on her bed. She looked around the room and saw piles of clothes, g-strings and tight tops. She saw the drug paraphernalia on her dresser. She watched as Raven was pumping in and out of one woman while another was taking care of her. Out of the corner of her eye, she saw the red flashing light of a camera.

Her practical side took over. She walked in, grabbed the camera and walked out, slamming the door as she exited. She didn't care if they heard her and she didn't care if they continued. None of the rest of it mattered right now. She was heartbroken and the last thing she needed was a sex tape leak of her client. Fuming, she took out the video card and threw the camera into Raven's room, letting it smash against the wall. She locked herself in the bathroom and flushed away the evidence.

Of all places, Raven had to choose *her* room. She let fresh tears come again. She was a spoiled, fucked-up diva. Having her cover blown had rattled Raven. She had chosen the typical route—lash out and hurt the one who cares so she didn't have to feel her own pain. Maybe she needed to shut herself off and experience something wild, so she found someone else.

Or she needed to reinforce her anonymity. Whatever it was, it was fucked up. And even more importantly than that, Raven should have been smart enough to see the camera.

Chris shook her head, wanting to be anywhere but where she was, but she was trapped. Eventually, she heard the women's voices coming from the end of the hallway. Goodbyes were said, but Chris couldn't bring herself to move. Of course, she wanted to be alone in her room, but it was tainted, and provided no sanctuary at all.

She could overhear Raven's chatter with the guys, her words overly animated and tumbling out of her mouth far too fast. Chris wanted to scream. Raven was going to have to grow up at some point and face her life as an adult.

Raven's footsteps approached the doorway of the bathroom and Chris could hear her ask the guys who was inside.

"Who else?" Chris thought, biting her tongue to silence her seething anger that wanted nothing more than to lash out at the one who had been so callous, so cold and so insistent in bringing upon her own destruction.

There was a knock on the door and she didn't want to move. Cognizant of occupying the only bathroom in the place, she took a look in the mirror and attempted to wipe what remained of her mascara off her face. She took a deep breath and vowed to be the bigger person in what was to follow.

Without a word, she opened the door.

"Hey," Raven said, nodding in her direction and giving her a lazy sideways smile. "What's up?"

Chris bit her tongue, willing herself to be strong against this cavalier behavior. She shook her head and walked to the kitchen to get water, so she had the chance to pass by her room. One glance at the space told her she still wouldn't want to shine a black light in there any time soon.

Ignoring the awkwardness, the guys continued their conversation and passed cards around the small table, ignoring Chris's presence. Feeling completely alone in the world, she made her way back to her room. Standing in the middle of it all, she didn't know where to begin. The bed was the last place she wanted to be.

"Hey Chris," Raven called from the doorway. Chris looked at the mess again, before briefly turning her attention to Raven. She couldn't meet her eye, so she turned away again. "Did I leave my phone in here?" Raven asked benignly.

Chris's anger mounted and she turned to face Raven directly. "Yeah, I'm sure it's in the same place where you discarded your clothes, and your dignity," she spat the words in Raven's direction.

"Why are you so touchy?" Raven asked unflinchingly.

"Of all the places, you chose *my* room," she said, careful to keep her words quiet but pointed. She didn't want to yell. "What the fuck was that about?"

"It's my bus," she said, shrugging her shoulders. "And I honestly didn't really look around too much. I was led back here and I followed."

"And what about the camera?" she said, narrowing her eyes. "How stupid can you be?"

"I don't know what you're talking about," Raven said, shaking her head.

"There was a fucking camera going," Chris said, throwing her arms up in the air. "You have to be more careful than that."

"Stop acting like my mother," Raven said, putting a hand defiantly on her hip. "And while you're at it, stop acting like a jealous girlfriend. You know the score between us. We don't have rules. That's what this whole thing was built on, remember? Living in the moment. Apparently you can't handle that."

"What I can't handle is you being an awful client," Chris said, determined to keep her anger in the right place. "You're right. We don't have rules. We never did and that's fine. I'm *not* a jealous lover. Do I wish you had respected me enough not to do it in here? Absolutely. I feel like you should have a shred of decency and be able to decide what's wrong and what's right. Do I wish you weren't strung out on something tonight so we could have a real conversation? Without a doubt. But it is what it is. There is no longer any video, because I destroyed it while looking out for you. And there *is* no more situation here. Don't worry. I won't threaten you by acting like a jealous girlfriend anymore. In fact, I am walking away from this. I'm done. I'll hand you off to someone else at the firm, or I'll suggest another firm."

"You can't handle it," Raven said again, taking a step closer. "You can't handle not being my one and only, can you?"

"You're messed up tonight," Chris said, shaking her head. "I'm not going to try to talk to you about logic or anything else. You probably won't even remember this conversation, so I'm wasting my breath."

She walked around Raven, grabbing the items still strewn about the room, and dumped them on Raven's bedroom floor. She grabbed her own baseball tee from the corner of Raven's dresser, so she could pack her things.

Raven still stood in Chris's room, watching her every move closely.

"Fine," Raven said, her defiance seeping through every word. "Go ahead and leave. Go ahead and run. Run back to safety where things aren't messy and people aren't fucked-up."

"Stop," Chris said, her voice a stern whisper as she felt it packed more of a punch. "Stop being a victim. Stop running. Stop hiding behind lies and false bravado. Right now," she paused letting her words hit their mark for the biggest impact, "you're nothing but a cliché. You're nothing of your own. You claim to be so different and you could be.

"You sang tonight about being bold. That's what you want to portray to your fans but it's a lie. You act like you're the world's only victim. You sit on your high horse and you hurt everyone in your path. We've *all* been hurt, screwed over, abused, cheated. We've *all* been victims. And instead of being the force you could be, you wallow in your victimization. You represent a litany of bad choices. You're determined to ride this cycle of screwed-up behavior and be nothing greater, nothing deeper, nothing more."

Raven opened her mouth to speak, but Chris shook her head. She was done listening to anything Raven had to say. She stripped the sheets, threw the pillows onto the floor and ushered Raven out the door.

"You don't know what you're talking about," Raven yelled, standing in the hallway.

"Of course I do," Chris said. "You're a cliché. *Be more.*"

With that, she shut the door, leaving Raven on the other side. She slid the lock into place and let herself slide down the door into a defeated heap.

The wretchedness of the situation took over, a clear reminder that she had failed. She had taken this job as a challenge, something she knew she was capable of. She had set out with no expectations other than that she would turn Raven's image around, that she would somehow help her to be more of who she really was.

Instead, all she had succeeded in doing was standing helplessly by while Raven destroyed herself, yet again. All their work was for nothing. It didn't matter how many rescue dogs she hugged, how many positive stories or how involved Raven was in things other than the music scene. None of it mattered, if she persisted in running around like a wild child.

Even though she had only been a part of the dynamic for a couple of months, Chris had been told that these outbursts and rebellious behaviors were not isolated incidents. Once the switch had been flipped, they could all expect more of the same in the coming days and weeks. There was little anyone could do to stop the train once it had started rolling down the tracks.

Chris wasn't going to stick around and take the abuse. She was the one who had reached inside, who had been let behind the fortress walls and that now made her the enemy. It wouldn't be long until Raven spiraled completely out of control. From what Paul and Frank had told her, this could last anywhere from a few days to a month or even longer. She wouldn't, couldn't stick around to watch it. It hurt too much to be in the middle of it, and given that her professional boundaries had already been crossed, it was best if she walked away now.

She glanced at the time, wishing she could call her boss now, but it was far too late. She thought through possible outcomes. Yes, she was walking away from a job, but she was doing so before it became an outright failure. There were times when clients and account managers just didn't mesh. They had all walked away in the past and this would be no different. She would explain the situation to Susan as best she could, but she felt confident she was making the right choice. After all, her boss had left it in her hands to decide when her work on the road was completed. Up until now, she had no idea when she was going home, simply because she had let herself get caught up in it all.

Now, it was different. The atmosphere had changed into something dark and cloudy that wouldn't ease for a long time. And it was no longer something Chris wished to be part of. She would leave here with her head held high and she would hand Raven's contract over to another manager. It would be as simple as that and if they chose to break the contract, that was their choice. She had done all she could do here.

Bracing herself on the dresser, she took extra care not to touch the lines of cocaine or black g-string. She emptied her belongings from the drawers, the closet and finally the bathroom. Once she had everything secured, she crawled into a ball on the floor, bidding the hours to pass quickly as the bus roared through the night.

She couldn't sleep. She tried to remember where they were headed next. Wherever, she was taking the first plane out of there. More than anything, she needed go home.

Still awake, she felt the bus come to a stop. It was daylight and she was ready. She typed up a quick email to Frank, letting him know that she would touch base with him once she was back in Houston and that they could discuss options for moving forward at that point. Making only one last attempt before exiting, she scrawled the words "be more" on a Post-it note, sticking it to Raven's door.

Whatever happened, she was heading home, back to where she belonged.

They had stopped at a gas station in Dallas. *Her* final stop. She breathed a sigh of relief that she was at least near a major airport. Not looking back, she walked until she came to a hotel and hailed a cab, her chariot back to normalcy.

* * *

The banging on her bedroom door drew Raven straight up to a sitting position. She yawned and rubbed her eyes, her head pounding with every movement.

"Just a second," she called, scanning the room for her clothing. When she opened the door, she was taken aback by Frank's expression. His jaw jutted out, his eyes angry and the lines in his brow deeper than normal.

"Do you want to tell me what happened?" he asked, keeping his tone neutral, even though everything about his demeanor screamed rage.

"What are you talking about?" she asked, walking out into the hallway, her eyes adjusting to the light. "I just woke up."

"I can see that," he said, looking her up and down. "I'm talking about what transpired here last night." His voice was low and fatherly. She could imagine him saying the things fathers say on television. *"I'm not mad. I'm just disappointed."*

"Last night is kind of a blur, to be honest, Frank," she said, wishing he would get to the point. "What are you referring to?"

"I'm asking why we now have no one to do PR," he said sternly, pointing to Chris's room. "You might not have noticed yet but she's gone. I want to know why. I warned you this would happen if you weren't careful, but you were so insistent on breaking the rules that we're back in the same boat. We're back at square one, without the one who had been helping you so much."

His words ran together for Raven as she tried to recall all the night before. Looking into Chris's room, she felt her heart plummet. He was right. She was gone.

"I don't know," she answered when nothing came to mind. "I'm sure I'll figure it out as the day goes on," she said, stepping past him to go get some water. Her throat was parched and she felt as though if she tried to say anymore, her sadness might manifest as tears.

"I'll call her later, then," he said, turning on his heel and walking for the door. "I'll ask *her* what happened and maybe you can let me know when you figure it out. Then, we can decide where we go from here."

Disappointment and anger dripped from his words and she was thankful when he finally left. She couldn't shake the profound disappointment in herself. This had been something she had wanted to make work and in her typical fashion, she had driven it right into the ground—even if she had no idea how or why.

Leaning back on the couch, she let the pieces come back. Someone had called out her name at the concert. Someone from her past had surfaced and found her. Or Chris had broken the trust Raven had placed in her. Her mind played tricks on her as she tried to figure out which to believe. Either she was right and it was a voice she recognized—a voice she had heard time and again throughout her childhood. Or it was a scorned past lover. Or Chris had told someone.

As she sipped her water, fresh fear and pain cascaded over her. She was no longer able to hide in her anonymity. She closed her eyes. No matter how she tried to fight it, she heard the voice again from years ago. She knew exactly who it had been out there last night.

It was the voice that had occasionally been nurturing, with bedtime stories and limited guidance. But it was also the voice that had, all too often, been the voice of rebuke, verbal assault and betrayal. It was the voice from which she had never heard so much as an apology or an explanation, the voice that took no note of shortcomings, the voice that had brought far more hurt than good into the world.

"*Erin!*" She heard it over and over in her mind, trying to recall the last time she had seen her mother. She remembered distinctly the way her bloodshot eyes had showed no remorse, as Erin was whisked away in a child protective services car. With her hands cuffed behind her back, her mother smiled, seemingly grateful that her only child was being taken from her. Even as a teenager, Erin knew what that meant.

It meant it was over. It meant that she was never going to see her again. Already toughened by life, the ten-year-old sat in the back of the car, willingly going wherever they had in mind for her. She had been sure it had to be better than life in this hellhole.

It hadn't all been roses, but it certainly *had* been better. And with each passing day, she had worked to make sure she never had to hear that voice, to see those eyes, to feel that heartache ever again. She hadn't had to, until yesterday. That *must* have been who it was. Luckily, it hadn't been a full-on encounter and she hadn't had to face her mother. Even so, it had been unnerving. And she knew the proclamation of love was a lie. It had always been a lie. "Erin" had been nothing more than a meal ticket and if her mother had resurfaced, it was surely money she was after.

She tried to recall what had happened after she got back to the bus. She knew she didn't go out. And as far as she could remember, Chris hadn't been around. Confused and desperately wanting to remember, she walked to Chris's room. She saw the heap of sheets and pillows on the floor, the evidence of drug use on the dresser. It all flooded back. The blondes. She tried to assure herself that she hadn't been in the wrong.

Chris could be hurt over it, but she had given no indication that they were in a relationship. She felt her defiance build as it had done so many times before, but she couldn't hold onto it. She wanted to be stubborn and stand by her choices, but she knew she had been at fault.

Then the rest flashed back, what Chris had said, the fact that Chris had seen her in action. Forcing herself to breathe, she made her way to her room, only to see a bright Post-it note hung on her door. She pulled it off, remembering having heard Chris say those exact words only hours before. "Be more." It rolled around in her brain like a ball in a pinball machine, flying through the air and hitting each stubborn wall.

She wished she could feel numb. But she felt a wave of guilt and heartache crash down on her, threatening to pull her under. She fell down on her bed, unsure of whether she should call and try to apologize or if that would only make matters worse.

Chris had been right to be angry. She had been right to be hurt. Raven was out of control and she knew it. For the first time, she let herself feel the weight of the sadness she had caused to not only Chris, but to all the other women before her.

She thought back to Chris's face, distorted in pain, mascara streaked. She had been crying and Raven had done nothing. Just like always. This time it hurt more, knowing that she had driven away the best person she had ever met.

Chris was special. Like a breath of fresh air. She was a good influence, and had seamlessly fit into Raven's life. She'd come in and tenderly opened the doors of Raven's heart, without prying and without force. That sweet, sincere smile never asking much or expecting anything. She was everything Raven had ever wanted and all of those things she didn't know she had needed. She was *everything* and Raven had fucked it all up.

She needed help. This time, she promised herself, she would get it. She would do what it took to be more.

She toyed with the idea of calling Chris, letting her know about her epiphany. But she tossed the idea aside. Chris deserved more. She didn't need an empty apology, words that meant nothing. She deserved to see that changes had been made. Raven wouldn't contact her until she had become worthy of Chris's attention.

She walked back into Chris's room, wiped up the lines, grabbed the drug paraphernalia and threw it in the trash. Sitting on her bedroom floor, the scent of Chris's perfume still lingered hauntingly in the air. If this is what rock bottom looked like, she had finally arrived.

CHAPTER SIXTEEN

Music streamed through her headphones, blocking out the surrounding aircraft noise and cocooning Chris into her own little world. She took another sip of her vodka. If she was honest, she wasn't sure which she faulted herself more for—believing Raven actually cared about her, or jeopardizing her career in such reckless fashion. It was an all-around failure. She knew as much. It had been inappropriate and had wrecked her professionalism—and all had been done with such poor judgment. She gritted her teeth, regret seething through her body. She shuddered, replaying her stupidity and her complete lack of regard for anything other than feeling good.

"*It'll all be fine*," she remembered telling her boss, assuring her that, whatever happened between her and Raven, it would all work out in the end.

She had been dead wrong and now she was going to have to pay the price, whether that meant finding a new job, swallowing her pride and working on Raven's account from afar, or being formally reprimanded once she was back at the office. Either way, none of it was going to be pleasant and it was all a direct result of her sheer stupidity, her denial and her willingness to go blindly into what was obviously a bad situation. And she criticized *Raven* for making poor life choices! Talk about hypocritical. This was her doing and she was going to have to bite the bullet with whatever came next.

She hit her call button on her console and waited for the flight attendant. She nodded silently when the well-meaning woman asked her if she was okay. There was no doubt she looked dreadful, with her puffy eyes and her disheveled clothing making it clear that she hadn't slept last night. She quickly drank her second strong drink, knowing they were close to landing. The music took her away again, this time not to another world—but to her reality.

Pink's "Crystal Ball" about missed chances echoed her thoughts. She moved her head to the soulful words, feeling them resonate within her and knowing that at least someone understood.

This was a reality she had helped to create. These were her choices, but she would stand by them bravely. She would apologize where necessary and not back down. She had taken a risk in getting close to Raven. And it had backfired. She was defeated.

For a moment, she looked around, wondering about her fellow passengers. They all looked so at peace, so calm. She wondered if any of them had a war raging within them, if any of them had experienced anything life changing in the past day. Regardless of the damage, there was no way she would ever be able to look back on the past two months and pretend that it hadn't shaken her to the core, that it hadn't changed her.

Steeling herself against heartache, she closed her eyes, knowing that she didn't have to have it all figured out just yet. She vowed that she wouldn't become hardened and jaded. No matter what, no matter if it hurt like hell, she was going to feel it, to let it take her to rock bottom if necessary, all so that she didn't become like Raven. She would do everything it took to keep herself from being so jagged and cold, so stubborn and determined to push others away. And so alone.

She was still the same soft-hearted, hard-working woman she had always been. Next time, she would be a little wiser. With growing confidence, she threw her trash in the bag as it passed by and readied her tray for landing.

Chris could feel the alcohol swirl in her brain, making it difficult to want to get up from the comfort of her seat. At the baggage claim, she felt her nerves tingle with their rediscovered passion for nicotine. Grabbing her bag, she headed for the curb. She lit up a cigarette, relishing one last moment. Breathing in deeply, she spotted Brittany's car parked in the loading zone. Reluctantly, she crushed the cigarette and threw it in the ashtray.

She waved, thankful that her friend was so dependable. With no trace of condemnation or curiosity, Brittany helped Chris with her bags, placing them in the trunk and gave Chris a long, welcoming hug. The warmth of the embrace almost shattered what little strength she had left and Chris felt the hot tears streak down her cheeks.

"I missed you," Brittany said, before pulling away from the hug and getting into the driver's seat. Chris followed suit, trying to regain her composure.

"I missed you too, by the way," she said, breaking the silence in the car.

Brittany smiled at her, reaching over to pat her leg. The movement was so simple but felt intimate. She thought about leaning over to kiss her. But she refrained. Half drunk and clearly a hot mess, Chris was not in any state to make a move on her best friend.

"You look a little worn down," Brittany noted, glancing out of the corner of her eye. "Are you okay?"

"I think so," Chris said, before shaking her head. "Actually, I know I'm not, but I also know that I will be—in time."

Brittany nodded, silently giving her support. She turned slightly in her seat. "Do you want to talk about it?"

Chris shrugged, knowing there were things she needed to say and knowing that this was a safe space. She didn't have to have her words exactly right. Aside from that, even though it would be difficult, it would be good practice for the meeting with Susan tomorrow. She needed to explain without tears. She let out a deep breath, preparing herself to try to distill what she had been mulling over on the plane.

"It was incredible," she said, looking off into the distance, remembering every moment. "It truly was like a work of art to watch play out. It was like fireworks. It all built with suspense and a slight hint of danger, weaving a pattern of fiery beauty across a night sky. But all too soon, it exploded, leaving behind wreckage and despair. That was really the only course it could have taken. It was beautiful. It was something that I'll never forget, but it had no way of lasting."

"Are you talking about her or this experience?"

The question was simple, but it made Chris's stomach somersault. "Both," she said, letting out a deep breath. "The gig itself was a once-in-a-lifetime thing. It was like the championship of my career, something people dream about. It was my biggest challenge and I have to say I did a damn good job. Mostly… But just like going to war, I suppose there are bound to be some casualties at the end of a hard-fought battle."

"What's the damage in this battle?"

"My heart," she answered, letting Brittany in on the secret she had tried so hard to conceal. To her credit, Brittany didn't flinch. "My heart and my pride. I got too wrapped up in it all I guess. I thought she cared the way I did and deep in the back of my mind, I realize now I was holding on to this stupid misconception that, whatever came, we would tackle it together. We had made such a good team and professionally, I made great strides. She's never had positive publicity like this before. In that arena, it was a win. But time will tell if it lasts, or if it was for nothing. My pride has that to hold onto. I can rest assured that I did everything in my power, even when my judgment was clouded by my feelings. My heart, though, will be battered and bruised for a while. But it will heal. It will just take some time."

Brittany nodded, but the pained look in her eyes was clear. "I want to kick her ass," she said. "She has no right to ever make you cry. I don't care how big and bad and untouchable she thinks she is."

"I had a hand in this too," Chris said, shaking her head. "I appreciate you always having my back. You're the best friend I could ever ask for, but this was partially my doing. I let her get away with it, by letting her slide on not having to commit to changing. As far as she was concerned, she was untouchable and I didn't challenge that. I should have known better than to let my heart get in the way of everything, but I went for it. I dared to feel. It sucks, because she's out there probably partying it up and I'm reduced to a pile of tears. But I'll recover just fine."

"I have all the faith in the world in you," Brittany said, letting out a long sigh. "If anyone is resilient, it's you. I'll still hate her though. And I'll still be here by your side every step of the way." She paused at an intersection. "What do you want to do? Do you want to go out? Do you want to find someone to take home and take your mind off things? Do you want ice cream and movies?"

Chris shook her head. "I'm a little partied out, I'm afraid. And I don't want to find someone else to distract. She meant more than that to me. It may have been nothing more than a good time to her, but it meant something to me. And I refuse to cheapen that memory by jumping into bed with someone else just to feel better. Let's just go home."

She almost broke down again realizing that, this time, there would be no pitter-patter of dog feet dancing with joy at seeing her, no one jumping into her arms to greet her and lick her face. She had lost her father. She had lost her way. She had lost another chunk of her heart. And she had lost the little dog she loved more than anything in the world. But this was her new normal and like the champion she knew she was at heart, she would overcome even this.

"Last time I heard from you, things seemed to be going well," Brittany said. The statement wasn't a question, and it held no judgment. "You seemed happy. Both of you did. I mean, I couldn't see your smiles in the picture, but you could tell that there was a sweetness in the embrace."

Chris nodded, feeling it all come back.

Chris shook her head. "We *were* happy," she said. "Nothing was established, of course, but it was blissful. It was easy and we seemed to just go through every day with a gentleness and bringing out the best in each other. Then, out of the blue, in a matter of moments, it changed irrevocably. Like something flipped a crazy switch in her head, she lost it."

"What did she do?" Brittany asked, her mama bear voice coming out again. "Did she hurt you? Did she get violent?"

"No," Chris answered quickly. "Not at all. It wasn't like that."

"What did she do?" Brittany repeated, articulating each word plainly. "I need to know."

Chris hardened her lips, forcing a deep breath out. She was going to have to get this off her chest—at least with Brittany. "We had been spending every night together. Every day too. We were so caught up in each other. She had been opening up to me, letting me see the parts of her that she keeps hidden. She made me think it was something important, and then when you called about Paco, she'd had a bad night as well."

She paused, looking out the window and wishing that some of what she had to reveal didn't hurt as badly as it did. "I knew we were in for a rough night, even before your call. Raven had opened up to me. She had shared some of her past with me—something that seemed so out of character."

She watched, waiting for Brittany's jealousy to flare. All she saw was genuine concern, so she continued. "We had this passionate connection. She shared details with me, including her real name. From what I gathered—and from online speculation—that's a guarded secret. Someone called her name out in the crowd that night. I'm not sure if it was an ex-lover, a family member who found her after all these years or someone else. Whoever it was, I know it had to have scared her and made her feel exposed. She's far more vulnerable than she lets on. She uses bitterness and fakes aloofness to push aside her fears and weaknesses.

I knew she would be volatile after the show. There's no way she would react any differently, given her history with blowups and incidents. I'd heard she lashes out. But I was prepared to be by her side, to make it better for her. Because of Paco, I was too late. By the time I sorted myself out and went to check on her, I saw things that I just can't forget. It was all a blur, but the memories are so vivid."

Brittany stopped at a red light and turned to face her, her forehead wrinkling questioningly.

"I rounded the corner to go to my room," Chris spoke but the words sounded foreign, as if she was recounting something in a court of law. Her voice was dry, cold, hollow and devoid of any emotion. "Instead of being in her room with her friends doing God knows what, she had chosen mine—for reasons I still can't figure out. She was in my bed. I mean, I guess technically it's hers. Everything is hers. She was in my bed, high as a fucking kite, having a threesome with a pair of blond whores. God knows where they came from. Her dealer I guess. I saw so many awful things that night, but worst of all, I saw that one of them had been filming the entire escapade."

"What the hell?" Brittany's voice was quiet, but it seemed to echo throughout the entire car, reverberating off the windows and replaying the sentiment that Chris had been expressing for the last twenty-four hours.

"I think she needed someone anonymous to make it hurt less," Chris said, explaining it away, her tone still hollow. "She had already called in reinforcements long before I disappeared. She didn't want me. That's all I can figure, unless it was just that being in my presence, in light of the pain she was feeling, was too real. It made it too personal, so she needed to just get lost in someone who knew nothing about her."

"That's unacceptable," Brittany said, shaking her head vehemently. "You are so much more than that and I know it sounds trite, but you deserve better than that. You're not some little plaything that she can throw around. She doesn't own the world. She doesn't own you. And unspoken or unlabeled or whatever, that's uncalled for. In fact, it's cruel. She doesn't get to rule the world as if nothing matters. Life isn't her big playground."

"She just got carried away, I think," Chris said, shaking her head. She didn't want to make excuses for Raven's behavior, but she had to see the situation clearly. She took a deep breath, steadying herself. "The thing is that I don't even think it's intentional anymore. I don't even think some of these things she does are even consciously thought out. She lives on a whim, always. Whatever feels right or sounds right in the moment is what she chooses. It's like an animalistic approach to life, truly primitive. Where the rest of us understand what's socially acceptable, she's decided that it doesn't matter."

"That's not healthy," Brittany said, shaking her head again as disapproval flashed in her eyes.

"It's not," Chris said, letting out a sigh. "Nothing about her life is healthy. But I don't think she's ever really been too grounded. I don't think she had the chance early on and later on in life, she adopted her own set of rules. When you're on your own at an early age, the rules are yours to make. And let's face it. When life is a party, where do you draw the line?"

Brittany pulled the car into their driveway and Chris breathed a sigh of relief. She was home. She paused, stepping from the car and letting herself drink in the fresh air as though it was her first taste of water in days. "When life is a full-time party, it's hard to know when to stop. When there are no rules, who's to say what's right and what's wrong? She has been surrounded by people all of her life who haven't told her when to stop."

"That doesn't make it right," Brittany said, helping her unload her bags. "There are some lines in life that you shouldn't *have* to be told not to cross."

"I completely agree," Chris said, "but someone has to teach you that." She glanced at the house, unsure how she would take walking through the front door without Paco. Pushing through the sadness, she continued the point she was making. "The thing is that she is so far gone that I don't even know if she thinks in those terms. She's on a pedestal to everyone and at the same time, she *is* the hot mess that everyone sees. She teeters somewhere between the two modes. She's the diva who holds the world in the palm of her hand, the one who can do no wrong. And she's also the one everyone expects to fuck up. It comes as no shock to anyone anymore when she does something crazy. There's nothing she can do to get a rise out of them. She dances the line between being everyone's goddess and everyone's screwed-up little sister. The dangerous part is that she doesn't give a damn and she has given up on caring what anyone else feels, needs, wants or expects. She has given up on being vulnerable. That night, it was like she transformed into some kind of party-hard zombie and I don't even know if she gave so much as a thought about me when she went off the deep end."

"You sound like you've given this some thought," Brittany said, opening the door.

The gesture warmed Chris's heart. If nothing else, she was home with someone who cared enough to take care of the little needs—picking her up at the airport, helping her with bags, caring about her problems…and opening the door. It was simplistic, she knew, but it still meant that she mattered. That was something she had been missing. She had been missing Brittany and maybe she had been missing her all along—on a deeper level.

"I had to so I didn't go crazy," Chris said as they made their way inside. Without Paco, the entire house had changed. It was still home, but it wasn't the home she had known. A single tear slipped from her eye as she carried her bags into her bedroom.

Brittany followed, still intent on hearing all that she had to say. "I have to understand why she could do something like that," Chris continued, needing to crystallize her thoughts. "I have to understand how someone with such potential to be an amazing person could be so cold, so removed from anything else. When we spent time together, it was as if she transformed into someone so alive, so raw and pure, so genuine. But she was able to just forget that and turn it off, as though she had never made love to me when in a vulnerable state, as though she had never laid not only her body—but her soul—bare in front of me, as though none of our connection ever existed. I have to understand her motivation or lack thereof, or I'll lose my mind. I'll start thinking that maybe I imagined it all. I don't want to do that."

"You don't want to forget?" Brittany asked, taking a seat on the edge of Chris's bed. "Don't you think it would be easier if we could just forget those things?"

Chris thought about that for a minute, as she sorted through her clothes, placing them in the laundry pile. "No, I don't," she said, shrugging. "You know as well as anyone that I've always gone back and forth between hating and loving this soft heart of mine, but I also know that I would be lying if I said I wanted to forget it all. I don't want to forget and I don't want to be bitter about it. That's why I want to try to see it from her perspective. If I just look at my side of it, I'll become cynical and angry and I'll hate her. I'll despise her for dragging me into this—even though I went willingly. I have to look at it from her perspective, so that I can hold on to what it meant to me—what I know it meant to her too, even if she's too fucked up to realize it or express it."

Brittany smiled at her with a knowing look in her eyes. "Come here," she said, opening up her arms for a big hug.

Chris complied, knowing that right now—probably more than ever—she would need this support. She fell into a warm, friendly embrace and feelings of warmth and of hope filled her soul.

"You're going to be just fine," Brittany said, stroking Chris's back. "You have this whole thing figured out, just like you always do. You're going to come out on the other side stronger and we all know that you're already ten times stronger than I am. I was a crying mess last night because I dropped my favorite bottle of perfume and you're standing here in front of me, staring at one of the most heartbreaking situations I've ever heard, telling me the ways that you'll take the pain head-on in order to grow and to learn from this. You're already taking preventative measures against becoming hardened by the jackass actions of others." She pulled back from the embrace and looked deep into Chris's eyes. The tenderness tingled Chris's heart strings. "You never cease to blow me away," she said quietly, the sincerity ringing through every word. "I truly hope you know that and hold onto it."

"Thank you," Chris said, nodding in agreement and letting the words resonate. Brittany was right and she *was* going to hold on to the fact that she was strong. While her wisdom was lacking these days, she knew she was strong.

She took a seat on the bed next to her best friend and turned to face her. "Tell me a story," she said, lying back against the pillows.

Brittany giggled. "What kind of story?" she asked.

"I'm glad that you didn't question that I wanted a story," Chris said. "Instead you just ask me what I want to hear."

"It's what we do," Brittany said, turning to lie beside Chris.

Feeling Brittany's warmth beside her, she felt comforted. This was home. Maybe Brittany was meant to be her home. She eyed her best friend, taking special note of her beauty. She longed to roll closer and let Brittany hold her, to plant soft kisses on the top of her head.

"What if I tell you all about how the pretty little princess at my work broke a heel the other day and completely had a meltdown?"

Chris smiled. Brittany's question snapped her out of fantasy. She settled in and got comfortable, letting all of the pain, the analyzing and the worry about tomorrow fade as she got lost in the normalcy of a moment sharing silly gossip with her friend. There was nothing normal about what she was feeling though. Her heart fought with logic. She had messed up her life badly by getting involved with the wrong woman. She had to consider the possibility that things fell apart so she would finally realize what she had here.

They had always been open with one another, but Chris didn't want to hurt Brittany. She kept her mouth shut. Brittany's voice washed over her, reminding her that it *could* be the voice she listened to every day of her life. She wasn't in a place to make that decision yet but she knew she loved Brittany.

Imagining the future she could have with someone who actually loved her, who wanted her, who was steady, who was an adult—hope washed over her, helping her drift off into a much-needed, deep sleep.

CHAPTER SEVENTEEN

"What's gotten into you?" said Paul, opening Raven's door. Raven looked up from her bed. "You're in your pajamas. It's not even midnight. Who are you and what have you done with my little sister?"

"Hey!" Pete yelled, sticking his head into the doorway behind Paul. "Want to come have a beer with me?"

"No thank you," she said. She smiled. "Drink one for me please."

"You sure?" Joe asked, appearing to be standing on his tiptoes behind Pete. "We're out here solving the secrets of the universe and jamming some Zeppelin. You should join in the fun. It's therapeutic and god knows we all need the therapy of solid rock jams."

"Thanks guys," she said, shaking her head. "I have a headache and am calling it a night."

Pete and Joe nodded and disappeared back into the main area but Paul remained in her room. "Do you need some Tylenol?"

She shook her head and waved him in. "Come sit with me," she requested, moving over to make room on the edge of her bed.

"Do you want to talk about it?" he asked.

She hated that question. Clearly, if she wanted to talk about something, she would. Letting out a sigh, she pushed aside her irritation. Aiming it at him would be misguided. She knew the real culprit in this whole mess. She faced her every time she looked into the mirror.

"I fucked up," she said quietly, even though her words hurt. "Truth is, I'm not even sure that I should say that in the past tense. The fact is that I've been fucking up continually for so long that I'm not sure I'd know how to make a good decision if it was the only one left to make."

"We all make mistakes," he said, putting his arm around her.

She wanted to bask in the feeling of being protected, but she couldn't. Even so, she didn't move his arm. "It's more than a mistake," she said. "It's not like I colored outside of the lines or lost my car keys. I fucked up on a grand scale. I'm a walking time bomb. I always have been. We all know it and everyone else who has observed even a bit of my life should know it. But I didn't protect the innocent bystanders. I didn't protect her. I should have been better than that. She deserved more than being put in the line of fire and then just discarded as though she was nothing more than another person who was in the wrong place at the wrong time. I didn't just fuck up. I fucked up someone else's feelings, someone else's heart and probably someone else's career—for no reason other than I don't think things through."

He held her closer and the tears came. As sobs wracked her body, she whispered the words that she had been tossing around in her head all day. "I think there's something really broken inside of me. I want to get help."

She had thought she was prepared, but when Paul cried with her, held her, rocking back and forth, she thought she might just explode from the onslaught of feelings.

"Stop crying, please," she managed through sobs. "I can't take it."

"I'm sorry," he said, wiping his tears, getting his hands tangled in her mess of hair. "I just never thought I'd actually hear you say those words."

"Me neither," she admitted, feeling the weight lift from her shoulders. "I don't know where to start. I'm scared."

"I'll be here every step of the way," he said, pulling her in closer. "You know that there's no one in the world who is more my family than you are and you know I'd never leave your side."

"Thank you," she said, another wave of tears wracking her system. "I should have done this years ago. I don't know why I've been so stubborn. But I'm ready to change. I'm ready to feel. If the past couple of months have taught me anything, it's that I have to be more. She told me that plainly and I resisted. But she was right. Everyone has been right all along. I can't keep doing this—not to myself and not to those around me. I have to be more, or I'll disappear and no one will remember anything but what a mess I was. That's all I'll have to hold on to if I'm not careful. The fame will fade. The ability to make music won't last forever. Without that, who am I, other than another tortured soul who was too stubborn to be something more?"

"You've always been more," Paul said, his voice gentle and soothing, but clearly still chock full of emotion.

"No," she said, shaking her head. "I *could* be more. I *am* more, somewhere underneath all of the things I've become. Right now, I'm a scared little kid, still running. I'm nothing more than that little girl who used to hide out and hope that the pain would go to someone else, anyone else. The only thing that's changed is that people pay to listen to me sing. Other than that, I'm not more. But," she paused, taking a breath to affirm her resolve, "I could be much more and I know that now. I know that, within me, there is more and I'm ready for everyone else to see that as well. I'm ready to do it for those I've hurt and to avoid hurting others in the future."

Wrapped in his embrace, she let the silence stand.

As they sat, she let it all come back to her, every piece that hurt. She let her mother's dark brown eyes flash in her mind, remembering the way they had always held the power to break her. Forcing herself to breathe, she made her mind relive even the most painful events, letting them come and finally facing what they meant to her.

"Those things do not define me." She repeated the mantra over and over in her head, silently and finally facing the fact that she had let so many things control her and define her for too long.

When the sobs finally subsided, she turned to face Paul.

"I need to talk about it," she said, clearing her throat.

"I'll listen," he said, the raw pain clearly dancing in his eyes as well.

"I know you were there for most of it," she said, choosing her words carefully. "If it's too much to go back through it, I'll understand and find someone else."

He shook his head. "I'm here, no matter how many times we have to relive it."

It was the encouragement Raven needed. She took a deep breath, finally prepared to let the floodgates open. "I am not Erin," she said, her voice confident and smooth, much to her surprise. As she listened to her words, she heard a new woman, stronger and far more real than she had ever been. "I hate that name for all that it's associated with. You were there through the dark periods, the years where Erin was all that I was. I was my mom's greatest fuck-up. She told me a million times and I carried that with me.

"I was a mistake and I wasn't needed or wanted for anything other than child support. I was hers to use however she saw fit. When she needed food stamps, I was her cash cow. When that ATM ran dry and when my father disappeared, I was nothing but a scapegoat. I was there to take the beating from her clients, or boyfriends as she called them. And then I became someone else's problem."

Paul winced and held on. "I know," he said, nodding for her to continue.

"You were there in the aftermath," she said, a single tear sliding down her face. "You were there. You kept my secrets. You were there to remind me that I was worth something other than a buck or two. You saw it, so you know. You know who Erin was. You know who Erin was later on, when I was nothing that anyone would miss. There were days I disappeared from foster homes for three days before anyone checked on me. There were still occasional bruises, depending on if I was in private care or in a home. There were horrible days and you saw them all. That's who Erin was. But I have to realize that none of that defines who I am today. I've been acting like some kid who's afraid of the monsters lurking in the darkness. But the part I never appreciate is that I survived it. I survived it so that doesn't mean that I should be some shell of a person. That means that I should be stronger than anyone else."

When she paused, Paul looked at her, his blue eyes sparkling with questions. She nodded, giving him the opening.

"What does that strength look like?" he asked. "As far as I'm concerned you're the strongest person I've ever met."

"No," she said, quickly dismissing the thought. "I'm far from that. You, of all people, should see me as I truly am and know that I've been nothing but weak and cowardly. Yes, on the outside, I've got it all together. Sure. I'll buy that for a moment. But, is it a good thing to live life so isolated? Is bitterness a badge of honor? I've just been scared. That's the real truth. I'm not tougher or stronger. I'm running scared, terrified that I will need someone and they will leave me. I've been scared that maybe my mother was right about everything and I'm not good enough. I've been scared for my entire life and it's consuming me. I've let it drive me to this point where I have almost been ready to throw it all away. But I won't. I can't. I am *not* what my mother thought I was. I am not her and I am certainly not weak enough to let her continue to control me."

"When did you piece all this together?" he asked, when she reached for the glass of water beside her bed.

"Over the last couple of months, I've realized that I'm scared," she admitted. "It would wake me up some nights, when I was comfortably nestled in Chris's arms. I would wake up with my heart racing, afraid that I had finally caved, afraid that she would be the one to undo me. I would feel fresh fear whenever she would look at me with those bright green eyes, because, when she did, I felt magic flow between the two of us. I knew how good she was for me and I knew deep down that I just couldn't be enough. I let who I used to be and what happened to me dictate who I was now.

"And when I messed up, when it all came crashing down, I looked in the mirror and I saw my mother. It wasn't *my* eyes, but hers that looked back at me. In that moment, I knew I had no one to blame but myself. I let it get this far. I should have sought help a long time ago—and not the kind of help that comes in a bottle or a little baggie. I should have sought real help and tried to become who I can be—who I still want to be."

She paused, letting her words breathe the fresh air of truth into the room. "I have Chris to thank for helping me realize it. I'm going to do this partially to honor her hard work, but more than anything, I have to do this for me—for Raven and for all that she stands for."

CHAPTER EIGHTEEN

Strumming her fingers on the table, Chris waited in the conference room. Eight had come far too early this morning and had served as a wake-up call that she was going to have to get her life back together. There could be no more of this gallivanting around like she was a teenager.

As the fluorescent lights above buzzed, her head pounded. She remembered everything she had disliked about this room. But this was where she belonged, a world of suits and heels, meetings and deals, polite smiles and professional speak. She didn't belong on a dingy bus, laden with temptation, booze, drugs and good-looking women. This was her world and she had to readjust.

Drinking her coffee, she checked her watch again, wishing that time didn't seem to move at a turtle's pace when one was as nervous as she was. Her nerves tingled, as she made a mental note of how Susan was always on time. Currently, she was running seven minutes late. Odd. Of course, that could mean that traffic had been bad this morning, but it could also mean that she was dreading this meeting as much as Chris was. As the coffee hit her stomach, she thought she might vomit. The acidic, warm beverage danced with her butterflies and suddenly she felt like she had just gotten off a tilt-a-whirl.

When she finally heard the click-clack of her boss's heels down the hall, she took a deep breath, bracing herself. There would be questions, all of which she could answer. But it would be the parental-like look of disappointment and disapproval that she was pretty sure would do her in. The door opened and she tried to offer a smile at the familiar face. She could feel how fake it was.

"Good morning," she said, her voice hoarse from last night's crying.

"Good morning," Susan said, her tone giving no indication of how she was feeling. "It's good to see you back. It feels like it's been years not months."

"Thank you," Chris said, genuinely grateful. "It's good to be back."

Susan took a seat across the conference room table from Chris, setting her coffee cup on a coaster before clearing her throat. "Do you want to begin?" she offered, extending an open palm to give Chris the floor.

Chris's heart felt as though it might beat out of her chest, but she nodded, hoping she looked more at ease than she felt. "I know I got myself into this situation," she started. "I accept full responsibility for all of my actions, but I just had to come back. The situation had turned toxic and I could no longer be in that environment. You were copied on the email I sent Frank Karnes and I have hopes that we won't lose the account. The work we've done for them so far has been phenomenal, seriously head-and-shoulders above what anyone else has ever been able to do for her."

"I've seen," Susan said, nodding with approval. "It's been quite an impressive campaign. It's been odd not to be at the center of it, to have you out there on your own, calling the shots. And I have to say that up until the last few days, I've been very proud of what you've done. You really proved yourself."

"Thank you," Chris said. She knew she wasn't out of the woods. "I apologize for letting my professionalism slip on this one. I should have been smarter about it all."

She paused to take a deep breath and Susan put up her hand to halt the apology. "I won't ask you what you were thinking or why you did what you did. I get that sometimes things get out of our control. I know you know better than to make some of the choices you did, and I know that you're clearly remorseful. You know very well that we all hold ourselves to a high standard here and that I can't have everyone thinking that it's acceptable to do what you've done. I also know that we're all human. Most of the time we're overworked, stressed out, tired humans. We can be weak. When we're thrown into new situations and life changes—especially with everything you've been through with the passing of your dad—we sometimes let our judgment cloud.

"For that reason, I'm not going to dismiss you. The rest of the staff will think you're getting a stern talking to in here and taking a short time of leave. But I'm human too and we all deal with life's pain in certain ways. Consider this your 'get out of jail free' card. It must never happen again."

Chris had always wanted to be treated like the others. Although Susan often put her on a pedestal and she had been given special treatment after her father's death—getting more than typical bereavement time off to get her life in order—she always tried to level the playing field. She didn't want to be seen as the boss's favorite. But this time was different and she felt relieved. She should be fired. She knew that much and she felt her confusion mount. "Why?" she asked.

"You're an adult. I can't tell you who you can and can't date. Of course, you know it's inappropriate to date someone you work with and that's why we don't condone interoffice dating. However I've never formally put a limit on clients, mainly because it's never been an issue. I'm working with HR to see what we need to do about a new policy. Even so, you are an adult and you made a choice. God knows it's been long enough since you've taken time to date, so I'm happy you put yourself out there. Maybe next time, you'll take a different approach.

"I know how smart you are and I know how much you care about your career. You've always viewed the company as though it was something you were a part of—not just a paycheck. You've helped me sell business and you've taken pride of ownership, not only in the work that you do for our clients, but also in our brand and our image. I realize you let that slip here, but I know you're smart enough not to let something this serious ever happen again."

Her tone was warm and almost motherly, but very stern. Chris tried to process it all. The weight of Susan's mercy pressed down on her, making her want to cry all over again.

"I will be much smarter," she said. "I honestly don't really know what came over me. I lost control for a while and I just let things happen."

"Good," Susan said, nodding. "Now tell me what happened. I need to know, because I'll be taking over this account from here on out."

It was for the best, she knew, but it still stung. This was the campaign she had pitched, sold and built from the ground up and now she was handing over the reins completely. Not that she wanted direct contact with Raven, but she would have liked to have some say in how it was implemented.

"Okay," she said, clasping her hands together as she collected her words to try to explain what happened. "Things were going well. Raven has a temper, yes. We worked on taming it in public. She saw me as an ally, which is really important in dealing with her. Once that was established, we were able to strategize together and build a really successful campaign. We got close—very close, as you know. We trod the line as best as we knew how, but we got swept up in it. At least I did.

"The last night I was there was bad for her. Her past came back to haunt her in a very real way and instead of dealing with it in a healthy, adult fashion, she did some drugs and hooked up with a pair of groupies or dealers—I'm not sure which. I walked in on it all and I let my heart do the walking out. I knew it would have been fruitless to even consider staying. Once she had seen through how I really felt about what she'd done—how badly it hurt me—I'm positive we would have been back to being enemies. I would once again be demoted to the outsider PR girl who can't be trusted and the campaign itself would flounder. I figured it was better to disappear and to salvage whatever had been achieved. With me out of the picture, maybe someone else can make sure that we don't go backward."

"Okay." Susan compressed her lips. Cocking her head to the side, her half grin showed both signs of sadness and maternal protection. "I'll take over it all and you will resume your usual client base. We'll get things back to a normal ebb and flow eventually. For now, I want you to go home. I think you need a day or two to get your head straightened out. Use two of your vacation days and then come back next week ready to work and ready to move forward."

Chris stood, walked around the table and hugged her boss. "I know I shouldn't do that," she said, pulling back.

"It's fine. I get it."

"Thank you," she said, her eyes welling up. "I won't forget this and I'll make sure you won't regret it."

"I know. Take care of yourself. And for what it's worth, even though it was a weird situation to start with, I'm sorry you're hurting."

Chris nodded, unable to form words. She made her way to the door before she broke down completely. As she walked to her car, she waved politely at the receptionist and hoped she didn't look too much of a mess. Quickening her pace, she made a decision. She was going to get her life together, whatever it took.

CHAPTER NINETEEN

With each footstep pounding against the pavement, Chris felt the tension fade away. Months had passed and she was beginning to feel more like her old self. Even in the early fall, the morning sunlight warmed her skin and sweat poured from every inch of her body in the Houston humidity. She felt oddly free. Embracing who she was and all she had been through, she let the music speak to her soul.

"Fight Song" by Rachel Patten blared through her earbuds. She bobbed her head to the beat, knowing that it was cheesy, but still relishing its meaning. Now was, indeed, the time to take back her life. She had changed her Pandora stations. She had removed Raven's music from her go-to playlists to be never touched again, unless she needed some sort of cathartic healing.

She pumped her arms faster and sprinted the last of her run, pushing her body to the limit. Her muscles ached and her shins were throbbing, but she didn't care. When she came to a stop, she surveyed the neighborhood, smiling at its normalcy. It was as quiet and peaceful as when she left it. The quaint little cul-de-sac reminded her of something out of a 1950s film and it had often been hers and Brittany's joke that they were the perfect little family. Maybe one day they could be.

For the millionth time since she had been home, the concept of a relationship with Brittany resonated within her. It would be easy. It would be full of love. It would be theirs. Though the idea never sparked fireworks for her, it was comfortable. God knows, there was little comfort anywhere else in her life.

For the time being, she was focusing on bettering herself. Once she felt whole, she would broach the subject with Brittany. She had done enough damage to herself and others. And this was *her* journey to personal growth—whatever path that led her down. She needed to complete it on her own.

It hurt, but this life was hers.

* * *

"Raven shows rare emotional performance..." The headline jumped off the page, along with an above-the-fold photo of her sitting on a stool, playing her guitar, tears streaming down her face. The article continued, with Raven nodding along with the words.

"In a rare display of emotion, Raven left the crowd speechless. One of the most powerful performances of the year, giving us a glimpse into the often unknown world of the rocker's personal life.

"Given her recent changes in behavior, being photographed with a significant other and finally shedding some light on who she is behind the glitz and glamour, it seems as though America's beloved bad girl might finally be growing up and growing into her own skin."

She pushed the paper away, knowing that they had hit the nail on the head. Raven replayed how it was for her on stage that night.

Clear-eyed, sober, ready to embrace emotion. Although Albuquerque provided a typically rowdy crowd, it seemed to sense the sincerity of the moment. A hush fell over the audience, as she reached for a stool and ushered the band off stage.

Typically, she would play alone for one of her own ballads, but this time she wanted her night's cover to be something special and meaningful.

"This one is just between us—just between me and each of you," she had told them, looking from face to face in the crowd. She strummed the first note, looking out at the crowd. "This song hit me the other day. I've heard it a million times, and it's a little out of what I'd normally play for you all. But I think there comes a time when we have to face the music and realize it's not all pretty. There are highs and lows and this is one of those songs for realizing the lows, embracing them and learning to move forward."

She saw the crowd's approval and closed her eyes. This song was for each of them struggling and it was for her. Most of all, it was personal. Though she kept the notion to herself, she was singing for Chris, an acknowledgment that she had done wrong and that she was going to make a change.

The lyrics of Kid Rock's "Only God Knows Why" highlighted the struggle of finding oneself in the midst of life's pain. Lost in the music, she swayed as she poured her heart out in song. The cell phones and lighters swaying through the air urged her to continue. As the song spoke of being away from home, she wiped away her tears. There was no doubt that she had been gone too long. Not from an actual home as the song alluded to. Home was not a place. Home was the home inside of her, the place that Chris had brought to life, the place that she had spent so long running from, the place that she now had to find again on her own.

She leaned back on the couch, putting her arms behind her as a headrest while she reflected upon it all. It was long overdue, but she *was* growing up making the changes she needed to make. Turning her attention to the tour schedule, she smiled.

Two more days and she would be ready. Since the day Chris had walked out three months ago, she had been making great strides. She was clean. She was sober. She was real. She *was* more. It was time to show that to the world and it was time to show Chris the difference she had made in her lover's life, regardless of if it could possibly change her views of Raven.

* * *

Soft music playing and the curtains drawn, Raven looked at herself in the mirror. Her brown eyes held hints of gold, a color she had scarcely seen in them in years. They were clear. They were confident and they were ready. This time, they were not a brave façade. They were genuine. She smiled nervously at her reflection, biting her lip.

"Are you ready?" she heard Paul's voice ask softly from the doorway.

She turned to face him, nodding and then shaking her head. She shrugged. "I don't know, to be honest. It's all so confusing and terrifying."

"You'll be great," he said, walking across the space between them and giving her a warm hug. "You've come a long way, in a surprisingly short time."

"I had a long way to go and I'm still not done."

"Yes." He looked down to make eye contact. "But you're trying and that much is evident."

"I guess it's go time," she said, checking her watch.

"Let's do it. I'm here if you need any backup."

"I don't think she's going to shoot me, if that's what you're referring to."

His laughter eased her nerves. "Not at all. I meant that solidly in the wingman sense. Like, if for some reason, this doesn't work and you want to try our old barroom skills, I'm your guy."

"Thank you," she said, winking at him and walking out of the room. "It can only go up from here."

Raven knew that things could go solidly south today. It could make recovery that much harder to face. Even so, she was prepared to walk this road alone, if that's what it took. She straightened her shoulders and took a deep breath, holding her head high as she walked from the bus, emerging onto the street.

She again read the text message from Susan, her new public relations specialist, to make sure she was in the right place. This place seemed so ordinary, so unfamiliar. Yet it was the place that was "home" for someone so extraordinary, someone who had brought the "home" feeling to Raven's life. She breathed in deeply, relishing the sweet scent of baking. From another era, cinnamon and sugar mingled in the air, making the fall breeze ever more pleasant. It set her at ease, as much as it made her dream of a time and place where life might have been a little simpler.

"Be more." She once again replayed Chris's words, nodding her head to the words. She walked up to the house, verifying once more that she had the number right. After knocking, she stepped back, waiting and sliding her guitar strap into position. At the sound of footsteps, she felt her heart might beat right out of her chest. There was a pause in movement at the door and she imagined Chris was peeking through the peephole.

Chris must have seen the huge bus pulled up out front. Slowly, the door crept open and Raven gulped back the last of her fears. It was now or never. Time seemed to stand still. Raven peered into the depths of Chris's confused, sea-green eyes, realizing again just how much she had missed her.

"What are you doing here?"

"I told myself I wouldn't come to you until I was different, until I was in a different, healthier place. I'm there and I'd like to talk to you a bit, if you will give me the time I don't deserve."

"Why now?" Chris's eyes lightened as she turned her head, tilting her chin up slightly.

"I have some things you need to hear."

Chris cocked her head to the side questioningly. Raven cleared her throat, undeterred.

"I'm sorry," Raven said, her words catching in her throat. "I'm so sorry for all I put you through and I wanted to see you to have a chance to tell you that and to show you something."

"What?" Chris asked in a voice barely above a whisper. The lines in her forehead deepened and she crossed her arms around her chest, as if trying to protect herself from what was coming.

Raven took a deep breath and played. She ignored the ice cream truck driving down the street behind her and the kids playing down the street. None of it mattered right now. The world was just Chris and her.

"Untouched by the fire,
Unfazed by the tides,
Bolstered by independence,
Held together with stubborn pride,
Convinced I was climbing,
Convinced I had it all,
Never knowing it could crumble,
Never knowing I could fall;"

She strummed her guitar, letting her voice meld with each chord as she poured out her heart in song. She kept her eyes on Chris, never wavering.

"Some call it toughness,
Some say I'm brave,
Sadly I know now,
It doesn't matter what they say,"

Stiffening, Chris wiped away a single tear, causing Raven to play the guitar solo for a beat longer than necessary as she struggled to compose herself.

"No longer tough, no longer brave,
Naked in front of you I stand,
I've been swirling the skies for too long,
And now I have to land;
Coming home,
Coming back around,
For the first time,
Seeing it clearly now…"

As she sang the chorus again, Raven felt the tears stream down her cheeks and watched as Chris listened, nodding but now showing no sign of emotion. When she finished, she pulled her guitar off and set it on the sidewalk, before walking over to stand directly in front of Chris.

"That was beautiful," Chris said. Her expression was hard, even though her tears had formed.

"It was for you," Raven said, breaking eye contact for a moment to look down and gain her composure. "I've made a lot of changes and I know that's probably not ever going to be enough. But I had to let you know that you changed me."

"I didn't," Chris said, shaking her head. "I couldn't."

"You did. You were the only one with the power to do so. You made me feel and you made me human, instead of the monster I was. You brought me back to reality, something I'd spent my entire life running from. I need to thank you and I have to beg for your forgiveness. I acted stupidly, selfishly and as though I was the only one who mattered. I thought that's who I was, but you showed me it wasn't. You showed me who I really am and you were right. I'm more. I'm more than a rocker chick with a bad attitude and a selfish mind-set. I have a big heart and I just never let it show. I was afraid to, but you made me brave enough to show it, to feel it. Thank you."

"I tried."

"No," Raven said, shaking her head. "You succeeded. You have made me a better person and I can never thank you enough."

"What about the drugs and the drinking? What about everything else? Are you working on that?"

Raven nodded. "I'm completely clean and have been for a while. I may have a drink at some point, at a party in the future, but I don't need it right now. I needed time to get my head screwed on straight, time to realize all that I could be without leaning on the crutch of a mistaken identity."

"You sound like you've made a lot of progress. I'm impressed."

The words came across as cold and guarded. Raven felt the blow.

"I don't want to take up too much of your time, or to overwhelm you, but…" her voice caught as she felt the weight of the words she was about to utter. "I want you to know that you are the single best thing that's ever happened to me. I will go to the ends of the earth to let you know that, to let you know just how sincerely I appreciate you saving me. I know I was on a destructive path. I was always just one bad decision away from letting it all go, being another Winehouse or Cobain. I let too many things define who I was and you saw through that. You saw me, the real me, buried underneath the bad decisions. No one has ever done that and it left me bare. I have no excuses for the horrible things I did or the ways I hurt you, but I want you to know I would do it all over again if I could and make it right."

"How would you make it right?"

"I'm not sure," Raven said, looking down at her feet, before resuming eye contact. "I know I can't change what I've done. I can't go back and undo it. All I know is that, moving forward, I need you to know that I'm in love with you. I'm in love with the way you burn with a passion for people, with the way that you view the world, with the way that you don't back down from any challenge, with the way that you make everything around you more beautiful. I'm in love with all that you are and all that you do, from the way you crinkle your nose when you laugh, to the way that you sigh right before you have to put someone in their place and from the way you make me a better person, to the way that you know who you are and what you're doing in the world."

"Love?" Chris asked, her voice breathless, sounding like someone had knocked the air out of her.

Raven nodded. "Love. It took me a long time to even put a name on the emotion, since I realized I'd never truly felt it before. For anyone. I love you. And I know I don't deserve another chance, but I'm here begging that you'll consider it."

"I need some time," Chris said, tears now rolling down her face freely. "I'm sorry. I have a life here. I have someone who does love me and would love me fully—without hurting me at every turn. More than that, I have me. And I'm learning to stand up for myself and fight for what's best for me. I'm sorry. I don't know how to respond."

"You have no need to apologize," Raven said, even as her heart fell from her chest with the words. "If you change your mind, I'll have seats for you at tonight's show and I'd love to take you to dinner afterward."

Chris frowned, nodded and then shook her head, before turning around and bolting for the safety of her house.

Raven stood on the street, looking around the serene neighborhood and feeling the weight of her actions crashing down. She looked up at the sky and forced a deep breath. Whatever came, just as she told herself, she would deal with it.

No more running.

* * *

More inspired than ever, Raven was ready to rock this show, with more feeling, more raw emotion than any performance she had ever given—no matter who was or was not in the audience.

Backstage, she looked into the mirror, enjoying what she saw. Yes, she was still the same girl she had always been with deep brown eyes, high cheekbones and long, flowing dark hair. Even her eye makeup and wardrobe was the same as usual, but there were notable differences—differences she was proud of. This was who she was supposed to be. This was real. Smiling, she straightened her shoulders and walked confidently down the long hallway leading to the stage. She knew that, one day, if it was meant to be with Chris, it would happen. And if it never did, she would be okay on her own.

"Go get 'em." Frank came up beside her, patting her on the shoulder and giving her an approving nod. His smile stretched across his face as he looked her up and down. "I'm proud of you."

"Thank you."

"Anytime. Go make me even prouder when you bring the house down." He winked, nodding again before ushering her behind the curtain. She smiled, letting the warmth of his words wash over her. This was it. This was her life and it was becoming one she was proud to live.

Closing her eyes, she waited as Paul addressed the crowd. Per her request, he was taking some time in the spotlight, welcoming the crowd and getting them amped up.

"Houston? Who's ready to get down tonight?" She heard his voice boom throughout the stadium, bringing about a wave of cheers and shouts. "Yeah? You ready to do a little partying? Maybe have a drink or two, get so swept away in the insanity of a mind-blowing rock song that you throw caution to the wind and make those bad choices you've been dying to make?" He laughed at the whistles and shouts in response. "Yeah, that's what I thought and that's why we're here. We're going to rock it so hard tonight that you're going to forget about everything, anything that holds you back, anything that stresses you. Let it all go, because tonight it's all about the music."

An eruption of cheering reverberated off the walls and Raven wished she could see his smile. This exposure was something she wanted him to have more often.

"Well folks, I'd love to stay around and chat, but I've got to get to work. And I've got to give this stand up to the girl you've all been waiting on, the girl who is more like a sister to me than anyone on this planet and the girl who holds the power to send you all into a daze that will feel more like orgasmic shock than anything you've ever felt—just with her voice and her performance alone. Without any further ado, I present you with the one, the only, RAVEN!"

As his voice boomed out, she smiled, strutting onto the stage and smiling at each face in the crowd as she passed.

"Thank you for all of that," Raven said, winking in Paul's direction. "Just so y'all know, I paid him to say that."

As the music started, she closed her eyes, moving her hips with the beat and feeling it rise within her. Belting out the opening lyric, she let her eyes drift to the seat that had held her heart's focus since she walked out onstage.

Chris was there.

Staring up onstage, her facial expressions changed every second. There was a brief smile, followed by an eyebrow crease, followed by a look of sheer confusion. Raven moved closer to the edge of the stage, walking in her direction. Her heart skipped a beat as she got close enough to make eye contact. Dropping the mic down by her side, she completely missed the second line of the song. With her mouth open, she gazed into Chris's deep green eyes, a slew of emotions hitting her like an avalanche. Chris smiled back, even though she was clearly feeling the same confusion. Judging from her tears and furrowed brow, she was feeling every bit of the intensity of the moment as Raven.

Time seemed to stand still as Chris began to nod her head slowly, mouthing the word "yes." Raven felt her heart soar, as its pace quickened and her face broke into a huge grin. The moment was cut short, when she felt Paul slide up behind her and put his arm around her. She noticed he had stopped playing when she turned around to face him.

She looked around at the sea of bewildered fans. She spun the microphone stand around in her hand swiveling her hips and bringing her attention back to the show. Clearing her throat, she raised an eyebrow at the crowd. "Sorry about that, guys," she said, still unable to wipe the stretching smile off her face. "I'm sure if you all could have seen what I can from here," she added, pointing the mic briefly in Chris's direction and winking, "you probably would have stopped for a moment too. I mean, have you ever seen something so inexplicably beautiful that it strikes you to the core, makes you lose all sense of direction and lights a fire inside your soul? That's what I'm seeing right now and I have to tell you that I'm sorry for messing up the song. I'll do it over again for you. Love just gets us sometimes and it's all we can see. Rest assured, though, I'm going to sing for you all and you're going to get to feel the depths of my love for this incredible woman and then I'm going to just soak up her presence after the show. For now, let's get going!"

The audience broke into cheers and a number of "aw" sounds swept through the crowd, but none of it mattered. The only reaction she could see was the beaming smile lighting up Chris's face and shining light into Raven's heart.

* * *

The music was a cover band playing oldies. Pacing back and forth along the halls backstage, Chris wrung her hands and then ran them through her hair. She turned on her heel and eyed the exit sign. There was still time to run. She turned back, looking at the dressing room door, where she knew Raven was changing. Torn, she stood so she could view the doorways. With eyes darting from side to side, she looked like a deer in the headlights. She glanced at the exit sign with one, last lingering gaze, knowing that her time was running out.

"I really didn't think you'd show up," she heard Raven's voice behind her and she jumped.

"You scared me," she said. She turned back around to face Raven, looking at those deep brown, melt-me eyes and let out a sigh. "I didn't think I would either," she admitted, after a pause.

"I'm glad you did." Raven's voice sounded honey-smooth and the corners of her lips lifted up into a smile, making Chris remember how soft they felt against her own.

"Me too."

"Can I ask why you did?"

Chris gulped, looking back at the exit sign before turning her feet and squarely facing Raven. "I came because there was no fighting it." Raven crinkled her brow, looking somewhat hurt. Chris held her hands up, buying a minute to get her words out correctly. "I can't stay away. You know that you're irresistible to me, just like you have been from day one. Trust me, I've taken time to sort out what I really feel. It's not an addictive thing, or some kind of superhero complex. It's not that I want to save you and can't walk away. It's that you legitimately enrich my life. You opened and unearthed feelings within me that had lain dormant for far too long. You opened my eyes to a world of life lessons, even as you were fucking up. You changed me—for the better, at least up until that crazy night."

"I'm so sorry," Raven said, pain filling her eyes.

"No, stop. Not now, anyway. I know you're sorry and truth be told, I was surprised to hear that admission of guilt, that sincere apology. But I know that's something you don't do all the time, so I take it as significant."

"I will own my actions from this point forward," Raven said, placing her arms gently on Chris's shoulders.

The touch made her tingle and she wanted nothing more than to fall into Raven's arms. She pulled back, forcing herself to focus. "I have more to say."

Raven nodded, taking a step back and bracing herself.

"It's not bad," she said, longing for Raven's touch again. "It's not bad at all. I just know that we both have a lot of personal growth still to come. I know this won't be easy and I know that there's a lot we still have to figure out—both about ourselves and about each other.

"We met under rough circumstances and when I was slightly vulnerable. I was still shut off. I was in the process of letting people in again after the heartache of losing a trusted lover and my father. Huge losses. But I've learned you're never quite as vulnerable as the moment you go from closed off to slightly open again. That leaves you cautiously optimistic. All it takes is a few kind words or a promising glance to blow the slightly ajar door wide open and leave you bare. But I know that—despite the issues we have to work through—I want to work through them by your side, not apart. I know that today you said some really strong words and I want you to know that I feel them as well."

"You love me too?" Raven asked, unable to hide her smile.

"I do," Chris said. "I've known it from the moment you first let me see those sneak peeks into your heart. I've known it from the day I watched you call and help Ryland out. I've known it for a long time, but I was scared. How do you love the one unobtainable girl on the planet?"

"You love her and you see who she is. Eventually, I guess she sees it herself."

Chris nodded. "Exactly. I don't know what the future may hold, or what shape this takes, but I came tonight because my heart wouldn't let me stay away."

"And what about that woman who loves you?"

"I love her too. But it's different." Chris sighed and shook her head. "She's safe and she's important to me. She's someone I'll always love. She'll always be dear to me. But try as I might, I can't make myself fall in love with her. I guess some things aren't meant to be. And some things just don't make sense. That's kind of how this is. It doesn't make sense to me to come back here. But I know it'll be worth it, because I love you, Raven Daniels."

"And I love you, Christina Villanova." Raven moved closer, wrapping her arms around Chris and placing a soft kiss on her cheek.

As their bodies joined in a tight embrace, Chris was sure of only one thing—this was just the beginning of their wild adventure. But no matter where it took them, she was right where she wanted to be.

Bella Books, Inc.

Women. Books. Even Better Together.

P.O. Box 10543
Tallahassee, FL 32302

Phone: 800-729-4992
www.bellabooks.com